CANDLE IN T

'Down with the traitors!
Down with the enemies of the People's Republic!'

In the midst of the hubbub Ling An walked in silence. When they came to the field at the end of the road they were halted and made to kneel in a long row, their hands still bound together behind their backs. The order was given to fire, yet Ling An scarcely heard it. The sky above her was dark and heavy, but glory surely lay ahead.

CLARE WYATT's compelling story is set in rural China, where she herself lived and worked for twenty years. It is closely based on real lives and events, although the characters in the book are entirely fictional. The story begins at the time of the Boxer Rebellion and ends in the violence of the communist revolution. Against this troubled background the family saga unfolds, focused on the love, faith and courage of one woman — Ling An.

CANDLE IN THE STRAW

Clare Wyatt

Published by
Lion Publishing plc
Sandy Lane West, Littlemore, Oxford, England
ISBN 0 7459 1833 6
Lion Publishing Corporation
1705 Hubbard Avenue, Batavia, Illinois 60510, USA
ISBN 0 7459 1833 6
Albatross Books Pty Ltd
PO Box 320, Sutherland, NSW 2232, Australia
ISBN 0 7324 0202 6

First edition 1990

British Library Cataloguing in Publication Data
Wyatt, Clare
Candle in the straw.
I. Title
823'.914 [F]

ISBN 0 7459 1833 6

Printed in Great Britain
by Cox and Wyman Ltd, Reading

CONTENTS

天比人大

A candle standing in the straw
Shines lonely in the deepening night.
It slowly burns and dwindles down
And dies amidst the tangling straw.
But as it dies the straws catch fire
And from that dying flame there grows
A fire that lights the world around.

1

THE VILLAGE

From the distance, the way to the village is clearly to be seen. It passes through a deep cleft in the hills which roll like the blue waves of a deep sea against the pallor of the sky. The traveller, however, finds it difficult to find his way to the cleft, for there are no roads, only rough tracks in that part of China, and to that particular village even rough tracks do not run. There are only paths, which run along the fields, following the edges of the terraces cut out of the loess which fills the valleys. However, once the cleft is reached, the way is clearly visible, for a deep gully runs through the narrow valley, and the only way through lies along it. It has been so well trodden by all who have passed that the rock is smooth and shining, and the path is almost a road.

It is said that at this point an old woman returning to the village from the market was once attacked by a robber. Hemmed in by the steep hillside on the right and the deep gully on the left, with not another soul to be seen or within earshot, even supposing there had been enough strength for screaming in her old cracked voice, the aged woman in desperation drew out the new kitchen knife which she had bought in the market and attacked the robber. He, supposing that such an old woman would have been an easy prey, was taken by surprise and, stepping back, fell over into the gully, where he broke his neck. The old woman returned to her home and was comforted by the villagers, and her courage and fortitude were praised. But she was never happy again, for her days and nights were continually haunted by the ghost of the robber; and so in a very short while she died.

Now this is a very strange story to tell about anyone who lived in that village, for the place had an evil reputation, and no traveller would enter it if he could avoid it. Indeed, it was said that on one occasion a wayfarer in ignorance of his danger ventured into the village at a time when all the men were away, tending their crops in the stony fields of the terraced hillsides. The women of the village set upon the traveller and, having murdered him without any difficulty, proceeded to quarrel over the possession of his scanty belongings.

Fortunately travellers were few and far between, for the village was remote from any place of importance. It is difficult to imagine how anyone in the beginning could have had the courage to scratch the first fields out of those stony hillsides. Even to this day they appear like a small patchwork quilt flung down upon a barren waste of hills. Perhaps in those days the hills were covered with trees, their roots retaining the water so that it flowed in little streams into the gully; but the trees were all cut down long ago, there are no streams singing as they run down the hillsides, and the gully is as dry as a bone, the valley as silent as a desert.

There is very little water in the village. The one well which serves the whole community is dried up for the greater part of the year, so the water has to be obtained from a well three miles away. In winter snow is gathered from the hillsides and melted in the sunshine to provide drinking water for human beings. Sometimes, if any water is left over after washing clothes, it is given to the ox to drink. In one small bowl of water a whole family washes.

Unfortunately snow, like everything else there, is very rare. This has been known to be a cause for divorce, when a bride has come from a village where there was an ample supply of water. One does not have to be very squeamish to dislike using the water in which half a dozen people have already washed.

It is not surprising that very little washing is done. Some miles away, there is a deep hole where rainwater collects in the summer. Although before the following spring there is little more than an inch or two of water lying over the thick black mud at the bottom, yet the village women manage to find enough to wash clothes, beating them with wooden washing pins upon the flat stones at the side. When even the last two inches of water have evaporated, then they come with lengths of handwoven cotton cloth and steep them in the mud, which dyes them black. So great is their desire for cleanliness that there is rarely a day when one or two of them are not seen squatting on their heels by the washing stones, sousing their washing in the inky water.

If the pool should be deserted, then one or two of those tall spare women will be seen hobbling on their tiny bound feet along the road between the pool and the village. For even in this lost village of fierce people, there is vanity and a respect for custom, and so every woman binds her daughter's feet, crippling them and giving the girl an ungainly carriage. The peasant woman works in the fields and hobbles to market on feet which are in her eyes as beautiful as those of any fine lady who spends her days smoking opium and playing mah-jong.

Who were the first settlers in that valley? Were they the scattered remnant of some defeated warlord's army? Did they flee to the hills for refuge and, recognizing at last that their cause was lost, become bandits, marauding the villages in the more fertile districts, retreating to their remote hills at night? Is their fierceness a heritage from a far-off generation which has been fostered by the struggle to live on such a penurious soil through long ages of poverty and even famine? Be that as it may, their reputation was bad, and very few people other than the inhabitants ever saw the short straggling street and the thatched stone cottages clustered about it.

One of these cottages was remarkable in that a tree grew outside it. It was the only tree of any size in the village, and it was valued because it not only gave shade but also bore edible leaves. Only this last fact had kept the villagers from cutting it down for fuel, as they had done to all the other trees in the neighbourhood. Edible leaves are a relish to people whose diet is mainly porridge made of millet or corn or, if these fail, sorghum. Even beans and sweet potatoes were luxuries to these people. So the tree was allowed to stand, and it cast its shade over the well outside the gate of the house and over the yard between the gate and the door opposite it.

There were three rooms in the yard, surrounding its three sides, each with its door opening into the yard where some puny hens were scratching in the dust. There were also a covered shed, where there was a millstone, and a lean-to shed against one of the rooms, which from its blackened appearance and the volumes of smoke proceeding from it twice a day was obviously the kitchen.

In one of these rooms one evening in early spring a woman was sitting upon a bed nursing a young child. The child was sick and, from the mother's anxious expression and her almost frantic peerings at the child's face from time to time, it was clear that the child was very sick indeed. As the child's breathing, which was hoarse and noisy, became more and more audible, the mother's anxious peerings beneath the folded quilt which partially covered the baby's face became more and more frequent. And from the deepening frowns of anxiety upon her face it was evident that she was not reassured by what she saw. Indeed, the pale pinched face and blue lips and little gasping breaths from the half-opened mouth would have made a more hopeful heart than hers despair.

The room was cold, the spring wind fluttered outside the paper panes of the window, now only a glimmering rectangle in the darkening room. The cold from the beaten earth floor crept up through her feet and made her legs stiff and heavy, but she was scarcely aware of this, so much greater was the chill of despair in her heart, for she knew in the depths of her soul that this child would die like all the others she had borne. She was an unlucky woman, and there was no help for it.

Presently the faint light from the open doorway was blocked by someone standing in it. She looked up and saw her mother-in-law, an old woman leaning upon a stick.

'Is it not time for the evening meal?' she said. 'How much longer am I to wait? What use are two daughters-in-law to me? Your sister-in-law is grinding the millet. You go now and light the fire.'

'The child is very sick,' said the mother, 'and if I do not nurse it, it will get cold.'

'And what is that to me?' replied the mother-in-law. 'It will die anyway, like all the others. And what is it but a girl anyway? Truly it was a bad thing, getting you for a wife for my son. Six children have you borne, and all of them are dead. Four of them were girls, too. What good are girls, eating the food in this house while they are young and marrying into somebody else's family directly they are old enough to be useful! Let it die . . . a weakly child will become a sickly woman, and then we shall have difficulty getting her married. Put the child down, go and light the fire and cook the millet. This isn't the first child you've thrown to the dogs.'

At this parting shaft the mother could no longer restrain her tears; but the habit of obedience to a typical mother-in-law was so strong that she stood up, carefully wrapped the quilt around the child, laid it on the bed, and went out of the room.

Outside it was dark. From the shed came the sound of grinding. Her young sister-in-law was walking around the millstones, her stomach pressed against the stick attached to the stones, pushing it as she walked and turning the stones one upon the other. From time to time she stopped to sweep the flour into a bowl. As the mother passed the shed on her way to the kitchen she called softly to her, 'How is the child?'

'Bad,' said the mother, stopping. 'It breathes like all the others. I fear it will die.'

'If we could do something . . . ' said the sister-in-law.

'What can we do?' said the mother. 'We have done everything. The child has been needled by old Sister-in-law Wang, and even though she thrust the needles into its neck, still the bad spirit remains inside, and the child chokes as it breathes.'

'If we lived nearer the city, we could go to the yard of healing. There is a neighbour in my mother's village who had a hardness of the soles of her feet. At last she could bear the pain of it no longer, so she cut off the hard lumps with the points of her scissors. The next day her foot swelled up like a gourd, and the day after that her leg was swollen and red as far as her knee. So hot was her fever she talked nonsense all night long, and no one could sleep. So in the morning her sons put her into a basket and carried her to the yard of healing, and there was a foreign devil of a doctor there, who cured her without even cutting off her leg. In a month she walked home without even the help of a stick.'

'Ah,' said the mother, 'but your village is only ten miles from the city. Here it is thirty miles, and a bad road. Two days at least it would take to get there. Besides, it is no use to think of it. Mother-in-law will not permit it. Not even for a boy would she allow such a thing.'

There was silence between the two women for a moment as the sister-in-law swept the flour into the bowl. Then she said, 'It is a long time since you went to your mother's house. Ask Mother-in-law to let you go home, and then . . . There is no one to take you: if you go tomorrow, you could go alone. Brother-in-law is away. Husband will not be back for two more days. Ask tonight, and start early tomorrow while the roads are still hard with frost.'

'But my mother will not know I am coming.'

'That does not matter. You will not go there; you will go to the city and take the child to the yard of healing.'

'Thirty miles is a long way to walk. Can I get there in one day?' said the mother.

'No; there is an inn at the village where you leave the mountains and come down into the plain. There you must spend the night. If you rise up early the next morning you can get to the city by the evening.'

This was so daring a prospect to both women that for a moment neither had anything to say. Neither of them had ever left the village unescorted by some male member of the family, and neither had ever spent a night in an inn. The most they had done, in the years immediately after marriage when it was customary to visit their maiden homes, had been to stop at wayside inns for hot water to drink and occasionally a bowl of hot millet porridge with spinach or lumps of sweet potatoes floating in it.

'And where will I get the money for that?' said the mother.

'Money!' said the sister-in-law. 'Coppers! how can you get coppers? Wait! I will think of a plan. Go and light the fire. Mother-in-law mustn't know that we are talking. I will think of something.' And pressing her body against the stick she continued her walk around the millstones.

2

THE YARD OF HEALING

The late afternoon sunshine lay like a sheet of gold upon the hard pale earth of the yard inside the main entrance of the hospital. The shadow of the cross upon the roof over the gate and the long dark shadows of trees patterned the gold. The gateman sat in his lodge in the porch, leaning his elbow on the table. He gazed through the little window which looked out into the gateway and down a flight of wide steps to a road leading uphill from the East Gate of the city of Erh Shih Ch'eng past the hospital to a pass in the mountains behind. There was an open Bible on the table before him, but he was not reading. He could scent an emergency from afar and, as he looked down the road, he knew that the woman hobbling up the hill was a soul in need. Indeed, he needed no second sight nor sixth sense to tell him that, for unaccompanied women carrying babies did not travel along that road so late in the day unless they were coming to the hospital. The outpatients' rooms were closed. The last patient had departed. He reached up for the key and waited for the woman to arrive.

A poor thing she was, too, when she came. The embroidery on her shoes was hidden completely under the dust that had gathered on them. Sweat was pouring in rivulets down her face, which was nearly as dusty as her shoes, and so thick was the dust on her hair that he could not tell whether it was grey by nature or black. Outlandish speech she had, too, and he could not understand at first what she said; but he could see that the child was very sick, so he unlocked the door of the outpatients' room and told her to sit down and wait while he went to fetch the doctor.

She was glad to sit down after walking so many miles. If only she had not come too late! She hardly dared to lift the flap of the quilt which covered the baby's face. There were pictures on the walls of the room, but she did not see them, nor would she have understood them if she had, for they were foreign pictures, crowded with figures and drawn with western ideas of perspective. But she saw nothing, for at that moment nothing existed for her but the tiny bundle in her arms, coughing and gasping for its very life.

There was the click of a door opening and shutting. She looked up and saw a foreign devil standing before her . . . a woman devil with eyes as pale as glass and hair as dry and grey as a ghost's.

'The doctor has come,' said the old gateman.

The doctor began to speak; but so great was the woman's fear that she could not understand a word that was said to her. She looked in desperation at the gateman, and he, as his custom was on such occasions, began to act as interpreter.

The doctor unfolded the quilt and examined the baby. 'Pneumonia,' she said. 'And practically no hope,' she added, to herself. For she knew that the child had been brought to her too late, and there was very little she could do.

'The doctor says,' said the gateman, 'that this child is very sick, and it may not be possible to cure it. It may die, but if you take it away it will certainly die. Leave it here in the hospital and the doctor will do what she can to cure it, and it may be that it will get better.'

The woman said, 'I have only a few coppers. I am very

poor, but I will give them all and I will work too, washing and sewing, if you will cure my child.'

'Don't worry,' said the gateman. 'I will find you a place to sleep tonight.' And he led her away to his wife, who gave her a large bowl of millet and chopped cabbage to eat and, having lent her a thick blue-and-grey plaid quilt, left her to sleep on the kitchen *k'ang*. So tired and exhausted was she that in spite of sorrow and anxiety she fell asleep almost immediately and slept like a log until the morning.

But in the women's ward in the hospital there was little rest for the patient, the nurse and the doctor. At about two o'clock the doctor, knowing that all that could be done had been done, left the child to the nurse and went to her room to sleep, for she had a hard day's work ahead of her.

The nurse sat by the child's cot. Many children had she seen in such a state, and many children had she seen die even in that same cot, for the people seldom brought their children before they had tried upon them the remedies which had been handed down from one generation to another . . . remedies which, alas, were often worse in their effects than the disease they were supposed to cure. Nevertheless, this same nurse and doctor had snatched many a child from the jaws of death, breathing the heat of fever out of his gaping mouth. So, as she sat watching the child, the nurse still kept a vestige of hope in her heart; but as the night wore on, she saw that there was no hope at all, and the child would not live until the morning. In fact, just as the first cock crowed in the darkness and the flame of the candle fluttered in the wind which stirs in the air before dawn, she knew that the child had only a few more minutes to live.

She got down upon her knees to pray for the little soul going out of this life. 'Poor child,' she said as she held it in her prayer in the light of the presence of God. And then, as she waited, kneeling on the cold concrete floor, love surged into her heart and lifted her heaviness, and she knew what she must do. Quickly she must do it, too, for time was short.

Hastily she poured some water into a basin and warmed it with some from the kettle. As she poured a little on the child, she said, 'Ling An, I baptize thee in the Name of the Father, and of the Son, and of the Holy Ghost. Amen. Now you will not be lonely, little soul,' she said as she rose to her feet. 'Now you can go and play with the holy innocents in the gardens of paradise.'

A pale light was creeping into the sky, and suddenly all the cocks in the neighbouring yards began to crow. A dog barked, a servant walked past the window softly in his cloth shoes, and the water buckets clinked as they swung from the end of his carrying pole. 'Another day,' said the nurse to herself, yawning and suddenly tired as she looked away from the cot to greet the nurse who had come to relieve her. 'There is nothing more to do,' she said. 'It is only a matter of minutes now,' and she went away to her bed and slept until nine.

'It is only a matter of minutes,' she had said; but the minutes passed, and the child stopped gasping and fell asleep. The blue pinched look faded from its face and the chill went from its hands. Warmth crept through its body as hour upon hour it slept the deep sleep of utter rest.

The cocks awakened the woman. Throwing off the blue plaid quilt she thrust her feet into her dusty shoes and would have gone to her child in the hospital there and then, but the gateman's wife said, 'Well, but you must wait. I will make you a bowl of millet first to warm you, and then you shall go.'

'Good, but I must go now,' said the woman, 'for I am very anxious.'

'They will not let you in so early,' said the gateman's wife. 'It is the rule. They are very strict. You must wait until nine o'clock.'

'Nine o'clock?' said the woman. 'When is nine o'clock?' For there were no clocks in her village.

'Soon,' said the gateman's wife, 'very soon. If you will help me grind this millet, the time will come quickly.'

So they went out into the yard, to the millstone. The gateman's wife asked polite questions about the woman's family so that in courtesy she had to answer them, and although the heaviness could not be lifted from her heart, yet she was able to endure it.

At last the gateman's wife said that it was nine o'clock and the woman could go to the hospital to see the child. She hobbled as fast as she could on the heels of her tiny feet past the gateman. He was occupied with the admission of a young bride who had taken a dose of arsenic and had just arrived accompanied by her mother-in-law, her husband, two of his brothers, and half a dozen neighbours and he did not see her as she crossed the yard to the ward where her child lay.

She crept softly to the door and looked in through the glass. The nurse had just come on duty again and was standing by the cot, amazed to find the child still alive and apparently much better. She looked at the mother and, putting her finger on her lip, motioned to her to come in quietly. The woman came in.

'Ah!' she said. 'She's better! My little child is better!' and she got down on her knees and knocked her head upon the floor at the nurse's feet. 'You have healed my child,' she said. 'Oh, you are good; oh, you are very good!' and the tears poured down her cheeks. 'Now I must go home; I must take the child home.'

'Not yet,' said the nurse. 'You must wait a few days. The child is better, but it has no strength. It might get ill again if you take it home now. Wait a day or two. Sit here and watch her, while I see to the other patients.'

At this point the baby opened its eyes, and the nurse began to chatter to it, calling it Ling An.

'Ling An?' said the woman.

'Yes,' said the nurse. 'She has a name now. I gave her a

holy washing and a new name. When she gets bigger you must teach her about Jesus.'

'Jesus?' said the woman. 'What's Jesus? I have never heard of Jesus.'

'Never mind now,' said the nurse. 'Later, I will teach you.'

So the woman sat down by the cot and watched the nurse, who did many strange and wonderful things to the sick people lying on the beds. By and by the doctor came in, dressed in a white coat.

'Poor foreign devil,' said the woman to herself, 'she must be in mourning. Who can have died? Perhaps it is her husband, for her hair is so white she is too old to have parents still living.'

Then she looked at her baby and thought, 'Truly, these people are good people. How kind they are here. I will stay a little longer and hear about this Jesus. It must be something very powerful. Ling An . . . Ling An . . . that must mean Receiving Peace . . . a good name. Whoever heard of such a thing, giving a name to a girl? And such a name . . . like a boy . . . Ling An!' she said softly to the baby, and again to herself, 'Ling An . . . Ling An.'

Even as she was thinking, there was the sound of footsteps outside; the gateman's voice was heard, calling to someone to stop. The door-handle rattled, and through the glass panes of the door the face of her mother-in-law appeared. She looked more and more angry, as being unused to doors with handles, she was unable to make her way in. She pushed it and shook it and pulled it, but did not think of turning it. The nurse, fearful that the noise would awaken the child, rushed to the door and opened it. The mother-in-law pushed her aside, went to the cot, picked up the baby, rolled it up in the cot quilt, and marched out without saying a word. The mother followed, fearful and trembling.

Outside, the great yard was full of sick people coming and going from the clinic, and it so happened that at that moment the crowd was increased by a group of ten wounded men from a warlord's army which had been skirmishing in the neighbourhood. The gateman, who had followed the two women, was obliged to leave them and see to the speedy admission of the wounded men, for the warlord was powerful and it would not do to offend him. The mother-in-law, carrying the child and followed by its mother, darted into the crowd. The two women became indistinguishable from the other people and made their way to the gateway. And that was the last the hospital saw of the two women. As for the child, she was to come through that gateway again, but not until more than half a generation had passed.

Later on in the day, the nurse and doctor took counsel with the priest of the parish. It was not the custom of the church to baptize the children of non-Christian parents without their consent, but as this particular child had been truly baptized, the church must see that she was properly taught and brought up in the Christian faith. Somebody must go to the village to visit the family and see what could be done. But when enquiries about the village were made, it was found to be so far away that anyone who went there from the city would be obliged to spend the night in the village, and its reputation was so evil that the priest would not consent to send anyone there, nor dared he go there himself. Of course, this decision was made only for the time being. It was hoped that when conditions improved, someone might be able to go there. But conditions did not improve. Political unrest became turmoil, and for many years travel even to places nearer than that village was hazardous.

The doctor grew old and retired to her own country. So did the nurse. The priest died, as also did the gateman. Yet there remained in the church register the name Ling An. And far away there was one person who did not forget.

The nurse, morning and evening, remembered the child

Ling An in her prayers. As she prayed, she saw in her mind the tiny baby face, and this image persisted, although when she thought about it she reckoned as the years passed that the baby must be a child, then a young girl, and then later a woman. 'Or it may be,' she would think sometimes, 'that she died long ago, for her grandmother certainly took her out of the hospital's care far too soon.' But she went on praying, even when she grew so old that the past was mixed up with the present so that she could not always remember where she was, and called the people around her by the names of her Chinese friends who had been dead for many long years. Then sometimes she would think, 'Ling An? Who was Ling An? I can't remember that person, but it must be someone who needs my prayers.' So she went on praying for Ling An.

And in the village, all unknown, God was working in the heart of a child who did not know that she was any different from the people among whom she lived.

3

THE GRANDFATHER

Ling An did not die, although there were several times during her childhood when she might have died. Puny as she was, she survived the various fevers which beset children, the rigours of climate and ill-nourishment. This caused some surprise among the neighbours who were acquainted with her mother's ill-luck in the rearing of children. But Ling An's mother was not surprised. For all ailments, from measles to smallpox, she had one infallible remedy. She would take out the hospital quilt of knitted patches and wrap it around the sick child, for she believed that anything that came from that place of healing must have healing power in itself.

Afterwards, when Ling An had recovered, she would fold it carefully, wrap it in a folding-cloth and hide it away in the bottom of her red bride's chest, and as she did so she would tell Ling An how she had carried her to the Yard of Healing in her arms, and how the strange foreign devil of a doctor had cured her when she was dying and the nurse had given her a name.

'Do the other girls here have names?' she would say. 'Of course not. Girls do not have names, but you have, because the foreign devil gave you a name.'

In her heart she really believed that the name had

healing power too, and that as long as Ling An used it, she would be healthy. She did not talk of these things to anyone except Ling An, for it was not wise to remind her mother-in-law of that episode, although when her next baby, a boy, also survived the hazards of childhood, her mother-in-law treated her less harshly.

So ten years went by, and Ling An grew strong and healthy. Then one cold windy day towards the end of the year, a pedlar came through the village. His goods were packed in bundles which hung down each side of his mule. He came leading the mule with one hand and clapping his pedlar's drum with the other. Pedlars so seldom passed through the village that this was quite an event, and soon the whole village was gathered around him. As the women examined his embroidery patterns and bits of cloth and skeins of silk, he quietly asked them for a certain Li Chou Shih. Li Chou Shih was Ling An's mother.

It happened that she was making biscuit bread on a griddle and, as that is an occupation which requires full attention, she had not been able to leave her work to gather with the other women around the pedlar. The women told him of this, and thrust Ling An before him, saying, 'This is her daughter.'

The pedlar looked at Ling An and said, 'Tell your mother that her father is very ill, and likely to die.'

Ling An ran straight to the lean-to shed which was the kitchen of their house, where her mother was sitting in the smoke, with one hand feeding the fire under the griddle with dried leaves, and ladling large spoonfuls of biscuit bread mixture on to the hot iron griddle with the other.

When Ling An told her what the pedlar had said, her mother went on with her work, for poor people cannot waste food. Not until the last spoonful had been baked and added to the top of the pile of flat circles of biscuit bread did she get up from the floor and wipe her hands on the towel that hung from a string stretched across a corner of the shed. Then she went out to find the pedlar and ask him more. There was not much he could tell her, for he had been given the message as he passed through the village where her parents lived, and that had been two whole days ago.

They set off early the next day. Ling An's grandmother had given her permission with reluctance, but to refuse to allow a daughter-in-law to visit a dying parent would be against public opinion even in that village. Moreover, in the twelfth month there is very little to do on the land, and men are idle. So early the next morning Ling An's father escorted his wife and daughter to her parents' village.

As they had no reason to linger on the way, they made the journey more quickly than the pedlar and arrived late in the evening of the same day on which they had set out. Ling An's grandfather had already taken a turn for the better, but as they had come so far and their visits were so rare, and perhaps chiefly because Ling An's father wanted to go on into the city where he could do a little profitable gambling, it was decided that Ling An and her mother should remain until her father returned from the city and took them home again. It might be in a week's time, perhaps even a little longer, but in any case before the preparations for the New Year, late in January, began.

Grandfather was one of those gentle people who are to be found in all countries and in all walks of life, who seem to have been born with less original sin than most of mankind. Sinful they are, like all men, but their sins are generally sins of omission rather than commission, for they seem to have an instinctive repugnance to evil. Where there is light, they reach out for it. In the dark places of the world they glow quietly and steadily, gentle lights to their own generations. Generally they are so unworldly as to appear simple to those who think themselves wise. Seldom are they rich, for everything they have they share with those poorer than themselves. Often in countries where animals are valued only for their usefulness, these gentle people treat them as companions, and are loved and trusted by both tame creatures and wild, in a way which seems a wonderful thing to ordinary men.

People remembered that Grandfather would remove stones from the paths so that people should not fall over them. There was a brightness of light that shone in his face and attracted all young children, and he had a still serenity which drew all those in trouble to open their hearts to him. Ling An loved him at once, and the two became inseparable.

In a day or two, Grandfather was up and about, and he and Ling An would find a sunny place by a south wall, sheltered from the wind. There they would sit together through the warm noontide hours, telling stories and talking of many things.

They were sitting thus against a boulder in one of Grandfather's plots of wheat, not far from the path, when a man came walking along. Ling An had never seen anyone so strange or so ugly, for as he came towards them she saw that his eyes were blue and his hair as yellow as ripe corn cobs. He wore a long blue gown like Grandfather's, the length of which was tucked up into a leather belt for ease of walking, and the shoes on his large feet were made of leather which shone in places where the dust had been rubbed off them as he walked.

Grandfather greeted him. 'Sit down, foreigner,' he said, 'and take a rest.' It was the common greeting of those parts, but no more than a greeting, and passers-by did not usually sit down and rest. However, this man left the path, came across to the boulder and sat down beside them. Ling An crept closer to her grandfather, her eyes growing wide with fear and wonder.

'The old grandfather is hot today,' said Grandfather, looking up at the sun.

The man smiled. 'That's not the old grandfather,' he said. 'That's the sun. The Old Heavenly Grandfather made the sun.'

'True,' said Grandfather. 'He made the sun and the moon and he sends us rain and makes the wheat grow.'

'Ah,' said the man, 'I see you know a lot about the Old Heavenly Grandfather. Let's talk about him.' They talked for a long time, and Ling An, already drowsy in the hot sunshine, fell asleep. When she awoke, the man was closing a small black book which he had been reading to Grandfather. He put it into his pocket and stood up.

'I'll see you again,' he said.

'See you again,' said Grandfather.

Then, seeing Ling An looking at him, the man thrust his hand into another pocket and brought out a little book full of bright coloured pictures. He gave it to her.

'A week tomorrow is Christmas Day,' he said. 'Christmas Day is the Lord Jesus' birthday. This book is about his birthday.' Then he turned away from them, strode back to the path and was soon out of their sight.

'That is a good man,' said Grandfather.

A week went by and the weather grew colder and rather dreary. There were days when the sun was not to be seen. The sky was covered with heavy grey clouds. It was past the time of heavy snow, but as none had fallen then, the villagers expected snow to fall from this heavy-laden sky.

One evening a group of half a dozen men appeared in the village. They stopped at the inn and later called on the village elder. They said that they were Boxers and that they intended to kill all foreigners and Christians.

The elder said that there were no Christians in the village and that they had not seen any foreigners. This news soon went around the village with more and more details added as it passed from mouth to mouth, so that that night every householder took more than usual care in barring his gate, and all the people retired to bed earlier than usual, starting with fright under their quilts at the most ordinary of noises.

In the morning Grandfather, against Grandmother's

advice, insisted on going out to look at his plot of land. Ling An's mother took clothes and a washing pin to wash clothes in the village pond. Ling An stayed at home with her grandmother, who had promised to teach her how to embroider the toes of a new pair of shoes.

It was Grandfather's intention to stop the young foreigner if he should come walking past his field again, warn him of the danger and advise him not to go through the village where the Boxers were waiting; but the young man did not come that way.

He had been spending Christmas with his sister at a town twenty miles away, and while there he heard that the Boxers had come into the district. At once he said that he must return to his church, which was ten miles beyond the village, so that his colleague should not be alone if the Boxers should come. He set off early, before daylight, and on the second day about noon he was near the village. So far his journey had been peaceful, and he had no reason to suspect the danger lurking there. He was in a hurry, and so instead of approaching the village by the path which went past Grandfather's field, he took a shorter route which led him through the other side of the village.

This road went past the inn where the Boxers were sitting taking counsel with the village elder. Even so, as they were fully engrossed in tormenting this poor old man as they tried to make him confess that there were Christians in the neighbourhood, the young foreigner might have passed through unnoticed. Unfortunately some children playing in the street saw him and began to call out after him, 'Foreign Devil, Foreign Devil!'

The six Boxers pricked up their ears and, leaving the village elder, they rushed out into the street and pursued the foreigner. He saw them coming and fled. He turned a corner and darted through an open gateway into a courtyard. It was Grandfather's house, but Grandfather was not there. Ling An looked up in surprise but, before she could say a word, her grandmother, seizing a broom, set about the foreigner and chased him out of the gateway. Ling An caught at her grandmother's arm to stop her, but it was too late: the young man fled from the yard; and Ling An, slipping out before her grandmother could bar the gate, followed after him.

The young man ran for his life. There seemed to be wings on his feet, but the Boxers were young and strong and swift. They passed Ling An, they caught up with the young man, and in an open field not far from the village they killed him. Engrossed in their evil deed, they did not see the child watching them in horror. She stood rooted to the ground, unable to move until they had passed her, swaggering up the road slashing the air with the wide curving blades of their swords.

Then she began to run, not back to Grandfather's house, but away from the village. She ran on and on, with only one purpose in her mind: to escape from so great an evil. She ran until it was dark then, curling herself up in the shelter of a wall of loose stones, in spite of the cold she slept the sleep of utter exhaustion. In the morning she went on and, sometimes walking, sometimes running, she reached her home early in the evening.

As for the young man, he lay in the field until people came from his church and carried him away and buried him in the church cemetery. Although his name was not Stephen, everybody came to remember him as Stephen. Even after a generation had passed, a teacher who could read more characters than most people, tracing with a long thin finger the characters of his name on his tombstone, said, 'There, see, Stephen. That's his name. His name was Stephen.'

Grandfather, safely behind his barred gate, said when he heard his wife's story, 'Wife, you should not have driven him away. He was a good man.'

Ling An was afraid for many days, and often had bad dreams at night. Sometimes, when no one was watching her, she would take out the little book and look at the pictures and think of the story that Grandfather had read to her. Sometimes she wanted to tear it up because it reminded her of the horror that she had seen, but always just as she took it up to tear it into little pieces, something seemed to stop her, and she would look at the pictures again for a while, and then thrust the book into the girdle that kept up her trousers . . . Until one day her mother saw the book.

'What's this?' she said. 'A Christian book! Daughter, if the Boxers find this here, they will kill us,' and she took the book from Ling An. So great was her fear that she did not dare add it to the thick pasteboard she was making for the soles of shoes, nor even to put it aside to burn with dried grass to cook that evening's meal. She fetched the tinder-box and struck a spark and burned the book then and there on the earth floor of the room.

Ling An, with tears in her eyes, watched the pages curl up in the heat, and all the bright colours of the pictures turn scorched and brown and finally black, until last of all there was nothing to see but a golden cross which was in the middle of the back cover. That for some strange reason took longer to burn away. But in the end that too turned black, and Ling An's mother swept the ashes away into a corner and stamped them into the floor with her tiny bound feet.

4

THE BRIDE

It was a hot airless night. Under a sky heavy with tomorrow's rain the frogs were clamouring in their muddy pools. Mosquitoes whined in the little inner room where Ling An slept. A blue cotton curtain in the doorway screened her parents' bed in the main room of the house; but as she lay sleepless in the steamy heat, Ling An could hear them talking together in low voices.

'Wang Chu Pin's son Yung Fu and our daughter would be a good match.'

'The girl is still young,' said her mother ' — scarcely fourteen.'

'It is a good match,' said her father. 'We shall not find so good a bridegroom later . . . an only son, and his father's business prosperous.'

'What business?'

'A butcher's shop, in the city.'

'It's a long way from here.'

'No more than a day's journey on a mule.'

'What about the young man's mother?'

'Just like the others,' was the reply. 'No better, no worse. Let's sleep.'

In the ensuing silence, Ling An shivered under the thin quilt in spite of the heat. That her parents had been discussing her marriage she had no doubt whatever. Like all the girls of her age in the village, she knew that marriage was inevitable and that she would have to leave her home and go to live in a family of complete strangers, perhaps many miles from her home. The girls were more concerned about their future mothers-in-law than about their bridegrooms, for in most cases they became the servants of their husbands' mothers. 'Just like the others,' her father had said. 'No better, no worse.' 'A day's journey on a mule' was a long way from home. 'A butcher's shop in the city.' Perhaps it wouldn't be so bad after all. Ling An, who had never been to the city, tried to remember all that she had ever heard about it, and with her mind full she fell asleep.

During the rest of that year and for several months after the New Year, Ling An was kept busy spinning the cotton thread which her mother dyed indigo blue and wove into cloth on the loom which almost filled one end of the main room of the house. Lengths of blue and white plaid patterned cloth were made up into quilts in the bright hot noons of late October when the beds were carried outside the house so that the cloth could be spread on them and kept clean from the dusty ground of the courtyard. Hard firm pillows stuffed with the excreta of silkworms for coolness and made with a hole through the middle for the sleeper's ear were embroidered at the ends by Ling An. A length of gaudily-flowered cloth for a pair of trousers and another of scarlet cotton for a jacket were bought from the pedlar. Shoes were made and embroidered by Ling An, her mother seeing that she mastered that craft thoroughly from its beginning of pasting old rags and paper together for shoe soles to the delicate intricacies of embroidering on the toes and sides of the uppers. The bridegroom sent a present of blue-enamelled silver ear-rings and hairpins. Ling An's fringe was allowed to grow long and pinned back to the rest of her hair, and her mother, who had been brought up in a more respectable village, kept her strictly within the walls of the courtyard, as she herself had been kept before her marriage.

The fortune-teller, who had cast the horoscope of the two young people and found them suited to each other, was consulted again to determine an auspicious day for the wedding. He chose a day towards the end of July.

Early on that day, while it was still dark, Ling An was awakened by her mother and dressed in the flowered trousers and scarlet jacket with a bright blue one on top of it. Her hair was done up in a bun on the back of her head. This took some time and had to be done more than once, as hair which has been hanging in a plait down the back for many years does not take readily to going up in the opposite direction. Neighbours had come in to help, and stood around offering advice, joking and laughing, and teasing the bride. Finally a spot of colour was put on Ling An's cheeks. The women all said, 'Good to see!' and she was left to sit quietly on the edge of the bed while they busied themselves with the arranging of the household goods which were her dowry and were to be carried in procession before the sedan chair which was to take her to her bridegroom's home.

As she sat there and thought how she was leaving home for ever and, except for rare visits of short duration, would not see her parents again, the tears ran down her cheeks and washed off the paint which had just been applied.

Suddenly there was a cry, 'The chair is here, the chair is here!' Instantly all was hustle and bustle, a mirror was tied to Ling An's waist, while her tear-streaked face was repainted. The silver hairpins were pushed again more firmly into the bun of hair on the back of her head, and a thick red veil thrown over her head and face. Then she was escorted, with many good wishes and last-minute words of advice, to the chair which stood waiting outside. The red curtains were drawn so that no one on the road could see inside. The men standing between the poles spat on the palms of their hands, picked up the poles, and set off.

Ling An knew that her father was coming with her but her mother would remain at home. The latter stood in the gateway and watched until the chair and the men carrying the household goods — the quilts, the washing-bowls each with a little grain strewn in the bottom, the red bride's chest and the tray with the teapot and four cups — were out of sight. Then, weeping, she went back into the house and was comforted by the neighbours.

It was one of the hottest days of the year. Within the red curtains of the sedan chair it was stiflingly hot. Discomfort and exhaustion rapidly replaced the sorrow of leaving her mother and her home behind. Even anxiety about the new life ahead of her was swallowed up in the drowsy lassitude which weighed heavily upon her. Remembering stories of brides who had been sent through the heat of summer to their bridegrooms' homes and been taken dead from the sedan chair, suffocated by the sultry heat, Ling An fought against the sleep which pressed upon her eyelids. But gradually she succumbed, nodding and waking and nodding again, and finally falling into such a deep sleep that nothing awakened her until she came in the late afternoon to her bridegroom's home.

5

THE DEBT

The Wangs' butcher shop was on the main street of a small walled city, not far from its South Gate. Like all the other shops, the front was entirely open all day long, and swarms of flies entered without hindrance. The shop itself was small and dark, and not much meat was to be seen there, but behind the shop was a larger room where the carcases of pigs and sheep were hung from hooks in the roof. From this room the smell of raw meat pervaded the whole house — a smell which later was to bring back memories of the early days of her marriage to Ling An whenever she smelt it.

The Wangs at this time were doing well. There was always plenty to eat, and life was much easier than in Ling An's maiden home. There was always something going on in the city: customers brought news and rumours. Travellers from other towns passed up the street to the inn. When the travelling theatre arrived and took temporary possession of the theatre outside the South Gate, Ling An accompanied her mother-in-law, carrying a bench to sit on so that they could see the actors performing plays from the ancient history of the country.

Her mother-in-law was not unkind, in fact she was almost easygoing, and Ling An's young husband seemed a pleasant enough young man. To Ling An, young and inexperienced as she was, all seemed safe and happy, and she could not understand why her father-in-law was so annoyed when his son stayed out late at night, nor why he should be so angry with his wife when she returned from visiting a neighbour, especially during the New Year holiday, when surely such things should be permissible. Old Mr Wang seldom addressed his daughter-in-law, but when he did he was always kind, which made his behaviour to his wife and son seem all the more strange. Ling An pondered the matter while she sat at her spinning-wheel and finally concluded that as he was so thin and always had a bad cough in the morning, he must be ill. That seemed to be the reason why he was so easily annoyed with his wife and son and always looked so worried when he sat by himself in the dark little shop waiting for customers.

Ill he certainly was; and when Ling An's first child, a boy, Li Hai, was five years old, he finally took to his bed, and young Wang was left in charge of the shop. For the first few weeks, he directed his son from his bed, but at the end of a month he rapidly grew worse, and after a few days he died.

For the first few months life went on as usual. Then the mother-in-law started visiting her neighbours again. The visits were of very long duration. Young Wang also spent long hours away from home, leaving Ling An to mind the shop. He would return late at night, red in the face and often very excited. Afterwards when he awoke late in the day, he would seem moody and depressed. Then at last Ling An knew that these two were gambling, and she began to be terribly afraid.

The butcher's business, lacking a master, soon deteriorated. A carcase of pork went bad before Ling An was able to make it into sausages, for she had two children to care for and a third soon to be born. The smell of meat became so strong that customers who mounted the steps from the street and stood on the threshold changed their minds and went away without buying anything. The carcase hung on its hook in the inner room, and the smell pervading the shop was so bad that the rumour spread through the city that the Wangs were selling bad meat. From that time no customers came into the shop. Young Wang, now having nothing to do, left the house every morning and came home late at night. His mother went out every afternoon. Only Ling An and the children were left alone with the terrible smell. Finally Ling An became so nauseated that her mother-in-law took notice and said to her son, 'Your son's mother cannot abide the smell of the meat. You must do something about it.' Only then did young Wang take steps for the disposal of the carcase of pork. By that time the business was ruined.

During the next five years, things went from bad to worse. Young Wang and his mother gambled all day long. All that old Wang had spent his life in saving and amassing was gradually gambled away. The money he had saved went first, then the land he had bought, until finally there was scarcely more left than the house and shop on the street in the city. When all but the last of the land was lost, the old mother had a stroke and died in a few hours. Ling An could not help feeling relieved, not so much that there was one mouth less to feed, but that there was one pair of hands less to gamble.

By this time Ling An had borne seven children and lost two of them. Tetanus took one of them a few days after his birth, and measles took the other scarcely two years old. Her elder son Li Hai, who being the eldest was usually called Lao Da, was ten years old, and his sister nine; her second son Lao Erh was two and his two younger sisters fifteen months old and two months old. Good healthy children they were, with golden skins and fine black silky hair, clear eyes, and straight limbs. They were as fine a brood as any parents could desire, but their healthy appetites had to be satisfied. With the shop closed and no money but the uncertain income of a gambling husband, Ling An was hard put to it to find enough for her family to eat.

Late one afternoon in the fourth month, Ling An was sitting in the empty shop, busy at her spinning wheel, when an old man mounted the steps from the street and, instead of standing politely in front of the counter, came boldly through the entrance to the space behind it.

'Is this not the shop of Wang Chu Pin the butcher?' he said.

Ling An looked up at him in amazement. For a moment she thought that he was the ghost of her father-in-law. Then, as she scanned his face and figure, she saw that this was a far more substantial man than her father-in-law had ever been in life. Old as he was, his back was straight, his eyes bright and clear, and his white hair sprouted from his head like a well-bristled brush.

'Where is my brother?' he continued.

'My father-in-law died five years ago.'

'And my sister-in-law?'

'Mother-in-law died last year.'

'And my nephew, your husband?'

Ling An's eyes fell.

'He is out,' she said, and was ashamed to feel the hot blood rising in her face.

'There was a meat shop here.' Ling An looked at the floor and said nothing.

The man went into the inner room where the meat used to be hung and saw the empty hooks. He went into the two rooms at the back where the family lived, his bright eyes darting into every corner and missing nothing. Then he came back into the shop, sat down in the black wooden armchair, took out his pipe, and filled the brass bowl with a pinch of tobacco from the bag which hung at his waist.

Ling An gave Lao Da a copper and sent him for a kettle of boiling water. When he returned, she made tea and poured out a cup for the old man.

Then she began to remember what she had heard about

her husband's uncle, the elder brother of her father-in-law, who had gone away in his youth, soon after her husband had been born, and never been heard of again, so that all the family had supposed him to be dead. Now, knowing who this man was, she began to feel fearful for her children, for this vigorous old man was the head of the family. What would he say to the ne'er-do-well gambler that was his nephew and her husband? How she wished that young Wang would return.

But dusk came and still he did not appear. She went into the kitchen and cooked the millet for supper; she carried a bowl of it to the old man, who continued to sit, sucking at his pipe, in the shop. When it grew late and he still showed no signs of moving, Ling An closed the shutters, brought him a quilt, and laid it on top of the counter.

'Has not my nephew Yung Fu returned?' he asked. Ling An busied herself with the quilt, too ashamed to answer him.

Young Wang stayed out all night. This was not the first time he had done so, and Ling An remembered that each time it had happened young Wang had lost heavily. Now surely there was nothing left to lose except . . . and of that Ling An dared not think.

Very early in the morning, even before the time of cocks crowing, there was a sound of brawling in the street outside. Ling An got out of bed, lit the lamp and went to the shop door, but the old man was already there. He opened it, and two men stumbled across the threshold; both were red in the face, and their breath reeked of the sorghum spirit they had been drinking. One was young Wang, the other a man whom Ling An had never seen before. Young Wang tried to push him out of the shop, but the other was too strong for him.

'It's mine,' he kept saying. 'It's mine. I've won it, and now I'm here I shall stay.'

He seized young Wang by the throat and began to throttle him. At this, the old man set upon the stranger, and with a vigour amazing in one of his age, pulled him away from his nephew, pushed him through the open doorway, and hastily put up the shutter in its place. Then he turned to his nephew who was sitting up on the floor, carefully feeling his throat. From him he turned to Ling An.

'Daughter,' he said, 'we will talk of this later in the morning.' And climbing on to the counter, he rolled himself in the quilt and went to sleep.

Ling An helped her husband to his feet and led him away to the room at the back of the shop. There, as she gently massaged his neck, she told him news which sobered him immediately. However, it did not keep him awake long, and as he slept by her side, Ling An went over the events of the day, wondering what would happen, and how she could meet this new set of difficulties which were about to arise.

The old man lost no time. When Ling An took him some tea in the morning, he looked at her with his bright penetrating eyes and said, 'Daughter, the city is no place for your husband. You must go into the country. There are fields and houses belonging to our family. You must go to one of those, and keep your husband out of the city.'

Ling An said nothing, knowing that those fields and houses had been gambled away long ago.

However, when at last young Wang was awake and in a fit state for a family discussion, it was found that there remained a few stony fields and a two-roomed house in the village of Li Chia Chuang in the East Mountains, so remote and worthless that neither young Wang nor his mother had been able to get rid of them. Young Wang was sullen and ill-tempered, feeling like a polecat caught in a trap and knowing that there was no way out. There was nothing left with which to gamble, and he had no doubt that with his uncle in charge this last gambling debt in which he had staked the shop would not be honoured: for the old man, as head of the family, considered himself the master and first holder of the property and declared that he had no intention of giving it up.

Later in the day, the man who had been thrust out of the shop in the early hours of the morning returned with two other men, who had been witnesses of his deal with Wang Yung Fu. The old man received them in the shop, alone. They stayed a long time talking, while Ling An and young Wang sat in the room behind the shop, Ling An working at her spinning wheel, and her husband sitting moodily in the chair by the table. The visitors at first were truculent and rude, shouting and beating their fists on the table; but as the old man remained calm and unperturbed, gradually the men lowered their voices, and Ling An and her husband were able to hear no more than a murmur of conversation through the mud wall and closed door of the room.

At last the men left, and the old man called his nephew into the shop.

'I have settled your debt,' he said, 'and it has cost me much good silver. This property is now mine. You will take your family to our land in the East Mountains. It is not right that the house should be untenanted and the fields left fallow. My son and my daughter-in-law and their six children will arrive in less than a week's time. There is not room here for us all, and you must leave immediately, either tomorrow or the day after.'

6

THE FARM

The wheelbarrow squeaked. In the pocket between the handles there was a little tin of oil for the axle of the wheel, but the squeak was part of the wheelbarrow, and so the oil was seldom used. Indeed, the sound was welcome to a lone barrowman pushing his load over the paths along the terraces in the high silence of the mountains.

Young Wang was not alone. Ling An, nursing the baby, sat cross-legged on top of half the family's bedding. An Mei, nursing her little sister, sat with her little brother Lao Erh on top of the other half on the other side of the barrow. Lao Da, harnessed to the barrow by a rope around his shoulder, steered their course ahead while his father pushed from behind.

They had been travelling since dawn, and it was now already noon. The easy roads through the loess fields of the plain had been left behind, and now they were beginning to mount to the pass. It was a long time since young Wang had exerted himself in such a way, and his pantings and groanings at times almost drowned the squeaking of the barrow. The children were delighted at this sudden change in the uneventfulness of their lives, but they sensed their parents' depression and kept silence.

Before nightfall they reached the pass and spent the

night at an inn beside the road, a little below it. The next morning they set off again, young Wang feeling stiff and sore, and so morose that none of his family dared to speak to him.

'One more day of this,' said Ling An to herself, 'and then what will there be for us at the end of the journey? Hard work there will be, but how can a woman expect anything else?'

So it turned out; for when in the afternoon of the second day they arrived at the tiny mountain village, young Wang, weary and stiff, flung himself on the ramshackle bed which, with a rickety table, was the only furniture in the house, while Ling An and the two oldest children, Lao Da and An Mei, first cleared the rooms of the accumulated dust and cobwebs of years and then unloaded the barrow and carried their household possessions into the house. It would be a rough life, and there would be much hard work, but this was the life Ling An knew, and she felt her spirit rise within her, toughening her will.

Something of the same thing must have happened in the heart of her husband, for the next morning he arose a different man, cheerful and talkative. He and Lao Da went out to look at their fields and returned for their morning meal full of plans.

By this time, the other villagers had become aware that the house which had so long stood empty was once again occupied; and although it was the first house at that end of the village, most of the women suddenly discovered urgent reasons for visiting the fields beyond it, reducing the pace of their hobbling heels as they passed the open gateway and staring into the courtyard. The children, of course, crowded in without the least reluctance, and what could be more natural for a mother whose child was in the newcomers' courtyard than to come in to take it out, scolding it for making a nuisance of itself and then apologizing to Ling An. From such a beginning all the necessary enquiries could be made.

Soon the whole village knew who the Wangs were and where they had come from, and all this was duly reported to the village elder, who put on his long padded gown. Being the fourth month, it was past the time for padded clothes, but it was the only long gown he possessed . . . He called on the newcomers late in the afternoon.

Young Wang's uncle had not sent them away penniless, nor without the materials and advice which his nephew, inexperienced in farming, needed for his new life. They had been provided with tools, seed and enough grain to last them until the crops they raised could feed them. There was even silver, secretly handed to Ling An to keep until they had arrived, enough to buy an ox and a wooden ploughshare.

The next three years were the happiest in Ling An's married life. Wang, too far from the city and his boon companions, settled down to regular work in the fields. The old man visited them occasionally and, mindful of his responsibilities, saw that they had enough to live on with even a modicum of comfort; and to Ling An's relief his gifts were always in kind and never in money. He had re-opened the butcher's shop, and once more the business had become prosperous, even more so than under his brother's management. He saved money and bought land. Pleased with his nephew's apparent reformation, he even talked of moving him to a better farm.

This, however, never came to pass, for one day of steaming heat in July he was struck down with a fit of apoplexy and died in a few hours. His son continued to keep the shop in the city for several months and then sold it in order to buy what appeared to be a better butcher's business in the capital city. There he speedily went bankrupt, and lost not only the business but his father's recently-bought land as well.

Wang now began to drop his reformed habits. With his uncle dead and his cousin no longer there, Wang began to pay frequent visits to the city, from which he seldom returned in less than a week. Ling An and Lao Da between them farmed the land as best they could; but what produce could be spared from family consumption, Wang took to sell in the city and squander in gambling and drinking. Once more he became moody and morose. On more than one occasion he returned with his purse full of silver and blood upon his garments. Ling An began to fear that she was yoked not only to a gambler but also to a murderer.

The other people in the village began to avoid them. Long ago some of them, returning from their annual trip to the city to buy implements at the great spring fair, had brought back rumours of Wang's gambling habits, and although it was never mentioned, everyone knew that Wang's uncle had sent him as far from the city as possible in order to prevent him from ruining himself and his family any further. During the years when Wang seemed to have settled down to be a good farmer, the villagers had gradually accepted him; but now there were other rumours about him which they did not like. Gambling was a vice, no doubt, as every ageing father took pains to teach his son. Did it not bring families to beggary? But murder was another thing, and a murderer and his family were people to avoid.

7

THE GREAT FAIR

It was the fifth month. Already the orioles were fluting their golden notes as they perched high in the sycamore trees around the village. In the early mornings as the sun rose up from behind the hills in the east, the young birds cried with that harsh, rasping sound which is like nothing so much as a rusty key turning in an iron lock. In their cry there seemed to be no promise of the lovely fluting notes of their parents. The three-knock-carpenters, as the country people called the woodpeckers, tapped up and down the tree trunks; azure-winged magpies scolded from the tops; swallows were back again, swooping over the ponds where the women washed their clothes; and the cuckoo called with his four mocking notes across the fields of rippling wheat. Children were sent to sit by the crop and watch it, instructed to run immediately to their parents should any danger threaten the ripening harvest from hostile neighbours or stray domestic animals. They sang to the cuckoo in a rhyming chant, translating his replies as they came:

Where are you, young wandering bachelor?
On the mountain.
What do you eat?
I eat stones.

What do you drink?
I drink mountain water . . .

and so on and on until the cuckoo, tired of answering, flew away.

As the sun rose higher, the shimmering heat increased until the blue of the cloudless sky faded to almost no colour at all. Mirages of silver water flowed in the distance over the flat fields. In the wide river beds, no water flowed over the sand among the boulders. Yet along the narrow paths between the terraced fields, the hardy summer flowers appeared: long arrow-leaved dog violets, wild gloxinias, long sprays of a tiny yellow rose, and a wiry daisy, bitter to the taste. As the heat increased, little boys were allowed to run naked except for a pair of shoes. Their thick cotton padded garments were put away in chests and cupboards awaiting the time when the women would have enough leisure to unpick them, wash them in the ponds, and replace the cotton wool which made them warm in winter.

There wasn't too much to eat: the winter's store of grain was running low, as it always did before wheat harvest. All eyes were upon those rippling fields which were the promise of many good bowls of porridge and piles of steaming hot bread. In the more distant fields, platforms with small shelters on them were erected, so that a man from the family which owned the field could sleep there at night, keeping his crop safe from thieves.

Then, before the final ripening of the heat, the great fair was held just outside the West Gate of the city. Here were sold all kinds of farm implements such as scythes, winnowing pans, baskets of all shapes and sizes, straw hats, ropes of many thicknesses, and everything a farmer would be likely to need for his harvesting then and later in the year.

The drapers who spent most of the year touring the villages set up their stalls, piled high with bales of blue cotton cloth, butter muslin, white long-cloth, and flowery prints for children's summer jackets and trousers. There were stalls which sold skeins of silk and paper patterns for embroidering shoes and babies' caps. There were crockery stalls full of rice bowls and cups — but no saucers, and very few plates. Heavy teapots, large earthenware bowls, and gaudy vases were ranged in rows upon the ground. There were stalls where strange medicines were to be seen in tiny brown heaps, which when people bought them were wrapped in little white paper packets, tied one above the other. There were goldfish for sale and seeds of all useful kinds, lemonade in shallow pans, steamed dumplings, roasted sweet potatoes, giant red haws candied and threaded on sticks, stacks of white steamed bread, and bowls of noodles to assuage the hunger and thirst of the throngs of peasants jostling each other in the narrow alleyways between the stalls. There were wineshops where men with faces red and congested, their eyes bulging like goldfish, downed minute cups of the fiery spirit made from the local sorghum. Noisy places these, and avoided by the women.

The space between the church and the city gate, ordinarily wide and empty to the sky, was completely covered with booths and stalls. People going into the church were obliged to elbow their way through the crowds of country people dawdling by the enticing goods which in this part of the fair were laid out upon white cloths by the roadside. Here were the sellers of sugar of all kinds, white and soft and damp like snow, yellow like sand, or damply stuck in a yellow-brown mass. Here were the sellers of beans and grain. A little apart sat the man who sold anti-scorpion powder, with a bowl of live scorpions (whose stings had been rendered harmless) in front of him. From time to time he took a few of them out and let them crawl over his hands, to the horror and amazement of the onlookers. Some of them bought a few ounces of the powder to put into little embroidered bags which they tied to the upper loops of their jackets or fastened on the outside of their mosquito nets, for it was a good medicine to keep away obnoxious insects.

Above this scene of humming activity the sun shone relentlessly in the cloudless sky. The air became drier and drier, paper curled at the edges, metal objects were hot to the hand, people grew thirsty. The sellers of hot water at a few coppers a kettle could scarcely boil enough water to keep pace with the demand.

There was free tea in the church compound, and those who took time off to venture through the gateway were thankful for it. To step into that gateway was to step into another world. First there was the glimpse of the gateman sitting calmly inside the room on the right, smoking his long pipe with its tiny brass bowl. On the left there was the bookroom where Bibles were to be bought, and penny Gospels, printed in characters large enough for elderly eyes to read, which was a good thing, for who else but an old man would have time to read?

Beyond the gatehouse a cool avenue of trees shaded a stone path to the church. Kindly-faced men and women came forward and conducted groups of country people around the church, explaining the pictures and the crucifix, the font, and the altar. Outside, some of the teachers and pupils sang hymns to native tunes. Bright pictures of strange scenes with people in foreign dress were pinned up on walls, and stories were told. Strange and wonderful stories they were, about the Old Heavenly Grandfather, something to think about as a person plodded home again in the cool of the evening. Some people who could read bought a penny Gospel in the hope of learning more; but few of these were women, for it was rare indeed if one of them was able to read.

Ling An had little time to spare, and how could the mother of five children hobble fifteen miles to the city on her tiny crippled feet, carrying a heavy child in her arms? In any case, why should she? She had nothing to sell and no money to buy anything with. No one went from the village, but they had all heard about the fair and its wonders. The cloth pedlars who lost their way in bad weather and occasionally spent a night in the village told their tales to the crowd who gathered to see them, but seldom bought more than a few strings of red cotton for the girls' hair.

This year the harvest promised to be good, and the family field rippled in the breeze: the spring rains had come at the right stage of its growth and lasted long enough to nourish the roots. Moreover the wheat was not yet ripe enough to tempt any of the neighbours to reap it in the owner's absence. An Mei was old enough to mind the younger children in the house while her elder brother watched the field. Wang counted the silver in his pouch, his share of the proceeds when he and his companions had set upon the rent collector in the hills, robbed him of all he had, and left him to die among the barren rocks. There was enough and to spare. He decided to go to the fair and take Ling An with him to help carry back the things he would buy.

They started in the early hours of the morning, a long while before the sun rose. It was cool then, and all their neighbours were asleep, so there was no one to see them go. With luck, when they returned, no one might know that they had been absent, nor where they had been.

It was hard going for Ling An, hobbling on the heels of her tiny bound feet in their embroidered shoes, behind the broad blue-clad back of her husband. There was no real road down the mountainside, and in the darkness it was difficult to see where to put one's foot. Moreover Wang was inclined to be impatient, and sometimes went ahead so fast that Ling An could not see him in the darkness. When they got further from the village, he called to her softly and waited for her to come up to him. She was glad to see the sun come up at last, but by then the village was well out of sight, and they knew that they could not be seen by any of their neighbours. It was easier to walk when one could see where to put down one's foot; but the sun grew higher and hotter, and soon the sweat was pouring down their faces and there were dark damp patches on the backs of their blue cotton jackets.

After an hour or two, they left the mountains and came to flat land and a road running through wheat fields that looked much greener than theirs; the stalks were longer and the grains in the ear larger and fatter. Now they began to see other people on the road, clad like them in blue jackets and trousers; but most of these peasants looked fatter and less wizened than either of them. There were women among them, but many rode on mules or were pushed along on wheelbarrows by their husbands, and very often there was a sturdy little boy pulling the barrow along in front.

When Ling An saw these little boys, her thoughts flew back to her children left at home. Would An Mei remember to keep the young ones away from the well? Could the elder boy in the wheat field keep their neighbours' oxen and mules out of it? Many were the stories she had heard to explain this child's crooked back, that child's blindness, and another family's poverty. As she plodded along behind her husband, her mind was a turmoil of anxiety; and if she had dared to leave her husband in the road, she would have gone straight back to her home and her children. But she did not dare, and soon, as she walked with the sun scorching her back and her feet aching so much that she seemed to herself to be nothing more than one enormous pair of burning feet, the anxiety in her heart was lulled and suppressed under the overwhelming effort she was obliged to make to keep up with her husband.

At last they came to a suburb of the city, a number of small mud houses clustered outside the gate which was set deep in the massive walls. There were soldiers on sentry duty there and others watching from the walls above. Wang, with the instinct of the lawless, avoided entering the city, although the road through it was the shorter route, for that road went straight through to the West Gate, where the fair was. He turned aside to the north and walked around outside the city wall.

Ling An was grateful for the narrow strip of shade from the great stone wall towering above her on her left. On her right there shimmered the brown water of the moat, bordered on either side by tall poplar trees. They were not alone, for many of those who came down through the east suburb preferred the cool shade of the path around the moat to the hot dry dust of the city street.

At last, when the sun stood as high in the sky as ever it would that day, they came to the fair, and almost immediately they were swallowed up in the mass of people swarming in the alleyways. Ling An pushed and panted behind Wang, thankful that he was taller than most of the other men around him.

In the middle of the fair they came to a fine gateway where at last the crowd was a little less dense. This was the entrance to the church. Here Wang paused. There were only two landmarks in that maze of booths, the West Gate of the city and the church gate. With his instinctive fear of authority, he avoided the city gate. The church gateway, which he assumed to be the entrance to the mansion of some rich landlord, would suit his purpose well enough.

Ling An was a hindrance to his progress through that hubbub, and if he lost her and had to look for her, there would be a delay in starting the homeward journey; and if she should be lost, there would be nobody to carry his purchases. So he stopped in front of the church gateway and told her to wait for him there. As she stood there uncertainly before him, some little qualm of pity for her moved him to suggest that she might look at the stalls near at hand, but not go so far that she lose her way back, and that she must certainly be standing there waiting for him when the shadow of the roof falling upon the threshold of the gateway told her that it was three o'clock in the afternoon. Then he strode off into the crowd and was immediately swallowed up.

Ling An stood for a while in the shadow of the gateway, feeling at first too tired to move. The hot water seller at her side was pushing the bellows in and out to blow up his fire. She would have liked to buy a cup of hot water, but she had no money, and as she watched him she grew thirstier and thirstier, till she felt that her thirst was more than she could bear. Just as she was turning to move away and go to look at the bales of cloth arranged on a high bench on the other side of the gateway, two country women came and stood in front of the hot water seller. One was fumbling in the knotted handkerchief which served her as purse for the coppers to buy them a kettle of boiling water and the use of two teacups standing on a rickety table by the wall, when the other one asked, why spend coppers on hot water when there was tea given away at the church? So she put the coppers back carefully, and the two hobbled on their heels past Ling An, through the gateway into the tree-shaded compound beyond.

Had they been grand ladies dressed in long narrow gowns, Ling An would not have dared to follow them; but although she recognized their superiority to herself, she could see that they were of her own kind. The shoes upon their feet were made of black cotton cloth and embroidered no better than hers. Their ear-rings perhaps had been more expensive, but their jackets and trousers were of blue cotton, although cleaner and much newer than Ling An's. So she followed them, thirsting for the free tea and hoping that what they said was true and not an idle tale and that there would still be enough left for them all.

It turned out that there was no tea left in the enormous teapot standing on the table just inside the gate, for the man in charge was just then outside buying another kettle of water to make another potful. As they stood looking at the empty teapot, a woman like themselves came down the path and greeted them.

'No tea?' she said, lifting the heavy pot and taking off the lid to peer inside. 'But it doesn't matter. I will give you some of ours. Come with me,' and she turned to lead them up the path and into a little yard which opened to the right of an enormous building that stood at the end of the avenue of trees.

'Aiyah! What a fine temple!' said one of the women to the other.

'That's not a temple,' said the woman; 'that's a worship hall. It's a church.'

'Aiyah! Truly it is!' said the first woman, not liking to show her ignorance.

'I'll tell you about it,' said the kind woman as she led them into a cool room with whitewashed walls upon which many brightly-coloured pictures were pinned with little brass nails such as Ling An had never seen before, 'but first we'll have some tea.' And she took a large teapot out of a padded basket where it had been kept warm and poured tea into four teacups set on a tray on the table.

The three women sat down on one of the benches which seemed to fill the room and drank the tea gratefully with suitable sucking noises. When they had finished, she poured another cup out for each and, although Ling An knew it would be polite to refuse, she was so thirsty that she accepted.

'How kind you are,' the women said.

'Not at all,' said the woman. 'The tea is provided by the church.'

'You are good,' the women said.

'The church is good,' said the woman, correcting them. 'But listen: you drink this tea now, but you will be thirsty again.' At this Ling An, remembering her second cup, looked down at the floor; but the woman continued.

'Yes, you will be thirsty, but the Old Heavenly Grandfather will give us the water of life, and when we drink that we will never be thirsty again.'

At the mention of the Old Heavenly Grandfather, one

of the women looked out of the doorway at the sun, high in its place at noon, and said, 'Oh yes, the Old Heavenly Grandfather, we know about him.'

'Yes,' said the woman, 'of course you do, but you don't know all about him, and many of the things you have heard about him are not correct.' She looked at the woman who had looked up to the sun, and said, 'You call that sun up there the Old Heavenly Grandfather; but he is not the sun. He made the sun, he made everything, he made you. Everything belongs to him. You belong to him too. He loves you.' With that she took a stick and, pointing to some large black characters written on a sheet of white cotton hanging on the wall, she began to sing in a high voice through her nose.

There is only one true God.
That is the Old Heavenly Grandfather.
He gives me food.
He gives me drink.
He is always taking care of me.

'Come along,' she said. 'Sing it with me.'

At that the women looked at the ground and said, 'We can't read; we've never been to school.'

'Never mind,' said the woman. 'I'll teach you.' And with infinite patience she began to teach them character by character.

Ling An looked at the Chinese characters. At first they all looked the same. Then she saw that some were simpler. 'Heaven' for instance had a lot of space between the strokes that made it, as well it might, for surely heaven must be a spacious place if more than the multitude swarming outside in the fair were to be housed inside.

But the character for Grandfather was so full of strokes that there was scarcely any space between them. It was easy to remember if you thought how old a grandfather was and how many hairs there must be in the beard that hung from his chin.

They sang the verse again and again until in the end, although none of them would have recognized any of those strange words if they had seen them elsewhere, except perhaps the one for heaven which was easy and simple, all three had learnt the little verse by heart. Then the woman stopped and poured out another cup of tea all round, and while they were drinking it, they said, 'What a fine voice you have, not like ours.' And she said, 'It is not so,' and 'You are quick to learn,' and standing up again she began to teach them the second verse.

This was not so easy. It began like this:

There is only one Saviour,
Our Lord Jesus Christ,
Who gave his life
To save my soul,
To bring me into heaven.

The Old Heavenly Grandfather everybody knew about, although nobody they knew had ever told them such things about him as this woman had; but none of them had ever heard of this 'one Saviour', this 'our Lord Jesus Christ'. Who was he?

As the woman pointed to the characters, urging the three women to sing until they had learned that verse by heart also, Ling An noticed that she glanced from time to time at the pictures pinned upon the walls, so she looked too; and although at first she could make nothing of the strange shapes and colours, which seemed to her untutored eyes to have no more meaning than the patchwork coats that were made for young babies to bring them good luck, gradually she perceived that in all of them there was one man who stood out as different from everyone else. Although his clothes were not the same in all the pictures, she could see by his face that he was the same man.

'There,' said the woman, stopping at the end of the second verse and pointing to this man in one of the pictures on the opposite wall, 'that's the one Saviour, our Lord Jesus Christ.'

'Truly it is,' said the other women politely, but they looked as though they couldn't see anything, as indeed they couldn't, being unused to the perspective and clutter of foreign pictures.

The woman perceived this, and saying, 'Wait a minute,' she went into an inner room, and came out with a small framed picture.

'There,' she said, setting it down on the table. 'This picture is easy to see. Look, this is our Lord Jesus, the Good Shepherd talking to his sheep. See how he loves them, and see how they love him.'

Ling An looked at the picture. It was a reproduction of a picture of Jesus the Good Shepherd by a Chinese Christian, an artist who worked in the style of old Chinese art. In that picture the Good Shepherd was Chinese, his features were Chinese, his hair and his eyes were as black as those of any of her countrymen. He wore ancient Chinese robes, but he was unmistakably the same man whose face looked out from all the gaudy-coloured foreign pictures around the walls.

The sheep were broad-tailed Chinese sheep, and they looked up at him and he looked down at them with such love between them that it seemed to stream out of the picture and to fill the whole room with that peace and stillness which no human heart can ever feel in any other way except upon that stream of love that flows like a river from the heart of God.

Suddenly the silence was broken by the sound of loud singing outside under the windows of the room where they sat. The two women got up to go, and Ling An, who felt she could have sat there for hours, was afraid that to stay there alone would be impolite, so she arose and followed them. Outside, a man in a long blue scholar's gown standing in the midst of a little group of schoolgirls was singing a hymn in a loud nasal voice, and all the girls were singing loudly and flatly but with great zeal. A crowd of country people stood around them gazing in amazement, as well they might, for the scholars were girls, and who ever heard of girls raising their voices in public! Moreover, their feet were big and quite obviously had never been bound, and all the women were thinking, 'How will they ever get husbands? What mother-in-law would ever welcome them into her household!'

But some of the young men standing there thought differently. 'A girl like that, able to read and write, might be a useful companion; and if a wife with small feet could work well, what couldn't one with large feet be expected to do?' However, there weren't many young men with such thoughts. Most thought it queer and unnatural that girls should have such freedom, and so they were something to avoid. Anyway, since none of them could choose a wife for himself, what was the use of wondering?

Ling An stood a while and listened; and then, as the people, tiring, moved away, she went too, and took up her vigil by the gate, anxious lest Wang should come and find her missing and start off on the homeward journey without her.

So it was that he found her, standing where he had left her, as though she had never gone away from the spot; and a spark of compunction pricked through his heart because he had enjoyed the sights of the fair and not a few cups of wine while she had done nothing but stand by the roadside waiting for him. So he said, 'Come, let us eat,' and he led her away to a stall where they bought two large round dumplings bursting with meat and a bowl of thick soup with lumps of beancurd floating in it; and having bought these, he had nothing left of the purseful of silver with which he had set out that morning, for in two short hours he had gambled it all away. There was nothing for Ling An to carry, for nothing had been bought; but she knew better than to ask questions when she already knew the answers.

So when they had eaten they set forth on the way back to their home, Wang walking ahead and thinking that it had been a day used to no purpose, and Ling An hobbling behind him, her heart full of new thoughts that would occupy her for many long nights to come.

8

THE LENGTH OF CLOTH

Ling An, sitting at the loom, looked across to the open doorway. From the shadow of the lintel which had crept beyond the threshold into the room, she knew that the sun was lower in the sky, and the time would soon be halfway between noon and sunset. Soon she must leave her weaving, take a handful of dried leaves from the heap in the corner of the yard, and make a fire to cook the evening meal.

Little enough there was nowadays for cooking, especially in the second month of the year, when even householders accustomed to plenty dipped carefully into their crocks of grain. All the wheat was eaten long ago, and most of the millet. There was still some corn, and of course the seeds of sorghum, but people didn't eat that unless there was nothing else. The ground was still frozen hard, and none of the weeds which would make a welcome change from the everlasting porridge were pricking through the iron soil yet. The fields were striped with rows of wheat sown last autumn, the blades so dark they appeared to be black. It would be several weeks before life crept into them again, and into the dry white blades of grass still standing at the base of the walls of houses. Then the colour would creep up through the blades like a green blush.

Ling An looked at An Mei sitting spinning in the sunshine by the open doorway. She was well grown now and could not be allowed out alone in the village street. Her long black hair hung in a thick plait tied neatly at the top and at the end with two strands of thick red cotton.

'It will be time soon,' thought Ling An, 'to start training that fringe back from her forehead.' For soon they must find her a husband and send her away. Was she not already sixteen years old? She should be betrothed to some decent young man who did not drink wine or gamble, a young man with only a few brothers, so that his share of the land would not be too small. It would be little enough, Ling An well knew, for An Mei would be dowerless, and her father's reputation was nothing to recommend a daughter-in-law to a young man's parents. However, she was a good girl, obedient and gentle, well grown, and able to hobble elegantly on her tiny bound feet. She was clear-eyed and rosy-cheeked. She could spin and weave cloth, dye it and cut out coats and trousers and sew them. She understood the culture of silkworms. She knew how to cook the plain food that farmers eat. She could tend children and look after animals, and she was strong enough to labour in the fields beside her husband.

Ling An thought, 'I have done well with my daughter.' But she was sad, because now that An Mei was useful and a comfort to her, she must send her away. Then she thought, 'But she is only sixteen, and that is young to be a bride; perhaps she can stay a little longer, now that Lao Da is getting so big and strong and so useful in the fields.' As she thought of her eldest son, Ling An smiled. A fine lad he was, broad-shouldered and tall like his father, and a good one for work in the fields. But for him, the winter wheat in the field outside would scarcely have been sown, for as he got older, Wang Yung Fu became more and more lazy. He lay abed long after the sun was up and spent most of his waking hours drinking and gambling with money which came from some strange source which Ling An could only guess about and which brought such thoughts of shame and fear into her heart that she lay awake sometimes in the night until the cock began to crow in the darkness.

Good! Lao Da was a fine lad, a son to be proud of. He would cultivate the fields and take good care of his mother while his father did nothing. If they got good crops, perhaps they could sell what they did not need and put money aside for a dowry for An Mei; and later they might buy back some of the fields that Wang had sold to pay for his gambling.

'Ah!' she thought. 'I wonder where that boy is now,' as she remembered that she had not seen him since the morning. So she said to An Mei, as she rose from the bench in front of the loom, 'Where is your brother?'

An Mei said, 'I saw him go out with our father, a while before noon, and they went in the direction of the town; but who knows where they have gone?'

Then Ling An sat down again, for she felt the strength flowing down from her heart and out of her body; for why else would Wang go to the town except to drink and to gamble, and why would he take his son, if not to teach him to do likewise? She was like a woman climbing a mountain, who within a few steps of the top slips down again.

For so it was. All through the slack time of the year, when there is little to do before the ground thaws, men lie abed till late in the morning to keep themselves warm. Later, in the middle of the day, they sit in the sunshine under a wall facing south, their thick padded coats open to let the sunshine warm their bare chests. They smoke their tiny pipes of tobacco, and sometimes press a child to the warmth of their bodies, the edges of their jackets drawn up around its neck, so that only its head sticks out.

Wang and his son would rise late and, having eaten their bowls of porridge, would walk away to the town and not be seen again until long after the sun went down; and sometimes it was midnight before they returned. But when the spring came and the villagers went out to work in the fields again, even Wang Yung Fu and his son stayed home for a while and worked, and Ling An began to take hope again.

The cloth she had been weaving was almost ready to cut from the loom. A fine piece of cloth it was too: two jackets and two pairs of trousers it should make for An Mei to take with her to her new home when she married. The colour was good too, the thread having been dyed a fine indigo blue before the cloth was woven; it should wear and wash well without fading. Next, during the hot summer months, after the wheat harvest was gathered in, she would teach An Mei how to weave a cover for a quilt in a chequered pattern of blue and white and black.

Gradually the sun grew hotter. Men's backs turned a bright copper colour as they laboured in the fields through the long hours of sunshine. Then the harvest was gathered in, the wheat pulled up by the roots, the ears flailed and winnowed. Everyone helped: even the smallest child who could walk was useful in some small way. When it was all gathered and stored away, the fields were ploughed again and sown with beans, peanuts, tobacco, sweet potatoes, carrots or cabbages, and in the fields where the soil was poorer the cotton flowers in their pastel pinks and yellows were soon in bloom.

It was a hot, still afternoon when Ling An cut the cloth from her loom and began to fold it, ready to put away in the chest in the inner room. Wang was sitting by the table, pressing tobacco into the tiny bowl of his pipe.

'That will make a fine gown for me and my son,' he said.

'I had thought it would make two jackets and two pairs of trousers for our daughter's wedding,' said Ling An.

'Good,' said Wang. 'If there is enough for two jackets and two pairs of trousers for our daughter, there will be enough for two gowns for me and our son. There is time enough to weave cloth again for our daughter.' Ling An folded the cloth and put it away in the chest, for if Wang did not see it, perhaps he would forget the gowns, she thought, and anyway why should he wear a long gown, setting himself up to look like a scholar, he who couldn't even read the character for 'Heaven'? But in this she was wrong, for in a day or two Wang asked about the cloth again, and whether she had cut out the gowns yet.

So there was no help for it. She took her scissors and cut the cloth and made two long gowns for her son and her husband, while An Mei wept over her spinning, for she knew that the cloth had been woven for her.

Then, on a bright summer morning while the sky was still blue in the early light of the day, and shadows lay long across the fields already green with the newly sprouting seeds of the autumn harvest, Wang and his son put on their new gowns and went off to the town.

An Mei watched them as they went, for she wanted to know where they would go. Anger was in her heart, for herself and for her mother who had spent long hours at the loom and now must do it again, weaving another piece of cloth, which perhaps her father and her brother would take for themselves again. So she watched them to see if they would go to the town, for if they did, her anger would be justified. From time to time she had to turn herself away to look at the cotton thread she was spinning; but again and again her eyes returned to the two blue-gowned figures of her father and her brother, growing smaller and smaller as they walked steadily along the rough track towards the pass; and there, when they seemed to be as small as two matchsticks, they disappeared down the other side of the mountain; and that was the last that An Mei ever saw of her father and her brother.

As for Ling An, she had not watched them go. She took a straw hat from the hook above the bed and a hoe from behind the door and set off for the fields. If Wang did not want to work and took his son away to play, then she must do what they were leaving undone.

When they did not return in the evening, she was not surprised, for they had often returned in the middle of the night. When morning came and still they had not come, she was not alarmed; but by the second evening, she began to wonder whether something had happened to them; yet she took comfort in the thought that they were two together and could help each other. In all her thoughts she was more concerned for her son than for her husband, for Wang had long ago destroyed what little affection there had arisen between them out of the life of daily hardships they had shared together; and so, while she thought of the mishaps that might have befallen them, it was for Lao Da that she felt the greater anxiety. If one of them must be killed by robbers or compelled to service in some warlord's army, let it be Wang, she thought. If Lao Da came back to her without the evil influence of his father, he would become once again the good son that he had been before Wang started taking him away to the town.

9

THE SOLDIER

The days went by, and they did not return; and now there fell a great disaster on the village, and it was Lao Erh and his second sister Anping, scraping dried grass from the mountain side above the pass, who saw it first.

As they looked across the plain stretching before them into the far blue distance, they saw what appeared to them to be an enormous black snake, winding through the fields towards the mountain. Their eyes widened in fear, remembering the stories of dragons told them by the old women of the village as they nursed their grandchildren while their parents were working in the fields.

They were too frightened to run, and as they stood staring in horror, they saw that what appeared to be the solid body of a snake was really a long column of men, marching relentlessly towards the pass. Picking up their rakes and their baskets, for these are remembered by the poor even in the extremes of terror, they fled to the village and told their tale.

Immediately the noonday somnolence was broken, and suddenly every household was bustling with activity. Anxious parents herded their marriageable daughters together and saw that they were taken away to the far side of the mountain and hidden in a place where it was hoped no soldiers would come. Crocks of grain and sacks of beans were hastily stowed away, clothes and bedding were packed into bundles and thrust among the rafters of the roof. Oxen and as many hens as could be caught were led away out of the village as fast as they could be made to go.

Lao Erh and Anping broke the news in their own house. Their mother had gone to the field to work, and only An Mei was at home, spinning and minding Anming, who was playing with a thin hungry-looking kitten in the yard. An Mei immediately sent the two children to tell her mother, one to run quickly, and one to follow with the ox. Then, having barred the door, she set about hiding their meagre store of grain. For she, like all the other villagers, knew that this column of men marching up the mountain must be a warlord's army or a horde of bandits. It did not matter which they should turn out to be. All soldiers were bandits and all bandits were soldiers, and their effect upon villages was the same. For at this time there was much unrest in China, following the death of the old Empress and the setting up of a new government under Sun Yat Sen. Warlords and their armies fought up and down the country ravishing the land and causing much suffering to the bewildered peasants who generally did not know what it was all about.

In this village An Mei knew that they would be the first family to be stricken, for was not theirs the first house in the village and the nearest to the pass? So she hurried, doing what she knew from old women's tales had had to be done in that village many times in the past, but so far never in her lifetime.

Having hidden the grain, she seized a quilt and began to roll up in it all the winter clothing of the family. She thought that she might be able to hide it under the bed, on the far side against the wall, and then if her mother did not soon get back, she would take Anming and flee with her to the field, before the soldiers came into sight.

Even as she was rolling the quilt on the bed, though a hole in the torn paper window at the side of the house she saw the first soldiers come over the pass and knew that it was now too late to escape. Most girls would have fled and been caught, for nothing moves a soldier to chase and capture more than something running away from him; but An Mei had heard tales, and she remembered and knew what could be done.

She unrolled the quilt and took out of it Anming's red padded jacket, and hung it outside the house on a nail by the door. Then she rolled Anming in the quilt and told her to go to sleep. This done, she crouched beside her on the bed, peering through the holes in the torn paper of the window. If they came to the door, as surely they must, she would mumble like an old grandmother and refuse to open it; but if they looked through the window, they would see she was nothing but a maiden, and break down the door; and what they would do after that she knew only too well. So, trembling all over, she seized the quilt from Lao Erh's and Anping's bed and wrapped herself in it, pulling it over her head so that her face was almost hidden. In the dark room, if she did not get too close to the window, perhaps she would not be seen too clearly.

This she had scarcely done before the first soldiers arrived in the village street. She heard them come to the door, their soft shoes stamping the earth. Then they hammered on the door, as though they would break it down, and shouted, 'Open the door! Open the door!' An Mei got off the bed and stood by the door and answered in a voice so thin and cracked that it surprised even herself, for fear had tightened the muscles of her throat and dried her mouth, so that she spoke like an old woman and had no need to act like one, as long as she could keep out of sight.

'Do you not see the red jacket of a child, hanging by the door?' she said. 'We have smallpox here.'

At that Anming began to whimper with fear. 'There,' she said, 'you have wakened a sick child. Go away.' The soldiers grumbled among themselves; one of them was for going in. He said he had had smallpox and was not afraid of it; but the others were afraid, and they said, 'It is only an old woman and a child. There are other houses, and if we do not hurry before our comrades come, there will be nothing left.' So they shuffled away in their soft shoes, down the dusty path.

But the man who had had smallpox stood on the stone lintel and waited a while, until he heard An Mei cross the room to the child on the bed. Then he stooped down, and cupping his face with his hands to keep out the light, he peered in through the crack between the folding doors and saw that it was no old woman who comforted the child, but a comely young girl. Nor were there any spots or scabs on the face of the child that was now crying too lustily for anyone weak with a fever.

Then he felt in his pocket for a stub of pencil, and wrote on the door in large characters, *Beware. Smallpox. Keep Out.* Then he set his seal below it. He walked softly around the house to the window at the side and found the hole in the torn paper; and putting his mouth to it he whispered, 'Do not fear, maiden. I will see that no harm comes to you. Keep the door barred, and do not open it to anyone.'

An Mei, with her arms around her little sister, stared at him; and then as he smiled to reassure her, she felt the hot blood rushing to her face, and bent her head to hide the blush; and when she looked again the man had gone. She sat still on the end of the bed, and listened as the soldier walked away.

But, she thought, what shall I do if they come here as they pass through the village? How long can I do this, without being known? But it turned out to be easier than she feared, for all the men recognized the sign of the red jacket and the seal and avoided the house.

As she sat there trembling and holding Anming close to her lest she should cry again, she heard the men shuffling past the house. The dust they raised in the road made a thick yellow cloud that began to come in through the crack between the two halves of the door. So thick and yellow it was that she feared at first that someone had set fire to the house and that it was smoke.

All through the village there were shouts and cries as the soldiers broke down the doors and foraged inside the houses for the hidden stores of grain and beans. Hens squawked in the road as soldiers chased them, and pigs which hadn't been driven off in time squealed as they were seized and killed. Dogs barked frantically as they saw the houses pillaged, until they were beaten and kicked to death.

Then, as the sun went down, the men gathered together in the pillaged houses and ate the food they had stolen, food which would have been life for several months for the families to which it belonged. Having eaten well, they settled themselves to sleep on the beds and on the earth floors of the houses, while their sentries paced around the village.

It was a dark night, and there was no moonlight. As Ling An crept over the stony hillside, she could hear no sound from the village street. A long time she waited in the silence, on the hillside behind her house, until she heard the sentry come to the end of the street and start on his return. Then she hobbled as fast as she could to the side of the house where the window looked out on the road to the pass and called softly to An Mei to unbar the door. Once inside, with the door barred again, they waited for the sentry to return. Then, as his soft footsteps faded away, Ling An leading Anming by the hand and An Mei following with a bag of wheat rolled in a quilt fled from the house to the safety of the hills.

But they had not gone unseen, for the sentry was the man who had had smallpox, Chang Pao Ying. He had seen Ling An slip into the house and knew from her hobbling gait that she was a woman and no doubt the mother of the girl inside. So, when he had paced a few yards down the street, he stood in the deeper darkness at the side of the road and watched them come out and disappear in the darkness.

10

THE VISITOR

The soldiers did not stay long; there was too little in that village to feed so many men for more than a day. So early on the second day they left, taking with them all the grain which they had not eaten.

The villagers, from their hiding-places on the hillside, watched them go, and when they were sure that they would not be returning, they crept back to the desolation of their houses. In most cases, there was nothing left; even Ling An's house had been ransacked after she had left it. Only bundles hidden high up in the rafters had not been seen. There was no livestock. Every pig and every hen had been eaten. Even the level of the water in the well was lower. No one had been killed and no young men had been forced into the warlord's army. No maidens had been molested, because all the village girls except An Mei and her little sister had got away in time, and even they had been saved by a ruse.

Ling An and her family were the heroes of the hour. The two little children had given the warning. An Mei had saved herself and her sister. And Ling An had braved the invisible terrors of darkness and the tangible danger of the warlord's army to rescue her two daughters. Yet although the villagers were thankful they were all alive and their houses were intact, there was scarcely anything to eat, and everyone would go short until the autumn harvest could be gathered in.

As the weeks went by, it seemed to be a doubtful blessing that they had all survived, for if there had been fewer to eat there would have been more food for each one who was left. The young men went away to the town to earn what they could, pulling rickshaws and pushing wheelbarrows and spending their strength in whatever manual jobs they could find. From time to time they returned to their parents, bringing what little food they could buy, and with it they brought news of the warlords' armies that were fighting up and down the country. Then parents looked at their daughters and said, 'Last time we were fortunate, and no harm befell our maidens; but what will become of them if another army should come this way again?'

So those girls who were already betrothed were sent away to their new homes, and for those for whom hitherto nothing had been arranged, middlemen were called in so that suitable husbands could be found for them. Although this was done for the safety and happiness of their daughters, there was benefit in it to the whole family, for it was customary for the bridegroom's family to give the bride's family a gift of silver, and with that, food for all could be bought to keep them alive until the harvest could be gathered again.

Now Ling An wished even more that Wang had found a young man to marry An Mei, for it was no longer safe for anyone in that village which was so close to the pass, and there was no man now in Ling An's family to protect his womenfolk and work for them when all their meagre stores had been taken by soldiers. Loath as she was to part with An Mei, who was a woman now and a companion to her, yet she knew she must do it for her daughter's sake. In the depths of the night Ling An lay awake, turning the matter over in her mind and wondering where she could find a young man who would marry a girl who had no dowry, whose father was a gambler and a drunkard.

One by one, the girls left the village, until An Mei was the only maiden left. Even little girls of thirteen had been sent away to their future mothers-in-law to wait in their homes until their future husbands were old enough to marry them. An Mei had no wish to leave her home and her mother and, although she knew of the danger, she did not worry about it; but sometimes as she sat spinning, she thought of the young soldier who had protected her and smiled at her through the torn paper in the window.

He had moved on with his comrades, and all that summer had fought many battles and pillaged many villages foraging for food. But when the plain was flooded and it grew near to harvest time, it was impossible to fight, and the men grew restive. And every day some of them escaped and returned to their villages. The warlord, thinking of the winter to come, disbanded all but a few men of his army and sent them away to their homes to help with the harvest, ordering them to return again to him in the spring.

Chang Pao Ying returned to his parents in the village across the river, which was fortified like a medieval castle; and great was the rejoicing when he walked in through the gateway, so footsore as to appear lame, late one September evening. For Chang Pao Ying was no professional soldier but the only son of his parents. He had been caught as he worked in his father's field and been pressed into the warlord's army when it had passed that way in the early spring. No one had dared to hope to see him again, and here he was alive and well and with all his limbs intact. His parents wept for joy, and all the village rejoiced with them; but they were afraid, for what had happened once could happen again and, if it did, could such good luck happen to them twice?

And so, a day or two later, his father said, 'Son, it is time to think of marriage. I am old, and I wish to see a grandson before I die, and your mother is too old to work in the fields, and she needs a young woman to serve her in the house.'

To which Pao Ying replied, 'Father, there is a maiden in a village in the mountains that overlook the plain. All the people there are poor, but she is strong and healthy and resourceful. Besides,' he added with a smile as he remembered, 'she is as brave as a tiger.' And he told his father the story of how An Mei had tried to save herself and her little sister, and of what he had done to help her. His father sat there listening, his finger on the tobacco in the bowl of his pipe, and his lips puckered around its stem, his eyes half closed as his mind assessed the virtues of this possible daughter-in-law.

'Well,' he said, 'and what is the name of this young maiden?'

'That I do not know,' replied his son, 'for I spoke to her only once, through the torn paper window, and she did not speak to me; but the village was the Li Family village, and this family only were called Wang.'

'Good,' said his father. 'I will make enquiries.'

So the weeks went by, and it was time for the autumn harvest. All the villagers went out to the fields and worked from the first light of day until the sun went down, and there were some who worked even after that. In every house someone was left behind to watch it. In some families an old grandfather or grandmother too old to work stayed behind, in others a few children were left to play in the courtyard; but in Ling An's house no one was left, for all were needed to bring in the harvest. Lao Erh and Anping did their best, but they were only children, and the strength of men was not yet in their thin brown arms, which were little more than skin and bone. So Ling An and An Mei laboured from morning till night. The harvest was poor, for the rains had come late in the season. On the hillsides most of it had flowed away in rushing torrents to the plain, where the fields had been flooded so deep that in some places only the sorghum, growing six or seven feet from the ground, was tall enough to lift the heads of grain clear of the water.

One September afternoon, as Ling An sat with her children in the yard, rubbing the grain from the cobs of Indian corn which they had gathered that day, the dog began to bark and growl in its throat. Then it ran to the gate and stood with its legs apart and its head thrust forward in the middle of the gateway, and barked until it seemed that its voice must come right out of its body.

Ling An rose from the ground where she had been sitting and, calling, 'Dog!' in a stern voice, she hobbled to the gate. There she saw a middle-aged woman neatly dressed in a blue jacket and black trousers and a black headband with a green jade ornament on the front of it around her head. She was carrying a staff in her hand, and the small embroidered shoes on her feet looked as though she had walked many miles over the dusty mountain tracks.

'Is this the house of the Wang family?' she said.

'It is,' said Ling An. 'Come in and rest a while.'

The woman came in while Lao Erh held the dog, and Ling An led her into the house and made her sit in the carved armchair at the left of the table, opposite the door, because she was a guest. Then she bade An Mei boil some water and, calling Anping, she found some coppers in the corner of her purse and sent her to buy some tea from the next house, which sometimes sold hot water and tea to the few travellers who passed that way.

The woman said, 'My name is Chang and I come from the Chang Family village beyond the river.'

'Aiyah!' said Ling An. 'What a long way to come. You have not walked, surely?'

'No,' said the woman, 'I came on a wheelbarrow which is waiting for me below the pass. I have walked only from the pass.'

'What about the barrowman?' said Ling An, rising from her chair to call Lao Erh to go and bring him to the house.

'Please sit down,' said the woman. 'Do not call him. My business is private, and I have come here quietly to talk to you alone.' At that, Ling An sent Lao Erh, who was standing staring and listening in the doorway, back to his work of rubbing grain off the corncobs. Presently Anping came back with a tiny paper packet of tea, and An Mei put it all into the teapot and brought it into the room. Ling An poured out a cup and gave it to the woman. She set it on the table and did not drink it.

'A fine girl that is,' she said. 'How old is she?'

'Seventeen,' said Ling An, as she tucked a raw carrot into the pouch of Anming's pinafore and told Anping to take her out into the yard.

'A well-grown maiden with feet like lotus buds,' said the woman, looking after An Mei as she walked out of the room.

'I see that she still wears her front hair in a fringe. How is it that she is not yet betrothed?'

'Times are bad,' said Ling An, 'and her father is away from home.'

'True it is that times are bad,' said the woman, 'and it is safer for a maiden in such times that she should be wed.'

'That's true,' said Ling An. 'But who will wed a girl who has no dowry?' For Ling An knew now why the woman had come, and she thought it would be well that the woman should know that they were poor and that An Mei could bring very little to her husband.

Then the woman unfolded the handkerchiefs which she had been carrying so carefully, and took out a photo of a young man staring straight in front of him with never a smile on his lips, and said, 'His name is Chang Pao Ying.'

'Chang Pao Ying,' said Ling An, 'Chang Pao Ying . . . I have heard that name before. Chang Pao Ying? Where could I have heard that name before?'

'On our doorway, Niang,' said Lao Erh, who had been standing unnoticed some time by the open door, listening to the conversation. 'One of the soldiers wrote his name on our doorway, under *Smallpox. Keep Out.* Do you not remember old Grandfather Li read it out to us, when we came back after the soldiers had gone?'

'So it was,' said Ling An, 'but doubtless there are many men called Chang Pao Ying. It is a common name. It cannot be the same man.'

'It is,' said the woman; and she told the tale of what Pao Ying had done for them on that night.

'Well,' said Ling An, 'it is a good beginning; but I must consider the matter. A thing like this cannot be settled in a day. It is my daughter's life that is concerned.'

They talked for a little while longer, and then as the shadows were growing longer, the woman finished the tea in her cup and got up to go home. Ling An called Lao Erh to look to the dog while the guest was going; but he was in the kitchen, telling An Mei all that he had heard.

11

THE PARTING

It was winter. The frozen ground was hard as iron. The camel-coloured fields were striped with rows of wheat which had been planted in October and, having sprouted for a few inches, had been frozen black when the frost grew strong in December. Now they could not grow above ground for a while, although their roots might grow beneath, but with the first warm rains of spring the green colour would come back into the leaves, like the blood returning to the cheeks of one who has been ill for a long time.

On the hills, the grass was sparse and yellow. Lao Erh and Anping, with their bamboo rakes and wicker baskets on their backs, were forced to go further and further afield in their search for fuel to cook the two meals of the day. There was seldom any snow, and when there was, Lao Erh and Anping with all the other children in the village went out to gather it in baskets and buckets and bring it home; for even snow had its uses in that mountain village.

The rivers and streams had all been dry since the summer rains had ceased, and the water in the village well was so low that there had been days when the villagers had been obliged to walk six miles to the next village for water, and there they had to pay for it. So when they awoke in the morning and saw the hills around them lying white under the leaden sky, everyone rejoiced. Now each could have a good wash, even clothes could be washed again, the animals could be given enough to drink, and nobody need trudge six miles to the well in the next village.

There was no ox tethered to the ring in the wall of Ling An's house to lie in the road chewing the cud. After the autumn harvest there had been little enough to feed a family, let alone an ox. There were taxes to be paid, and money to be found to provide the things which must be made for An Mei's wedding. So when she had ploughed the field for the winter wheat, Ling An had sold the ox. It was such an old ox and its bones were so near its skin that it hadn't fetched much money, and Ling An took comfort in the thought that if she hadn't sold it then, with so little to eat in the winter it might have died anyway, and then she would have had neither ox nor money. They had been sad to see it go, for it was nearly as old as Anming, and although it was only an animal, and so rated in their minds along with inanimate objects such as houses, chairs and tables, they had grown fond of it.

So the ox had gone, and now An Mei was going too. Although it was so cold, Ling An was up before daylight. An Mei was already dressed in a bright blue silk jacket which she wore over a red cotton padded one, the sleeves of which could be seen at her wrists. Instead of the gaily-embroidered pleated skirt which brides from more prosperous families wore, she had on a pair of scarlet trousers patterned with enormous peonies and huge daisies in many gaudy colours. On her tiny feet were shoes embroidered by her own hand, and on the table beside her was an embroidered headband which she would wear when Ling An had succeeded in putting up her hair into a flat bun on the back of her head. Into this were inserted the enamelled silver hairpins which, with the ear-rings dangling from her ears, had been a gift from her bridegroom.

The room was full of women giving advice, for An Mei's

abundant hair recently washed with soda did not take well to being pinned in a bun, and had to be done several times and well covered with gum before it would stay in place. An Mei said nothing. Her heart was too full of sadness. This was the end of her life at home. From henceforth she would not belong to her mother.

She knew little enough of her bridegroom, although in that she was more fortunate than most brides, for she had seen him, and knew that he was pleasant to look at. She had also heard him, for had he not told her not to be afraid? And from that she knew that he was kind; but what of her mother-in-law? What kind of woman was she who would control her now instead of her own mother? So she was sad and a little afraid; and then she was wondering how her mother would fare now that her daughter was leaving her, for in the last six months mother and daughter had grown very close to each other. Still, there were three other children to keep her company; but the two eldest of these, Lao Erh and Anping, scarcely ten and nine years old, were only children, and too young as yet to share their mother's fears and anxieties and give her the loving sympathy with which An Mei had comforted her mother since their father and their elder brother had left them in the summer eighteen months ago.

The women crowded around her. 'Ah!' they said. 'Good to look at! A beautiful bride!' and some of them joked about her mother-in-law; but most of them were kind, remembering their own sorrow when they had left their maiden homes. The bed was piled high with the thick cotton padded quilts which An Mei had made during the autumn. A red wooden bride's chest full of new clothes and embroidered shoes stood on the end of the bed. Two enamel bowls stood one inside the other on the table. In the upper one were gathered a teapot and four teacups and four rice bowls with four pairs of chopsticks. Into the lower bowl Ling An poured a few grains of maize, millet and wheat, so that it should not leave the house empty and, for good luck, that it might always hold plenty.

Now there was a shout outside, and the women near the door looked out and said, 'It's the chair.' And sure enough it was the sedan chair with its red curtains and two men between the poles, and with it a man with a carrying pole and two baskets to carry the bride's chest and the bedding.

Now Lao Erh went into the inner room where he slept and came out with his new black cap with a red button on the top on his head and a long blue cotton gown that came down to his ankles and made him look for all the world like a little scholar. Ling An looking at him felt her heart swelling with pride, and then the tears stung her eyes as she remembered her elder son, who should have been here to escort his sister to her new home instead of this child.

The room was full of bustle as the chest and the quilts were passed out and arranged in the baskets so that everyone they would pass on the road could see them. An earthenware pot of glowing charcoal was put into the sedan chair to warm it, a mirror was tied to a string around An Mei's waist. A red veil was put over her head, and she climbed into the chair and sat down. She lifted a corner of the veil and looked at her mother, and then down at her shoes to hide her tears. The curtains were drawn that no one might see her on the way. The men took up the poles, and Lao Erh took his place behind the man with the pole and the dangling baskets, bringing up the rear as the man of the family escorting his sister to her new home.

Ling An and the women watched the little procession until it reached the pass and disappeared over the other side. Anping leading Anming followed with the rest of the children until they were tired of running. Then the women slowly drifted away, and Ling An went back to the empty silence of her own house.

12

THE CHARCOAL FIRE

At last the long day was ending. The guests were beginning to go. Through the open doorway, the cold air flowing into the room was as refreshing as a cup of cool water from the bottom of the well on a hot summer's day.

Since Pao Ying had lifted the veil from her face and had led her to his parents to bow in respect, and the two had drunk together the cup of wine and had become man and wife, An Mei had sat in silence, listening to the guests and trying not to smile at the jokes which they made in their efforts to make her laugh. All the village had followed the sedan chair as it went down the street; and when it stopped at the bridegroom's gate, they had crowded so close to An Mei that only those nearest to her had caught a glimpse of her as she was led through the gateway into her husband's home. So then, eager to see more, they had thronged the courtyard, jostling each other in their eagerness to see the new bride who was to become one of themselves. One small child, carried in the arms of his mother, even poked a finger through the newly-papered window of the bridal chamber; but nobody saw this happen, and if anybody had, nobody would have been concerned, though two or three women following close behind made use of the rent in the paper to peer inside and exclaim to each other at the cleanliness of the room and the beauty of the quilts piled up on the bed.

It was to lead her to this room that Pao Ying said to An Mei, 'Come,' and she rose and followed him.

There were two rooms in the house on the west side of the courtyard, which were to be Pao Ying's and An Mei's home. The inner one was small and had only one small window in it. There was no door in the doorway between it and the outer room, but because of the intense cold a thick quilt had been fastened over the entrance. The window had been newly papered, and the cracks between the window frame and the mud walls had been neatly closed with strips of white paper. A bright picture of five rosy babies was pasted on the wall, and another of a cat gazing upwards at a mouse nibbling some grapes on a vine hung on the wall behind a small table. In the middle of the bed, the quilts were spread over an enormous wicker frame, under which there was an earthenware bowl of glowing charcoal.

To An Mei it all looked bright and cosy. How fortunate she was, she thought. She knew that she would love her husband and that he already loved her. His old parents too were kind, and she would have pleasure in serving them well. Oh, what a lot she would have to tell her mother when she paid her first visit home in three days' time!

Just as Pao Ying stretched out his hand to put out the lamp, he saw the rent paper in the window.

'Look,' he said, laughing, 'another window with a hole in it!'

An Mei smiled. 'But we must cover it up,' she said, and knowing the ways of village people, she added, 'because people will look in and see us in the morning.' So Pao Ying got out of bed and found a piece of thick paper, folded it, and tore it to the size and shape of the window pane, and pressed it against the wooden frame.

'There,' he said. 'There is no wind on this side tonight. It will last till tomorrow, and then I will paste a new piece of window paper in.'

On such small obstructions as this apparently trivial incident is the course of life deflected and sometimes dammed and brought to an end. Nobody knew that the charcoal had been made from the wood of the thorny date tree, and so while they slept, the room slowly filled with deadly carbon monoxide gas; and as no air could enter the room from outside, since the window and the doorway were closed and even the cracks in the wall had been stopped up, there was nothing else for Pao Ying and An Mei to breathe.

The family slept late the next morning, and it was winter anyway and foolish to leave a warm bed before the sun was high enough to take the chill out of the air; and who would want to disturb a bridal pair early on their first morning as husband and wife? So when the old parents and Lao Erh, who had been sleeping in their house, awoke, they did not disturb them. But by noon, when they had not appeared, and Pao Ying's mother with her ear close to the paper window could hear no sounds inside, she became a little alarmed, and sent Lao Erh to awaken them with a pot of tea.

This Lao Erh found impossible to do, and he came running in fear and said, 'They won't wake up, and their faces are as red as fire!'

The old parents did what they could, carrying them out into the centre of the courtyard where they could breathe the cold clean air, if they were still able to breathe. After a while, Pao Ying stirred, and a little while later opened his eyes, and although he shut them immediately in pain, they knew that he would live; but An Mei never stirred, and her eyes never opened again, and at last they knew that it was too late, and there was nothing more to do; and someone must take Lao Erh back to his home and tell Ling An what had happened to her daughter.

Then Pao Ying's mother lifted up her voice and began to wail, and all the neighbours came running to see what was the matter. The women vied with each other suggesting remedies, and many were tried, but none of them were any use, for what medicine is there that can bring the dead back to life again? So at last they stopped, and stood around in silence, shaking their heads.

Then Pao Ying's father said he would take Lao Erh back to his mother and tell Ling An what had happened to her daughter. So his wife paused in her wailing and opened a drawer and brought out her husband's padded leggings which were like a pair of trousers without a seam, made for ease in walking in a long padded gown, and bade him put them on; and as she was tucking in the ends of his blue ankle cloths, the neighbours stood around him telling him to be careful and to go slowly and to rest, and to remember the child if he would not consider himself.

Lao Erh, white and shaken, wept with his head in the bosom of a woman who had had many children of her own and still had love to spare for a strange child who needed to be comforted.

At last they were ready, and the old father stood up and tucked the front of his long gown into the girdle of cloth tied around his waist, and took his staff in his hand. The kind woman wiped Lao Erh's face with the sleeve of her jacket and bade him be a good boy and a comfort to his mother. Then they walked to the gateway of the courtyard; but when they got there, a sudden faintness and dizziness assailed the old man, so that he had to put out his hand and support himself against the wall. The neighbours crowded around and said, 'Old Brother! You must not go. You must stay home and rest,' and, when he would not be convinced, one of the neighbours said, 'Besides, your son may need you when he awakens fully and understands what has happened to his bride.'

And the old man thought, What if some evil should befall my son after we have saved him from this tragedy? What if sorrow should guide his hand to do harm to himself? And he thought of the well in the courtyard, and his son's sword hanging on the wall, and the block of arsenic in the shed against the east wall of the yard. So when his wife took hold of his arm and led him back to the house, he went with her and sat down on the chair by the table and sighed, for he did not know what to do; and Lao Erh stood uncertainly in the doorway and waited.

Then the headman of the village elbowed his way though the crowd in the room and stood before the old man and said, 'Elder Brother! I will take the child back to his mother and tell her what has befallen her daughter. You must stay here and take care of your son. It is better that such things should be done by a third party.'

All the villagers, when they heard this, said, 'You heard that, Elder Brother. It is better for you to stay here and take care of your son. Your wife has enough sorrow already without having you ill.'

So Pao Ying's father stayed; but not so much because of his neighbours' advice as because when he stood up the room reeled round him, and he could not walk without falling. His wife made him lie down on the *k'ang* and covered him with a quilt, patting it close all around him so that no draughts should get in between its heavy folds and his body; and a neighbour took some long dry stalks of sorghum and pushed them into the hole in the side of the *k'ang* and made a fire inside it to warm the bed; and while they were busy in this way, the headman took Lao Erh by the hand and led him out of the house.

As for Pao Ying himself, in the late afternoon he awoke and his head was clear; but his arm ached as it would ache for many days to come, where the dead weight of An Mei's head had rested upon it all through that night. Then, feeling the soreness of his arm, he turned, and not finding her there, he sat up suddenly and shouted for her. The old woman who was sitting by him and had had such experience in other people's sorrows as well as her own told him gently what had happened; and when in the strength of his grief he would have leapt off the bed and done himself harm, she forced him down with her old gnarled hands and bade him be quiet if he did not wish to kill his father, who was ill with shock and grief; for well she knew that a second sorrow can sometimes soften the first.

It was late in the afternoon when the headman led Lao Erh out of the house, so he took him to his own home and kept him there that night; and the next morning as soon as it was light they set off for Li Chia Chuang, Lao Erh's village. They got there about noon. Ling An was alone in the house, for Anping was away on her daily task of gathering dry grass for fuel on the bare hillsides, and her little sister was playing hopscotch on a neighbour's threshing ground with other little girls at the end of the village.

'Tomorrow, at this time,' thought Ling An, 'Lao Erh and An Mei will be back again, and An Mei will be telling me about her new home.' Even as she smiled at the thought, she heard Lao Erh's voice calling her, as he ran across the yard. Hurling himself into her arms, he burst into loud sobbing.

'What is it?' she cried. 'What is it? What has happened?' She pushed Lao Erh away from her and held him at arm's length, but he could not restrain his sobbing. Then she shook him a little, but still he could not speak. The doorway darkened, and she looked away from the child's face and saw the headman standing there.

'Your daughter, An Mei . . . ' he began, but Ling An knew what he could not bring himself to say.

'Oh my daughter!' she cried, and would have started wailing, but the man stood there silent in the doorway, waiting to speak, the tears running down his weather-beaten face, making two clean furrows through the dust of the journey.

She bade him sit down in the left hand chair by the table, sat down opposite him, and heard his tale; and when he had told all and there was no more to say, he got up to go, for it was a long journey back to his home. Then Ling An sent Lao Erh to buy some noodles and a small packet of tea, and when he had brought them, she went into the kitchen beside the house and cooked the noodles and made the tea, and brought them to the man and made him eat; and after that he bade her goodbye and went on his way.

Then Ling An brought a bowl of noodles to Lao Erh, but she would not eat any herself. She watched him eat, and then she heard his tale. It was the same as the head-man's, and so she knew that the story was true in every detail. She clasped him in her arms as he stood beside her, and the two of them wept together; and so they were weeping when the sun sank low in the sky and the little girls came home and found them. Then Ling An arose and cooked the evening meal, and Lao Erh besought her to eat, so she did for the children's sake, although the food was salt with her tears, and her heart was heavier than lead.

As for Pao Ying, in a few days he recovered his health of body; but his heart was so sorely smitten by the loss of his young bride that his parents feared that the deep melancholy into which he was sinking would lead him to destroy himself.

'I fear we shall lose our son,' said the old woman one night when she and her husband lay awake listening to Pao Ying tossing and turning on his bed. 'He has not slept for a week, and eats scarcely half a bowl of millet in the morning. If this goes on he will die of the Old Sickness.'

'True,' replied the old man, 'if he lives that long; but I fear he may kill himself in his grief, and then we shall have no son to carry on our family and to pay reverence to us and our ancestors when we die.'

'What can we do?' said his wife.

'In the morning I will tell him that his conduct is not filial. We shall see what that will do.'

However, the next morning, before his parents had had time to broach the subject, Pao Ying announced that he was going away again.

'Where will you go?' asked his father.

'I will join the Nationalist army.'

'Oh my son, are you going to leave us again?' cried his mother.

'Yes, Niang. There is no help for it. There is too much time for thinking here. It is so quiet and peaceful, and if I think, I grieve, and if I grieve I do not want to live.'

'I know,' said his mother, 'but all sorrows soften in time. You must be patient.'

'Let him go,' said her husband. 'Our son is right. It is quiet here. He needs a busier life to fill his mind. Let him go for a while. There are no wars now. There is peace. It is a good time for a young man to be a soldier. Let him go for a few months, and he will come back to us again and be a good son to us.'

So they let him go, although their hearts were heavy as they watched him walking away in the early morning light of the next day.

13

THE EVICTION

The great padlock on the door of the house was locked, and the key hung from the fastening of Ling An's blue jacket. They were all in the fields. Anming was gathering edible weeds that grew around the edge of the fields, and Ling An and the two older children were ploughing the field in which they would sow beans. As they had no ox, Ling An had harnessed the two children to the plough, and they were dragging it up and down the field as she pushed and guided it behind. When they began, they had laughed and played, lowing at each other like two oxen, nudging each other with imaginary horns, but now they were getting tired, and trudged across the field in silence. Ling An was thinking that soon they must stop for a rest. She knew that after half an hour on their backs in the shade of the cedar tree at the edge of the field they must all start working again.

Spring had come late that year, and the gentle rains that generally thaw the frozen fields in the middle of March had not fallen until the end of the month. So now all the villagers were in the fields ploughing. Great black heaps of dried night-soil which had been airing against the walls of the courtyards in the streets were disappearing as the owners spread the precious fertilizer over the fields. Beside those which remained, old grandmothers would be sitting, mounting guard as they wound the cotton they had spun from one spool stuck into the side of their shoes to another that they twisted in their hands.

The black heaps, the white cotton, and the blue jackets of the old women against the buff colour of the walls with the clear blue sky above made a picture of bright, sharp colours; but the man who came riding a mule down the village street had no eyes for that. At the gate of the Wangs' house, he dismounted and, having fastened his mule to the ring to which the ox had formerly been tethered, he pushed open the gate and went in. At the sight of the padlock on the door of the house, he hesitated for a moment, and then, clenching his teeth, he tugged at it with his strong brown hands, wrenched it out of the rotting boards of the door, and went in.

He glanced quickly at the room and the inner room at the left, and then went out to the gate and looked up the road. In a few minutes, two wheelbarrows appeared. On one side of the first sat a middle-aged woman, nursing a small child. On the other seat three children were sitting. The wheelbarrow behind was piled high with boxes and bundles. The barrows were being pushed by two stalwart young men who were so like the man standing in the gateway that anyone could see that they were his sons. A little way behind them, a third son led an ox. They all turned into the gateway, and then the man barred the gate from the inside, so that none of the old women, who had left their heaps of night-soil when they heard the squeaking of the wheelbarrows and gathered on the other side of the road opposite the house to watch these strange goings-on, were able to see what went on inside.

The man and his wife and his three sons went into Ling An's house and, having gathered all that they could find, made a heap of it by the gate; and when nothing more was left, the three sons opened the gate and put the things outside in a pile against the wall of the yard, while the man and his wife unloaded the wheelbarrow and took their own things into the house. Soon there was the smell of smoke as the woman set about making a fire to cook a meal.

Up to this moment, none of the old women had done anything but stare. They were all of them well advanced in that process of withdrawal which eases the sorrow of final departure. They stood together, watching, as in their young days they would have stood watching the performance of a play put on by a troupe of travelling actors, if by chance any should ever have come by that village. What they saw was interesting, but nothing to do with them. As they stood there gaping, with the spools of cotton twisting endlessly in their gnarled brown hands, Lao Erh, who had been sent back to fetch a pot of cold tea from the house, came running down the street, the key of the padlock dangling on a string from his hands. He pushed at the gate, expecting it to open. Then, unable to believe that it could be barred, he pushed again. It would not open. He turned and looked at the old women staring at him.

'What is it?' he said.

The old women stared and said nothing, and the white spools twisted silently in their fingers. Then Lao Erh was afraid, and turning from them, he ran up the street to tell his mother. The old women waited.

In a little while Ling An and the children appeared at the end of the street. When she could not open the gate, she banged on it with her hands and called, 'Open the gate!' but no one opened the gate. Anping and Anming began to cry; but Lao Erh climbed on to the back of the mule tethered to the ring in the wall and, reaching up, hooked his hands to the top of the wall, drew himself up, lay flat, and looked over into the courtyard of his home; and he saw the ox and the two wheelbarrows standing and the children playing and the man and his wife and their three sons coming and going into the house and about the yard as though it belonged to them. He climbed down and told his mother what he had seen, and then Ling An and the three children beat with their hands upon the gate and shouted till they were hoarse.

But no one would answer them and nobody came to the gate. Only the old women stood in silence, winding their white cotton thread. Only Lao Erh thought of the mule, and he untied it and led it up and down the road and Ling An shouted, 'Take the mule. That's right take the mule!' and the mule, disturbed by the hubbub, began to bray with the ear-splitting sound that only a mule can make. Then the man, cursing himself inwardly for having forgotten to take the mule inside, opened the gate and came out. He jerked the bridle out of Lao Erh's hand and pulled the mule in through the gateway, while his sons and wife stood watching him.

Then Ling An said, 'Let me come into my house. Who are you, and what are you doing here?'

And the man said, 'The house is mine and the land is mine too. Your things that were in the house are there by the wall. Take them and go away.'

Then he shut the gate, and Ling An heard the bar drawn across it, and the soft sound of their footsteps in the dust as the man and his family crossed the yard and went into the house.

Now anger swelled up in Ling An's heart, and she began to curse the man and his family in a loud voice as she paced up and down the street by the wall of her own courtyard. The little girls sat in the shadow of the wall and cried softly in terror; but Lao Erh found a rough place in the wall on the east of the yard, and lay flat on the top and pulled off little bits of mud and plaster and threw them at the man and his family when any of them came out into the courtyard.

So Ling An paced up and down cursing loudly until the sun went down and the villagers came home from the fields. Then she went to the headman and told him what had happened, and he came and called 'Elder Brother!' politely at the gate.

The man came out and bade him come inside, but as he barred the gate again, Ling An was not able to get in with the headman. After a while he came out, and Ling An knew by the look of him that he had nothing good to tell her.

'Elder Sister,' he said, 'the house and the land are no longer your husband's. They belong to this man.'

'How can this be so?' she asked.

'Your husband owed this man's father much money.'

'How could he?' said Ling An.

'Did not your husband gamble?' said the headman. 'Was he not fond of wine? Did he not spend all his days in the city?'

'Yes,' said Ling An, 'it is true. But he has been gone now with my son for over a year. If he owed this man money, why has he not come to claim it before?'

'Elder Sister,' said the headman, 'it was not to this man that he owed the money. It was to his father, and he was an old man and he has been ill for many months, and latterly he had become a child again in his old age. But now he is dead, and this man, his son, who was away from his home, has come back and found there is nothing for him to inherit but what was owing to his father. He has shown me the bill. There is nothing we can do.'

'I will not go,' said Ling An.

'Yes,' said the headman, 'you must go. Your husband owed more than the value of the land and the house. Have you not two little girls? You must go before he thinks of taking more from you, for I can see that he is a hard man with a heart like a pig, and he will have no mercy.'

When she heard that, Ling An felt her heart drop in her body like a ball of lead, and the strength flowed out of her soul like blood from an open vein. She loaded the bag of beans and millet on her back and bade the children pick up the quilts and the kettle and the bowls and the teapot and the rest of their few possessions; and then, clutching the cooking pot to herself, she and the children slowly went up the street towards the pass; and so they left the village.

The headman stood in the road and watched them go. He would have liked to have given them shelter for one night; but if he did that, how would he send them away in the morning? It was better not to begin something which he could not continue. Besides, there were the little girls. So he went home and told his wife; and she said, 'Well, Wang was not one of us anyway, and we are well rid of such a family.'

'But his wife and the children have done no harm,' said the headman, 'and in the summer when the warlord's men were here, the children were the ones who gave us the warning.'

'Well, and what if they did?' said his wife. 'Did not the eldest daughter marry one of the soldiers? They were in league with them, you can be sure. We are well rid of such people.'

'Well, it may be as you say,' replied her husband. 'But how do you know that this man is any better than Wang?'

'At least he is not as poor,' said the woman. 'Has he not an ox and a mule and two good wheelbarrows, and three grown sons to work for him? How long do you think those Wangs could support themselves without borrowing from us and never paying back. It is a pitiful thing, but there is no help for it. Do not fret yourself.'

The headman put a pinch of tobacco into the bowl of his pipe, and sat and puffed at it two or three times until it was spent, and wondered what Ling An would do. By the end of the summer, after the locusts and the hailstorm and the bandits had been, he had no room for Ling An in his mind because his own troubles filled it.

14

THE INN

The midday sun was high in the sky, and although they were still among the hills and high above the plain, there was no wind to temper the heat. They were all hot and thirsty. Here there were no villages where there might be wells of cool water, and the watercourses were all dried up again after the brief spring rains. At first the children, like any others, had enjoyed the novelty of sleeping on the open hillside and helping their mother cook on the stoves they made with stones and earth; but now the novelty was beginning to wear off. They were tired of climbing up and down the everlasting hills. They were hot and thirsty, and the bundles they carried seemed to get heavier the further they went. How nice it would be to get to their mother's old home and see the uncle and all their cousins whom they had never met.

Ling An would not answer their questions. All she would say was, 'Wait until we get there. Then you will know.' In fact she could not tell them very much, for she herself had never returned to her maiden home since An Mei had been a year old, and that was sixteen years ago; and during all that time she had heard no news of her brother.

For all she knew he might have died many years ago.

Even if he were living still, she was not sure that he would welcome her, especially now that she was bringing three children with her. After she had left her parents' home a girl no longer belonged to it. But where else could Ling An look for help? At least the little girls would be safe in that place, for no one would dare to come near it.

They were approaching the brow of a hill, and to encourage the weary children Ling An said, 'When we get to the top of the hill we will all sit down and rest.'

And Lao Erh said, 'Good. I can see two cedar trees. We can sleep in the shade.' When they got there, they threw themselves down in the shadow of the trees and all lay silent for a while.

Then Lao Erh, with the resilience of childhood, stood up and looked down the road on the other side of the hill. It looked almost the same as the road they had already traversed . . . no more than a rough stony track just wide enough for a cart. On either side of it the dusty hills, sparsely covered with grass, rolled away to the hot colourless sky. There were no patches of cultivation and no signs of human habitation, except one lone hut with a tree behind it and some low stone walls surrounding a few barren-looking fields, just below the brow of the hill.

'Niang,' he cried, 'look, there's a house down there! We could get some water.'

Ling An sat up, leaned on her elbow, and looked. 'Good,' she said. 'You and Anping take the kettle and go and ask for me.'

In a little while the children came back swinging an empty kettle. 'Niang,' they said, 'there is nobody there; but the place looks like an inn.'

'Perhaps they are out in the fields,' said Ling An, standing up and scanning the hillside. But she could see nothing but the heat shimmering over the dry land.

'If there is a house there, there must be some water somewhere. We will go down and see.'

So they gathered up their bundles and went down the

track to the house. Alongside the little stone-built house there was a lean-to shed, open to the road. In it there were some rough wooden benches and a few rickety tables at the end furthest from the house. Against the wall of the house there was a stove made of dried mud, with a box-bellows at one end, and several holes for kettles and pots, and a large hole with a pan over it for cooking grain. There was no fire in the stove, only ashes under the kettles, which were still warm.

'Is there anyone at home?' called Ling An; and again, 'Is there anyone at home?' as Lao Erh and Anping ran round to the back of the house.

As Ling An stood uncertainly in the shed, the children came back. 'Niang, there's a dead dog covered with blood at the back,' they said. Ling An felt the hair rising on her head. There was something strange in the silence.

'Come!' she said. 'Let's go!' And as they picked up their bundles she heard someone groan in the little house.

Fear fastened their feet to the ground. Their hands seemed to freeze stiff on the bundles; and as they waited, they heard the groan again. Then they fled from the place.

A little way down the road, they all paused for breath.

'Niang?' said Lao Erh.

'Yes, my son,' said Ling An.

'Was there someone there?'

'Yes, I think so,' she said.

'Was it a ghost?'

'I don't know,' said his mother.

'Let's go!' said Lao Erh.

Suddenly Ling An was aware of a strange compulsion to do something contrary to that which her whole being desired. Now, in fear for herself and for her children, she wanted only one thing: to get away from that place as fast as their legs could carry them; but she felt compelled to return to the house. Fears of ghosts and demons were uppermost in her mind, but her common sense told her that there could not have been a dead dog behind the house unless there had recently been someone in the house to whom the dog belonged. So, telling the children to stay where they were, she took the kettle and went back to the house.

Again she called at the doorway, 'Is there anyone in?' From the inside of the house there came a faint sound of groaning. Her knees felt like water, and her hands shook so that the lid of the kettle began to rattle in its hole, but she crossed the shed and looked into the house. It was so dark in there, and her eyes were so accustomed to the bright light outside, that at first she could see nothing. Then slowly the darkness cleared, and she saw something lying on the floor of the room. It was an old woman, her grey hair dyed red with the blood from a gash on her head.

'Aiyah! What has happened?'

The old woman opened her eyes. 'Bandits,' she said.

'Where?' said Ling An.

'Gone,' said the old woman.

'Where are the rest of your family?' asked Ling An.

'There is only me,' said the old woman.

'What!' said Ling An. 'Are you all alone in this place?'

'My son went away a long time ago, and my daughter-in-law died.'

'Aiyah! It is pitiful,' said Ling An. 'I will help you; but first I must call my three children who are waiting down the road.' So she went to the door and, as luck would have it, saw Lao Erh standing in the road close to the place where she had left them and looking towards her. It was not long before Ling An had the little girls sitting on the benches in the shed, while she and Lao Erh lifted the old woman on to the *k'ang*, and washed the cut on her head, and bound it with a towel which she found hanging from a nail by the window.

Then she went into the shed and lit the fire while Lao Erh pushed the bellows. When the kettle was boiling, she made a pot of tea, took a cup of it to the old woman, and lifted her up so that she could drink it. After that she washed the dirty cups on the rickety tables and poured tea for the thirsty children and herself. As she sat sipping the hot tea she thought that there was only one thing to do for that night at least. A person could not leave an old woman who was so weak from loss of so much blood. Bandits who had already been there that morning would not be likely to come there again; whereas if she and her children journeyed on, they themselves might fall into their hands.

She set about making the evening meal, and when they had eaten, she spread the quilts for the children on the two beds in the inner room; and then as the day grew dark, she lay down on the *k'ang* beside the old woman and slept.

The wound on the old woman's head took a long time to heal, and when, at last, after several weeks, she was able to climb down from the *k'ang*, there was so little strength in her legs that she was glad to lean on Lao Erh's shoulder and totter into the shed to sit for a while in the morning sunshine. She could do no work, and it was doubtful whether she would ever again be strong enough to run the inn and till the stony fields behind the house.

This she already knew in the depths of her heart, and so she was glad when Ling An showed no sign of leaving her. For Ling An had known, when she awoke on the first morning, that it would be many days before the old woman could be left alone again. So she had stayed and done what she could to keep them all from starving. She had found an old plough in the guest-room at the end of the shed, and with Lao Erh and Anping pulling it she had ploughed the stony fields and sown them with beans, sesame, and corn; sweet potatoes and carrots; cabbages and radishes; and even a few seeds of the cotton plant in the poorest soil where little else would grow. If they could keep themselves alive through the summer, there should be enough to keep them through the winter.

The road was a lonely road. Few travellers came that way, but when any did, they always stopped, because it was the first inn they had come to for many miles, and they knew that there were still more miles ahead of them before they came to another. So they stopped, called for tea for themselves and water for their mules, and rested their feet for a while. Most of them were people well known to the old woman: pedlars travelling from one tiny hamlet to another and poor farmers from the villages returning from the markets and fairs of the little towns at the foot of the hills.

Seldom did any strangers come to the place, and even less often was the guest-room at the opposite end of the shed occupied at night. For the surrounding hills had a bad reputation, and all travellers, in fear lest they should meet bandits and be robbed not only of what money they might have but even of their lives, hurried on to the ends of their journeys. There were even days when no one passed by, and the dusty track stretched dry and deserted across the hills from one pass to another.

Even so, there was one stranger who came by that summer whom Ling An was never to forget. It was June, and the sun was so hot that all the colour was burned out of the cloudless sky. The green tinge on the hills which had followed the spring rains had long ago turned to yellow. The children went out every morning and raked the grass and brought it back to be stacked in a great pile behind the inn. This was their only fuel, and it was used sparingly for cooking and boiling hot water for tea.

Although few travellers came that way more fuel was required than would have been used for an ordinary household; so when there was nothing else to do and Anping and the old woman were spinning while Ling An and Anming were weeding the crops in the fields, Lao Erh was often on the hills until late in the evening, raking the grass and tying it into a huge bundle which he carried across his back.

One evening, while still some distance from the inn, he came down from the hillside to the road, and there by the roadside he found a young man sitting with his back propped against a boulder. His face was as white as paper, and the ground beside him was red where his blood had soaked into it. At first Lao Erh thought that he must be a victim of the bandits, and his first instinct was to flee away as fast as he could; but as he stood staring the young man smiled and said, 'Is there still anyone in the inn by the pass?'

'There is,' replied Lao Erh. 'I live there.'

'Then I will come with you.'

Lao Erh, pointing to the red stain in the earth, said, 'But are you not hurt?'

'No,' said the young man, 'that's nothing. It's my cough.' And saying that, he coughed again and spat more blood on to the earth. Then he got up and began to walk slowly along the road with his hand on Lao Erh's shoulder; and so after a little while they came to the inn, and by that time it was already dark.

The young man slept in the guest-room that night and three nights after, for in the morning when he did not get up Lao Erh was sent to waken him, and he found him still in bed and his face flushed red with fever. When in a little while he got up and sat at one of the rickety tables, he looked so thin and ill that Ling An besought him not to continue his journey until he had rested a few days. As it happened he could not have gone very far, for that very same morning it began to rain heavily and did not cease for three days. He said he was a student and that he was going home to his parents because he had been ill. The old woman was sorry for him, but she was glad too that he stayed, for she needed money to buy tea from the pedlar the next time he passed by.

There wasn't much to do through the long summer days. The women and Anping had their spinning and weaving, but Lao Erh could not go out to gather grass on the hills while it rained so heavily. The young man took books out of his bundle and sat at the table reading them. He also had an inkstone and a brush, and sometimes he sat writing characters on yellow paper ruled from top to bottom with red lines.

Lao Erh stood by the table, fascinated by the strokes and hooks that came off the tip of the brush in the long fingers of this student. After a while he took a twig from the heap of fuel by the stove, and stooping down by the table, he began to copy the young man's writing in the dust of the earthen floor. When the student saw this, he laughed until he coughed and spat on the floor, and when he had rinsed his mouth with the cold tea left in his cup and spat again he took out a sheet of paper and another brush, gave it to Lao Erh, and showed him how to write 'man' with two strokes, and then how to make 'man' into 'big' with a third stroke across the middle, and then how to make 'big' into 'heaven' with another stroke on the top of that.

'You see,' he said, 'heaven is greater than man.'

When Lao Erh, with his tongue between his lips, had written all three characters, he took the paper to his mother and said, 'Niang, look! Man, big, heaven. Heaven is greater than man.'

'So it is! You'll be a scholar yet, my son.'

And the old woman mumbled, 'Heaven is greater than man. So it is. Heaven is greater than man.'

So Lao Erh went back to the table, and all that day and for three days after, he sat opposite the young man learning more characters and listening to the tales that the student told him between bouts of coughing and spitting.

On the fourth day, the weather cleared. The sun came out, and soon the steamy air was rising hot and heavy from the ground. The young student tied up his bundle of books, and paid his bill, and said, 'I will see you again,' and set out for his home; and what became of him they never knew, for they never saw him again; but Ling An was to remember him with sorrow for ever after.

For he had not been gone for more than a few weeks when Lao Erh began to shiver and shake in the fierce heat of July, and at night he would burn with fever, and waken in the morning bathed in sweat. The old woman pounded herbs to powder which she seethed in boiling water and gave him to drink; but nothing would quench the fire of the fever that was burning him up and melting all the flesh from his bones, so that in two weeks there was nothing left but skin stretched tightly across them. His once so merry little face was all eyes and teeth, and his arms and legs were scarcely thicker than stalks of sorghum. The travellers who passed by recommended many remedies, and one who stopped on his way into the town brought back medicines in tiny white paper packets from the medicine shop on his return journey.

Lao Erh swallowed them all, but none of them did any good. What could be the matter with him? There were no spots on his skin as there should have been if he had been attacked by any of the seventeen kinds of measles, nor had he the white skin inside the throat which was the dreaded sign of the diptheria that people called white-throat. The travellers shook their heads and said, 'It is Old Sickness, and there is no cure for it,' and Ling An remembered the young student and his racking cough.

Everyone said, 'Rest is a good medicine,' but they could not keep him in bed, and as long as he got up and moved about, and insisted on gathering grass although he hadn't the strength to go further than a few yards from the house, Ling An was hopeful that he would take a turn for the better; and to encourage her the old woman had many tales to tell of such sudden cures. But there came a day when Lao Erh could not rise from his bed. He stared wildly at his mother as though he did not know her.

Then the old woman said to Ling An, 'There is an old woman in the village of my maiden home. She is very skilled in curing the fevers of children by piercing with needles and pinching the flesh so that the demon which causes the sickness flies out in terror, and the child recovers. As no other remedies are of any use, would it not be good to try hers?'

The village was five miles away in the heart of the hills. So the next morning Ling An rolled her son in a thick quilt, and carrying him in her arms, she started her long walk over the hills. The ten-year-old boy weighed little more than a child of two years, and so, in spite of the heat, Ling An was able to walk at a good pace. By noon she had reached the village and was soon shown the old woman's house.

When the woman saw the child, she said that she did not think she could do any good; but when Ling An besought her with tears, she took out her needles and thrust them into Lao Erh's body, and gathered up the skin of his neck and pinched it so that large red patches appeared. She then pasted some thick black ointment on to pieces of black paper and stuck them on to his chest and back; and with that she said she could do no more. So Ling An thanked her, paid her the few coppers she asked, and started the long journey home.

When they were a mile from the inn, the sun was low in the sky, and Ling An's arms were weary; so she laid Lao Erh in the quilt on the grass and sat down beside him. He seemed better: there was recognition in his eyes when she looked at him. Perhaps, after all, he would recover. It was a quiet lonely place where they were. There were no trees, nothing but stones and sparse tufts of grass on the rolling hills. They could see the sun sinking like a great ball of fire in the sky. Their shadows were long and black on the grass. Lao Erh watched it as it sank slowly behind the hills, and the quiet sky grew bright with sunset.

'Heaven is greater than man,' he said, and turned to his mother. 'Love me, Niang! Love me, Niang!' he sighed, as if he knew that her love had power to keep him. She gathered him in her arms, and together they watched the colour fade from the sky; but all the human love in the world was powerless to keep Lao Erh now. So, with his mother's arms about him on the bare hillside, his brave little soul sped away, and Ling An was left desolate.

15

THE ORPHAN

Many miles away in the heart of the mountains there had been a village in a valley. Fifty or sixty years before, in a time of great unrest, the time of the T'ai P'ing rebellion, the villagers had built themselves a refuge on the top of a neighbouring mountain. The summit was ringed with a strong stone wall, and inside it each family had built its own hut of stones loosely piled on top of each other. From the distance, the mountain seemed to be wearing a crown made of grey stones, and it was not easy to see the narrow slit in the wall which was the only entrance.

There the villagers had taken refuge when the rebels had come and camped in the village at the foot of the mountain. Safe they had been behind their wall; but there is usually no water on the tops of mountains, especially in the winter, and soon all that they had was finished. Those who sallied forth at night to replenish the water pots were killed one by one by the soldiers waiting for them below.

The few gaunt women who survived the siege found nothing left in the looted village when they returned. Even the seed corn had been eaten by the soldiers. None of the women lived to see the spring, and from that time the village had been uninhabited. The roofs of the houses fell in, doors were blown down in the spring gales. Rain poured on to the floors of beaten earth and softened them in summer, and weeds grew up and filled the rooms waist high between the walls. The few travellers who passed that way hurried through its eerie silence in fear. There were some who were reported to have seen two or three haggard women in old-fashioned jackets washing clothes in a pool among the rocks. These, when addressed, had faded away before the travellers' eyes. In short, the village was said to be haunted, and was better avoided by all sensible people.

Now, after a generation had passed, there was unrest again. North was fighting South. Warlords and their armies raged up and down the land, ravaging the villages, plundering the fields, condemning the population to starvation and death.

Here, like a dog seeking a quiet place where he can rest alone, lick his wounds, and recover from a fight, a defeated warlord and his men sought shelter. They occupied the mountain refuge and the deserted village below intending to remain only one night, for in such a place there was no hope of obtaining any food; but the warlord had his wife and daughter with him. The haste of the journey, the rough jolting of the mule on the stony mountain paths, and the burning heat from the brazen sky that hung between the mountain peaks had been too much for the warlord's wife, six months pregnant. Her time had come upon her, and the dead child was followed by a haemorrhage which could not be stopped. No help was available. Indeed there was not even an ignorant woman to remember what others had told her and do what she could to stem the flow that was carrying life away from the woman's body.

The warlord, who had grown to love his wife, stood by helpless in his grief, and his little daughter knelt upon the floor and tried to warm her mother's cold hands in her own. The woman was not sorry to be going. To be always pregnant and to have nothing at the end of the pregnancy but a dead child, to be always tired, to be endlessly journeying from one place to another, never to be long enough in one spot to make a home: this was not a life to be preferred to the rest and peace to which she was now drifting. She felt the hot tears falling upon her cold hands. She opened her eyes and saw her little daughter and her husband, and she said, 'Husband, take care of our daughter. Find a woman to keep her company.' With that she closed her eyes and gave herself up to dying.

When Ling An sat alone on the hillside, two of the warlord's men had already been scouring the country for a woman for two days. It may have been an hour that Ling An sat there weeping over her dead child while the evening glory faded, and the darkened shoulders of the hills were clearly silhouetted against the pale sky. Perhaps it was not so long. When the human heart is drenched in overwhelming emotion, time stands still, and a day may pass in one moment.

Slowly within her consciousness there came the sound of mules' hooves among the loose shale between the rocks; and even as she became aware of the two riders now so near, she knew that she had heard them for some time already. She crouched low over the child, hoping that in the darkness she would not be seen. Then, as she shrank with indrawn breath and ears alert to every sound, the riders stopped before her. One leapt from his mule, pounced upon her, and pulled her to her feet.

'A woman,' he called to his companion.

'Good,' replied the other. 'She'll do.'

Ling An began to struggle to escape, and the second rider dismounted to help the first.

'What's this?' he said, as his foot struck Lao Erh. 'Another?' and he bent down to see. 'A child,' he said, 'and dead. Is this your child, woman?' he asked.

'He is,' replied Ling An, 'my son, and he is dead!' And forgetting her own plight she began to wail. The men softened a little. They had not been expecting this.

'Well,' said the first, 'it is a pity; but you can do nothing about it now,' and seizing Ling An, he lifted her on to his mule and set her in front of him. 'See to the child,' he called to his companion, 'and come on quickly.'

It was a long ride through the mountains. They rode up and they rode down, through narrow passes where the wind whistled, cold even on that hot summer night, through narrow valleys where the grass grew thick and green in the shadow of the hills, out on to bare hillsides where grass burnt brown by the sun was slippery as ice beneath the hooves of the mules. Ling An felt that there might be no end to the journey. She could hear the second mule trotting behind and guessed that the rider had buried Lao Erh among the boulders.

The man who held her so firmly did not seem unkind. He said, 'Do not cry, Sister-in-law. We will not harm you. We need your help.'

Ling An had no doubt that they were bandits, and so she said nothing about her children and the old woman. Although she had been taken, at least the little girls were safe for the time being. So she said nothing and would tell them neither her name nor the place where she lived. But how the old woman and the two children would fare without her she could not bear to think.

They rode up and they rode down. Sometimes she dozed, sometimes she wakened, and always there was the soft sound of hooves in the grass, of stones slipping away from under a hoof and rolling away down the hillside. They rode down and they rode up. The hills and the valleys rolled away for ever and ever. There was no end to them. Surely there would be no end to this everlasting night. Then the sky in the east grew light, the morning star paled and vanished. The sun leapt up. Shadows grew strong and black. Heat beat down upon their heads, but still they rode on.

At last they came to the foot of a hill which was crowned with a stone wall all around its summit. They began to go up towards a narrow slit in the wall. So narrow it was that it was scarcely visible from below; but as they got nearer, it widened, until when they dismounted before it Ling An saw that it was just wide enough for a man leading his mule behind him to pass through.

There was a sentry at the opening, and when they had passed him they found themselves in a village of stone huts swarming with men. There were no women. The two riders, pushing Ling An before them, walked briskly along the path between the huts to a larger one in the middle. A makeshift door of sorghum stalks hung askew across the entrance, and a man stood on guard beside it. At the sight of the two men and Ling An, he lifted the door and let them in.

Inside, by the dim light, Ling An made out two chairs and a table, and a vast mountain of a man sitting in one of them.

'What?' he said, as they stood before him.

'We have brought a woman,' the men said.

'From where?'

The men replied in detail. 'Fair enough. She won't be followed.' This, thought Ling An, must be a warlord. And in that she was right, for warlord he was.

'Sister-in-law,' said the warlord, not unkindly, 'we have had you brought here to take care of my daughter who is here with me, twelve years old, with no woman to keep her company. Her mother died three days ago. You will stay here and serve her and take care of her, and some day perhaps, when there is peace, we will take you back to your own village.' He led Ling An into an inner room to the left of the entrance, and there, face down upon the bed, sobbing hopelessly like one who has been weeping for a very long time, at first with violence and now with exhaustion, without strength to stop, lay a young girl . . . the daughter of the warlord.

16

THE EVANGELIST

The old woman was not alarmed when Ling An did not return to the inn that night. 'She has stayed with the Healing Woman, and will be here tomorrow,' she told Anping and Anming. The next day, when still she had not returned, the old woman said, 'Doubtless your brother is in need of more needling. Your mother is staying with the needler a few days.' And so she went on, reassuring the children from day to day, although deep within her heart the fear grew that something had befallen Ling An on the way to the Needling Woman or on her way back to the inn. So it was that when at last the two little girls realized their loss, they had already grown accustomed to it.

There was nothing they could do to find out what had happened. The old woman could not walk as far as the needler's village, and it was too far to send the little girls alone. She hoped that someone from that village would come to the inn; but no one did till after the autumn harvest, and that person had no news to tell of Ling An nor of Lao Erh. It seemed that she had vanished utterly.

The old woman and the two children did what they could in the dusty fields behind the inn, but it was a poor crop they harvested between them in the eighth and ninth months. Travellers were few and far between, and not many coppers went into the old woman's purse. Sometimes as she lay in bed looking at the few bundles of beans hanging from the beams, or when she took two or three handfuls of millet from the crock for the evening meal and saw how it was dwindling, she wondered how they could manage with so little through the winter. At night, lying awake while the children slept so soundly, she would feel her old heart pounding against her ribs, and she wondered how the children would fare if she were to die before their mother should return.

Die she did before the winter was over, in the second month of the new year, when the cold is most severe; and still Ling An had not returned. But towards the end of Candle Month the old woman's son and his second wife had come back to the inn, so the little girls were not alone.

For a while they were tolerated by the new owners. They were useful. Even Anming could be sent out to gather fuel from the bare hillsides. Anping was old enough to work all day in the inn and in the fields and was soon a little slave.

The man and his wife were not cruel, but neither were they kind; and as the slender stores of grain and beans grew lower in the crocks in the lean weeks of early spring, the woman began to grumble to her husband about the size of children's appetites and to hint at ways of getting rid of girls . . . children who had been deserted by their mother.

Then the man, egged on by his wife, began to make enquiries from the few travellers who stopped at the inn about a husband for Anping. They shook their heads and pursed their lips. Who would want a girl who belonged to nobody and had no dowry? Even a well-favoured girl in such circumstances would be difficult to marry off; and such a skinny scarecrow of a child only ten years old would be well-nigh impossible.

However, there came one day an elderly woman who said she knew of a family with an unmarried son, who being poor themselves might be pleased to receive such a plain-featured dowerless maid for a daughter-in-law. A little later in the spring she came again, and after she had left, the man's wife bought some flimsy Japanese cotton, stiff with dressing, and set Anping to making a quilt. A few cheap cups and a teapot and a basin were purchased from the same pedlar who had sold the cloth; and one fine summer morning, almost before the sun was fully risen, Anping said, 'I will see you again,' to her little sister, and set out for her new home.

As for Anming, bereft at nine years of age of all her family, she was given no time for grieving. From that day the woman expected her to do not only all that her older sister had done but also all that had fully occupied her days before. She worked from sunrise to sunset. Even on the rare days when the weather was too bad for fuel gathering on the hills, Anming was expected to sit at the old woman's spinning wheel, spinning the cotton harvested the year before from the poorest of the fields behind the house. Every mouthful of food was begrudged her. Gradually the merry dimpled little face grew thin and apathetic. The bright eyes grew dull and listless. With never a moment to spare from work, she lost all desire to play. Even at night, shivering under the thin quilt which was so threadbare that lumps of cotton wool were always falling out of the holes in the cover, Anming was too tired to weep. After a while she forgot all that had befallen her before.

Anping fared little better than her younger sister. The young bridegroom was two years older than herself . . . only thirteen; and both children were considered too young for actual marriage. Anping in the meantime became a slave to her mother-in-law, whose naturally bad temper was sharpened by poverty, perpetual hunger and middle age.

So the two little sisters were kept alive at least while their mother, forced to follow the warlord and his army, moved ever further to the west, until all thoughts of escape vanished from her mind. With her tiny bound feet in their cloth-soled shoes, it was impossible for a woman to walk so far back to her children, and she had no money to hire a wheelbarrow and a man to push her. Even if she could have stolen a mule from the army, she would not have known the way home; and for such a long journey she had no coppers with which to buy food for herself and a mule and to pay for shelter at night in the inns along the way. So she said, 'There is no help for it,' and set herself to the task in hand.

She cooked and washed and sewed for the warlord and his little daughter. To keep the child with her, so that she did not run loose among the soldiers, she set her to sewing and making her own shoes and embroidering the toes with silks worked over paper designs of flowers and butterflies pasted upon the cloth uppers of the shoes. These paper embroidery patterns she obtained from one or two friendly soldiers whom she had nursed in sickness, and they had got them from frightened villagers who had been thankful to get rid of the soldiers at no greater cost.

In this way also a spinning wheel had been acquired, and Ling An set herself to teach the child, Mulan, to spin the cotton which grateful soldiers obligingly looted from the fields as they passed by them in the late autumn. She would have liked to teach the child to weave; but a loom was heavy and bulky and, as they were continually moving from one place to another, would have been difficult to carry, and not worth the time and trouble of taking down and setting up. Besides, what would have happened to the unfinished cloth upon the loom?

Mulan knew nothing before Ling An came. From babyhood she and her mother had followed the warlord from place to place, never staying any length of time anywhere. He dared not leave them at his ancestral home lest they should be kidnapped and held as hostages to his embarrassment.

The wife had been a gentle, meek creature. Pregnant nine months in every year and Mulan her only living child she had gradually lost hope and spirit, and was always too tired to teach her daughter anything. As the child grew into girlhood, the mother and daughter, who never met any other woman, became very fond of each other, and were closer perhaps in each other's hearts than they would have been had they been living a normal life. This affection Mulan now transferred to Ling An, and loving her companion, with her days filled with interesting occupations, she began to blossom with good health, happiness, and beauty. Then the warlord, seeing this, was pleased and grateful. He treated Ling An with favour, and would bring her and Mulan presents from the loot his army foraged as they went through the land; but he never gave either of them money, nor did he ever relax the guard he continually kept upon them.

So the months went by, and soon a whole year had gone, and then another year; and still the warlord fled, ever further and further to the west; and as he fled, his army melted away from him until there were not more than forty or fifty men left. These, ill clad and ill shod, possessed nothing but their huge swords with the long curved blades. Every morning they sallied forth and foraged for food. They did not often kill, for the villagers fled immediately they approached and left the bandits (for such they had become) to forage freely through their houses. Loyalty had kept this last remnant of his army with the warlord; but now they remained with him not so much for reasons of loyalty as for the impossibility of returning so far to their homes. For they were all men from the east, and none of them had any money.

As they fled further and further westward into the heart of the mountains, their plight became desperate. Winter was coming on, and they had no warm clothing. Villages were few and far between, and the people so poor that there was little to be wrung out of them. They fell sick from exposure and semi-starvation. Ling An did what she could for them, but some of them died. As small bands of five or six men foraged in the hills, they began to grumble and discuss plans for escape.

'With a bit of money we could get a place on the train. Now if a traveller should pass this way we could rob him. Travellers always have money,' they said. But by this time, with prices on their heads, they had been obliged to flee to the most remote regions, and it was rarely that anyone except those who were at emnity with their fellows ever passed through that interminable sea of mountains.

But where some have gone in hate, others will follow in love; and so it was that on one frosty morning in late October, six men gathering dried grass on the slope above a bare stony valley espied a lone figure enter it and pick his way between the boulders towards the far end. As if travelling alone through such a place were not foolhardy enough, the traveller was singing at the top of his voice in a high falsetto tone:

Jesus is the Good Shepherd;
He leads his sheep;
He goes in front,
The sheep follow behind.
Night and day he will protect them all;
Those thieves and robbers
Can never steal them.
He leads them beside still waters,
He leads them on the mountains,
He calls them with his gentle voice,
He keeps them safe.

Through the clear frosty air his voice came up to the bandits crouching among the boulders. They heard every word. 'Those thieves and robbers can never steal them' came clearly through the sparkling silence.

'Come,' they said. 'Let's go.' And quietly they began to go down into the valley, three of them ahead of the traveller, and three behind.

Chang was a man not long past his youth, still strong and sturdy and capable of great endurance. He had no spare fat on his long limbs, but he never appeared thin to those who saw him. This was because the gaze of most people generally stopped at his face. It was a plain flat peasant face with a small fat nose, large full lips, and eyes slightly oblique. He was clean shaven, and the hair on his head was usually cropped close. So far there was nothing extraordinary about him; but the whole face was illuminated from within by a glowing radiance that shone out of him, a light such as people never saw on any other faces; for this man Chang was a whole-souled Christian, and it was not his own soul that shone through his face but the light of Christ who was in him.

As a child he had lived not far from a church where there was a school; but his parents were too poor to pay the small fee; besides, his help was needed in the fields. But one year the spring was late in coming. The mighty river that flowed past the fields was full of great slabs of ice that cracked and split as the current bore them away. The soil was hard as iron, and across the fields the thin stripes of wheat sown in the autumn were black and dry. There was no work to be done, and young Chang had time on his hands.

One evening he wandered past the church and, greatly daring, walked into the courtyard. A young catechist saw him and beckoned him into the church, and told him to sit down on one of the benches behind the font. He sat there awed by the size of the great church and the silence, and was just about to run out of the door when a huge bell clanged over his head. There was the sound of boots in front of him, and a priest in a white surplice followed by the friendly catechist came out from the apse behind the altar. They took their places opposite each other in the chancel.

The school children and a few other people immediately in front of Chang had risen to their feet and now sank to their knees. A rosy-cheeked kneeler on the women's side slid a hassock across the aisle to him and motioned him to kneel also. He did so while the unintelligible words of psalms and prayers flowed past his ears.

Then everyone sat down, and lo and behold the catechist opened a great book on a stand and began to read. It was the first lesson of evensong, and that day the lesson was from the book of Genesis, and it was the beginning of the story of Joseph. Young Chang listened spellbound, and he would have listened all night if the catechist had not stopped at the place where Joseph had been sold to the Midianites. 'That cannot be the end of the story,' he thought. 'I will come again when the bell rings and hear the rest.' So he began to come to church morning and evening, and listened fascinated by the wonderful stories that came out of that great black book on the stand.

Soon it was not enough for him to listen. He must learn to read. The catechist was friendly and started to teach him. A new road opened before young Chang: a road that would take him to heaven. A sheep in the Good Shepherd's flock, young Chang jostled along with all the other sheep of that congregation following where the Shepherd led. With his eyes on the Shepherd's back, young Chang waited for him to turn and look at him as he had long ago when those two disciples, Andrew and another, had followed him. Then one never-to-be-forgotten day he had turned and looked at Chang, and from that time sheep and Shepherd were never apart.

Young Chang had gone to school for a little while, just long enough to learn enough characters to read the Bible for himself and to write down the songs which he made about the Bible stories and set to the country music to which he had been bred. His shining face, joyful singing and burning zeal soon came to the notice of church authority, and he was sent to be the catechist of a village in a widely-scattered parish. Here, the love of Christ, which hitherto he had soaked up like a sponge and pressed upon all with whom he came into contact, flowed like a mighty river through his heart and out again — like a rushing torrent that would not let him rest.

It was soon discovered that he could not stay long in any one place. Compulsion was upon him to preach to every creature; and when he had done all he could for everyone in one place, he had to go on to another and preach to the people there. This rare gift for evangelism was recognized and accepted. Another man was sent to take his place as catechist, and Chang was set free to go where the Spirit of God should lead him. So now for most of his life he had been roaming the country and preaching wherever he went. His wife and children, safely housed with his parents in the house by the church, could always say whither he was bound. But exactly where he was on the way no one could tell, for he himself did not know when he set out what deviations from his route would be required of him.

Chang had set off for the north-west and was now heading due west, a great distance from his original objective. As he walked along in the fresh cool morning, sometimes he prayed and sometimes he sang.

The bandits thought that they had not been seen; but Chang had seen them before they had seen him and he put them into his prayers. He was not surprised to see three of them barring his way before him and to hear others closing in behind him.

'It's early,' he said. 'Have you eaten?'

'Have you any money?' said one of the men.

'Money?' said Chang. 'Well, I've got a few coppers. Would you like them?' he asked, as another thrust his hand into the girdle that kept his trousers up and pulled out his purse. Sure enough, there were only a few coppers in it. The man was disappointed and began to manhandle Chang. The men pulled off his clothes and examined them carefully for hidden notes. There was nothing. In the bundle he carried there was only an old quilt, forty or fifty single Gospels, a Bible and an exercise book full of songs and hymns which he had made himself.

'So!' said one of the men. 'A Christian! If he has no money his friends will ransom him. All these Christians love one another. Aren't they always talking about love? There must be a church near by. We'll find out and we'll hold him until they pay what we ask. Come, let's take him.'

'Good,' said one of the others. 'But what will our master say when he sees the man and knows of our plan? He'll hold him for ransom himself, and we shall not get even one copper of the money.'

'True,' said the others. 'We must hide him; but first we'll find out where his friends are.'

They led Chang away to a place where the rock jutted out from the hillside like two knees. In the depression between them was a tiny spring of water which enabled a few cedar trees to grow. Here they questioned Chang, but he would give them no information. So then they tied him to a tree and beat him; but still he would not tell them. At last they grew tired, and tying him up by his thumbs to the branch of a cedar tree so that his toes barely touched the ground, they went away and left him; and as they walked they heard him singing:

Jesus loves me, this I know,
For the Bible tells me so.

'The man's crazy,' they said.

'Well,' said one, 'we'll leave him an hour or so and cure the craziness.'

The sun was high in the sky. The bandits' hour or so had lengthened to noon. Chang's arms were heavy and numb. His feet ached with the effort to keep at least the tips of his toes on the ground. He had sung, he had prayed, and he had endured with the eyes of his soul fixed upon his Lord, whom he saw hanging on a cross beside him. Now a merciful unconsciousness had come upon him as he hung there with his chin sunken upon his chest.

It was thus that Ling An and Mulan found him. They had been making millet biscuits on a griddle all the morning and had used all the fuel. Now they were gathering more for the evening meal. They had seen the tops of the cedar trees from afar and thought that there would be sticks beneath them.

Mulan saw Chang first and ran white-faced and shaking to Ling An. They both fled from the trees on to the open hillside. Then again Ling An felt that strange compulsion upon her to do what her whole being revolted against. Taking Mulan by the hand, because she dared not leave her alone, she went back to the tree and crept closer to Chang.

'He is alive,' she whispered to Mulan. 'We must help him. Climb up into the tree and along the branch and untie the strings around his thumbs.'

With Ling An's help Mulan climbed the trunk of the tree, crawled along the branch, and untied the strings around the man's blackened and swollen thumbs, while Ling An stood below and supported his sagging body.

Excruciating pain as the blood flowed back into his arms and hands brought Chang back into consciousness. For a few moments he could not speak. Then, 'Quick,' he said, 'the robbers are coming back in a little while. Go away away before they come. They will kill you.' But Ling An would not leave him until by rubbing his arms she had restored his circulation and he was able to walk. Then she led him to a hiding-place among the boulders and bade him stay there until nightfall and then flee away as fast as he could.

Mulan had gathered up the Bible and books of Gospels scattered about on the ground. She tied them up inside his quilt and made a bundle of them. As they were about to leave him, Chang took a copy of St Luke's Gospel and gave it to Ling An.

'Sister-in-law,' he said, 'this is more precious than money. Read it and it will show you the way into heaven.'

'We cannot read,' said Ling An.

'Take it,' said Chang, 'and keep it until you find someone to read it to you.'

At that Ling An took the book and slipped it under her jacket, and they left the man crouching among the stones.

That evening Chang made his way down the hill and through the valley and, travelling all through the night, he came to a village where he was able to rest and recover, and later go on his way, preaching and singing, with many adventures which have nothing to do with this history.

17

THE CAVE

It was autumn again. The soft gentle rains had come and gone. Now the mornings were sharp with frost, although it was still hot at noon. Of the great army no more than a dozen men remained, and these with the warlord and the two women were camping in a cave in the hills high above a long straggling village in the valley below.

Here they had been all the summer, and the villagers were very tired of them. They had fed them at first from fear, but now that they knew how few of them were left they were no longer afraid of them. Moreover, the long cold winter lay ahead. They met together in the headman's house, and after much talking they decided to ask the men of a neighbouring village to help them get rid of the bandits.

Nobody had any weapons but the long spears adorned with red tassels, one of which was to be found in every house. One dark night, twenty-nine men, each armed with a spear, climbed the hill to the cave and, taking the sentry by surprise, overpowered him before he could shout a warning to his fellows inside the cave. Then they lit an enormous fire at the entrance and smoked out the inhabitants and killed them one by one as they ran out of the cave for air.

In the smoke and confusion Ling An awoke and, seizing Mulan by the hand, dragged her as she thought to the entrance; but dazed and shocked she ran instinctively from the fire which blocked it and fled to the back of the cave, where there was a narrow tortuous passage which led nowhere. It was however very high, narrowing to the top where it came out among the boulders near the summit of the hill. Here it was too narrow for the passage of a human body, even that of a small child. Escape that way was impossible; but air came in, and smoke could pass out.

Having got to the end of the cul-de-sac, the woman and the girl began levering themselves up the narrow crevice by their knees and elbows; they wriggled as far as they could and clung to the uneven sides, scarcely daring to breathe, burying their faces in the sleeves of their jackets in order to breathe as little as possible of the smoke.

After a while, the shouting outside the cave as the villagers pursued those bandits who had escaped them at the mouth of the cave died down. The crackling of the fire was silenced, and the smoke began to clear. Mulan would have come down from her hiding-place, but Ling An below her barred the way. She knew that the villagers would come into the cave to search it. So they waited, clinging like two bats high in the crevice.

In a few minutes, there was the soft sound of cloth shoes among the stones and a murmur of voices as the villagers came into the cave brandishing flaming sticks which they had snatched from the fire. They found the passage at the back, and two of them came and stood beneath the women, but neither of them thought of looking up. 'There's no one here,' they called to their fellows, and they went back to rejoin them in the cave. There they stood about the entrance discussing the event. Were all the bandits killed? Who had killed one? How many had escaped? Would any come back? Should they leave a guard? Should they block the entrance so that no one could come in again? It had been assumed that there were only about a dozen bandits in the cave, but nineteen of the villagers were sure that each had killed a man or severely wounded him. Five lay dead before the entrance to the cave, the rest were scattered over the hillside. In the dark it was impossible to find them. In the end the villagers decided to leave the cave and return to their villages. In the morning they would search the hillside for any who might be lurking among the boulders.

Ling An heard them beat out the smouldering fire, and then she heard their soft footsteps descending the hill.

She listened, and then let herself down in silence to the floor of the passage. Mulan followed, and both of them stood listening. There was nothing to hear. They crept into the cave, keeping close to the wall. They felt their way along it to the entrance. The ashes of the fire were warm under their feet. It was not quite so dark outside, and their eyes, accustomed to the black darkness of the cave, were able to see five hummocks where the dead bandits sprawled; but it was impossible to tell who they were.

'Father,' whispered Mulan. 'Where is Father?'

'Come,' said Ling An, pulling her past them. 'We've got to get away, before daylight.' They scrambled up the hillside, not knowing which way to go, only knowing that they must get away from that valley and its village and hide in another. So they went, tripping and stumbling in the dark.

Suddenly Mulan's foot was gripped by a hand among the stones, and she fell to the ground. Ling An fell with her, and before either of them could get up, they heard a hoarse whisper, 'Don't scream! It's I, Bao Erh.'

18

THE SURVIVOR

Bao Erh was one of the bandits whom Ling An had nursed when he was sick and brought through an attack of pneumonia.

A young man in his early twenties, he was the second son of a well-to-do farmer whose land lay next to that of the warlord far away in the east of the country. He had been sent to school and should have stayed there until he had finished his high school course, but he was no scholar by nature, and although he was not lacking in ability, he was seldom to be found poring over a book.

During one of the political upheavals of the time, he, along with other students of his school, demonstrated against the government of the country. Leaving their studies, they marched across country to the nearest railway station. There they boarded a train which took them to the capital, where they met contingents of other students from all over the country.

They marched upon the houses of the ministers who had incurred their disapproval, but these had already developed sudden illnesses and taken refuge in hospitals. The students threw stones at the walls of the houses, attempted to batter down the gates, with no success, shouted slogans until they were hoarse, and would have done a great deal more if it had not come on to snow. What made matters even worse was that the snow rapidly turned to sleet. Cold and wet, the students dispersed and made their way back to their schools.

There were many who had to walk back, begging their food as they went. For some of them with heavy colds this plodding through the mud under the cold wet sky was the beginning of tuberculosis, from which most of them died during the next decade.

In this, Bao Erh was more fortunate than most; he had never known poverty. There had always been more than enough to eat in his home. He had stamina; and when at length he returned to his school, he was no worse for his experience.

There was no question of punishment or expulsion by the school authorities. Since all the students had taken part in the episode they could hardly be expelled on their return. Indeed, the head of the school thought it wiser to say nothing whatever and treat the whole affair as though it had never occurred, especially as many of the teachers had accompanied the students.

Bao Erh's father, however, took a sterner view of the matter. In politics, as in all other serious matters, his policy was to live and let live. He had no wish to get himself involved in distant affairs, especially through his second son, a mere stripling who had had no experience of the world beyond his home and school . . . a young man who could not even manage a farm and was not married yet. How dare such an ignoramus meddle with affairs which he, his father, would not even begin to think about!

A servant with a mule was sent to the school to fetch Bao Erh, his books and his bedding. Once he was home, there was no question of his return to school. His enthusiastic description of his adventures met with cold disapproval. His father had two medicines to cure such nonsense: hard work and marriage. Hard work to exhaust surplus strength and fill up time; and marriage to tie a man down to the place where he belongs. Bao Erh was given duties around the farm, and negotiations were begun with the family of a suitable young woman.

This cure might have worked if the warlord had not made one of his rare visits to his family just at the time when Bao Erh was smarting under what he considered his father's unjust interference in his affairs. Moreover, one of his friends had just then told him that his prospective bride was no beauty. In fact, she had a squint. He kept his own counsel and made his plans. When the warlord left in the spring, Bao Erh was in his retinue.

'Where are you two going?' he said to Ling An when she had recovered from her fright.

'We were just escaping,' she said.

'Have you seen my father?' asked Mulan. Bao Erh had seen the warlord, his hands bound behind him, being led away by the villagers; but he did not think this was the time to tell his daughter such a thing as that.

'Yes,' he said, 'I saw him. He was alive.' 'Now,' he said, 'we must make plans and get away as fast as we can.'

'Not without Father,' said Mulan. 'We must wait for Father.'

'Yes, we'll wait for him,' said Bao Erh. 'So first we'll make for a cave I know on the far side of that mountain over to the east.'

He knew they would be safe there, because it was said to be haunted; but he kept that knowledge to himself. 'But first, while it is still dark, I am going back to the cave to see if I can find any of our things. We shall need quilts and the cooking pot. Once it gets light, it will be impossible to return to the cave. The villagers will be coming back.'

So saying, he stood up, and bidding Ling An and Mulan stay where they were, he scrambled down the hill as silently and stealthily as he could. He was back within an hour, with a large bundle on his back and the great cooking pot pressed by both hands against his chest and stomach. Cocks were beginning to crow in the village below. The two women took the cooking pot from him, and carrying it between them as well as they could, they began to climb around the top of the hill to the valley on the other side.

In the pale light of early morning Ling An saw that the back of Bao Erh's head was dark with congealed blood from a deep gash. His face was pale as ashes as he stumbled up the steep slope of the mountain on the far side of the valley.

19

THE NORTH GATE

The level of the millet in the crock was low. There was scarcely enough for one more meal for the three of them. Even now, after two weeks, Bao Erh still tossed and turned in the high fever resulting from the infected wound in his head, but Ling An was beginning to see hopeful signs of recovery. There must be something for him to eat when the fever left him. She must get him some red sugar. She turned the matter over in her mind as she sat beside him, pulling the quilt up over his shoulders when he tossed it off, patting it down all around the shape of his body to keep the warmth in, holding him down with all her strength when in delirium he attempted to get up and make for the entrance to the cave. That at all costs must be prevented, for if he were seen by any villager who happened to be minding sheep on the hillside all their lives would be in danger.

Clearly the small and slender Mulan hadn't the strength to cope with him while Ling An went to the village to buy red sugar. There was no help for it. Mulan must go to the village to buy the red sugar. Perhaps, though, it would be better for Mulan to go to the small walled city ten miles away. There she would not be noticed in the crowd, especially if she went on market day. Her feet were big, she could walk quickly, and she was so small that with a child's bonnet on her head and her hair done so that her pigtail came out through the hole in the top of the bonnet, she could be taken for a little girl of eleven or twelve.

Ling An and Mulan conferred together. Mulan was delighted with the prospect of getting out of the cave and away from its vicinity for a few hours. She would keep her ears open and bring back any news she might hear.

So early the next morning, Mulan set off, not by the road from the village but along the hills from which the road could be seen. She had Ling An's coppers wrapped in a piece of cloth, tucked into the top of her trousers. On her head she wore an old black bonnet, and from the hole in the crown her long pigtail, bound at the top and at the end with scarlet cord, dangled down her back. It was a clear cold morning, the sun shone out of the pale sky, and the thin dry blades of grass glittered like needles of gold. Every stone had its shadow, clear and black, and the folds of the hills cast their shadows blue upon the western slopes.

Mulan's spirits rose. After the shock and anxiety of the last two weeks, she felt a sudden release, such as a bird must feel when it escapes from a cage. The depression which had lain upon her so heavily since the villagers had attacked them and taken her father away vanished, and hope took its place. She would listen, she would hear good news of her father. He must have escaped. She was sure he had escaped. Of course such a wise strong man as her father must have escaped. How could it be otherwise? She walked along convincing herself that he had certainly escaped, and it might even happen that she would meet him in the city, in some sort of disguise. Then she began to worry whether he would recognize his daughter in the child's bonnet. Still she walked along happily, planning how she would cope with that problem when it arose. By the time she reached the East Gate of the city, she was sure that she would meet her father that day.

There was a moat all around the city wall. A great

number of country people carrying chickens, eggs, vegetables and fruit were walking through the East Gate and through the city to the South Gate where the market was held. Mulan mingled with the crowd. It did not take her long to buy the red sugar, some salt and the medicine which Ling An had told her to get. She looked at the shadow of the South Gate on the ground and saw that it was still early. There would be plenty of time to get home again even if she did not start her return until noon; besides, if she moved about it would give her father more chance of seeing her.

There was plenty to look at. Mulan walked up and down the narrow lanes between the vendors' goods laid out on mats and cloths on the frozen ground. There were so many things to see, such things to smell. Eyes, ears, and nose were hungry.

She stopped at the stall of a cloth merchant, whose goods were laid out on a trestle table. There were bales of bright coloured cotton, of plain indigo-dyed blue cloth, of white log-cloth, of blue homespun with a pattern of white flowers and butterflies for children's clothes, and bales of cotton printed with enormous flowers in bright colours for making quilts. As Mulan stood there, feasting her eyes on the unaccustomed brightness, two women stopped close by her and, after greeting each other, began to talk. Mulan listened. One was from the village near their cave. The other lived in the city. It appeared that they were sisters. The husband of the older one had been injured during the attack on the bandits. After answering her sister's enquiries about him the woman asked what had been done to the bandits who had been delivered to the city.

'What!' said her sister. 'Haven't you heard? They've been executed. You can see their heads hanging from the wall over the North Gate.'

'Aiyah!' said the other. 'When?'

'Last week,' replied her sister.

'All of them?'

'All of them, except the one who was never caught.'

'Well, I'm thankful for that.'

They went on to talk of other things. The ground began to rise and fall beneath Mulan's feet. The market revolved around her, sounds were muffled and roared together in her ears like thunder. She shut her eyes and put out her hands and steadied herself on the cloth merchant's trestle.

Fortunately nobody noticed her. The cloth merchant was too busy attending to a troublesome woman who wanted to buy only one foot of his most expensive cloth to make a baby's hat to notice a little girl about to faint.

The women walked away together, and Mulan opened her eyes and moved away. In her mind she repeated the women's words. 'All of them,' over and over again. Her feet moved beneath her, carrying her to the East Gate. 'All of them. All of them. All of them,' she said to herself as she walked, her feet keeping time to the words, 'All of them. All of them.' 'Except one who was never caught.' That was Bao Erh. But did the villager know how many there were?

'Except the one who was never caught.' . . . Father after he had escaped from them. Of course he would never be caught again. No wonder he couldn't come to them in the cave. He must be miles away by now. She must get back at once and tell Ling An and Bao Erh. There was no reason now to linger in the city. He would not be here.

Thus she got to the East Gate. Then, 'All of them. All of them,' she said. 'I must make sure. I must go and see. Then I shall know that Father escaped.'

So she followed her feet which dragged her as though they were not her own around the city wall to the North Gate. And there she stood irresolute, unwilling to lift her eyes to the gruesome things above. The wind was blowing from the north straight from the icy hills. Across the frozen fields it blew into the north gateway. The guards, stamping their feet, stood as far back in the shelter of the gateway as was consistent with their duty. A few country people came out, and with their heads bent against the wind trudged away to their villages to the north of the city. No one looked upwards to see what was above the gate. Then Mulan thought, 'There is surely nothing there. The woman was wrong. I didn't hear that terrible thing.' So she took courage and looked up.

They were there. They were all there; all seven of them. The wind was blowing their hair across their faces and into their staring eyes and their gaping mouths. Mulan looked at them all, one by one, and her father was the last in the row.

20

THE OLD MAN AND HIS WIFE

It was a long night. The cave was so far from any village that none of the early morning sounds came through the darkness to tell the inhabitants that daylight was approaching. Ling An had been awake for many hours, pondering the news which Mulan had brought. Fortunately Bao Erh was asleep when Mulan stumbled into the cave and gasped the tragic news into Ling An's ears. Shocked and horrified, she yet had presence of mind to warn Mulan to be quiet. Bao Erh was definitely on the mend, but such news in his weak state might be fatal and, even if it were not fatal, would prolong his weakness. They were all in the utmost danger, and their three heads would hang along with the others over the North Gate if they could not flee away from the district before they were discovered.

She wanted to leave at once, she and the girl together. Two women, mother and daughter travelling together, would not attract attention; but two women travelling with Bao Erh would share his fate if caught. In the morning she would fill the old kerosene tin which they used to draw water from the spring near by full to the brim, Mulan should gather a store of dry grass for fuel, and they would leave Bao Erh to fend for himself and get themselves as far away from the place as they could. He was weak, but he could manage by himself now.

Having made this decision, she had slept for a while; but not for long. The cold crept under the quilt which she shared with Mulan, and she awoke shivering and could not sleep again. Then, as she lay cold and comfortless in the darkness, there stirred within her again that strange compulsion which had so often directed her, and she knew that she could not leave Bao Erh.

So they stayed. Bao Erh grew stronger. The wound on his head healed. He no longer needed a bandage; but strangely his legs, which had not been injured, seemed to have no power in them; and until he could walk without help they dared not attempt to escape. The time dragged heavily, as Ling An and Mulan were afraid to leave the cave in daylight.

In the dusk of very early morning they fetched water from the spring and hastily gathered grass and leaves to burn. Only at night after it grew dark and there would be nobody on the hills did they dare to light a fire to cook a meal. Not that there was much to eat. The millet had been eaten. There remained only a few sweet potatoes and carrots and peanuts which Mulan had stolen from the fields at the foot of the hill during their first week in this cave. Now that the hard frosts had already begun, the villagers had gathered in these last crops of the year, and no more could be expected from that source.

During the daylight Ling An did what she could to repair their shoes. It was impossible to make new ones because there was nothing to make them with, no old clothes to be cut up and pasted together and dried hard in the sun to make shoe soles. The only old clothes they had were on their bodies. But shoes they must have for their journey. It was then that Ling An pulled out the book which old Chang had given them and which she had kept folded in four in the inner pocket of her jacket. The pages were made of double paper, and she began to tear them out.

'What's that?' said Bao Erh from the back of the cave where he sat huddled in his quilt.

'It's a book that a man gave me once,' said Ling An.

'Give it to me. Ah! A holy book. The Christians' book.' Bao Erh began to read aloud, 'There was in the days of Herod, the King of Judea . . . '

Ling An and Mulan listened. Sometimes they understood. Sometimes they could not understand at all. Bao Erh read until the daylight faded. Then he could see to read no longer, so he folded the book and put it into his pocket.

'I will read more tomorrow,' he said. 'You can make shoes with it when I have read it all.'

'That Jesus was a good man,' said Mulan.

'Yes,' said Ling An, 'I know.'

'You know?' said Bao Erh. 'How can you know? Can you read? Have you read this book?'

'No,' said Ling An. 'I can't read, but I know Jesus.'

'How can you know him!' laughed Bao Erh. 'All this was a long time ago.'

'Well, but I know him,' said Ling An; and that night, huddling with Mulan under the quilt, Ling An thought, 'It's true. I know him; but I don't know how I know him.'

When they awoke the next morning there was a thin layer of snow on the hills.

'It is the time of Little Snow,' said Ling An, remembering the calendar.

'Well,' said Bao Erh, 'but it does not always snow on that day.'

'Usually there are only clouds,' said Mulan.

'It is our bad luck,' said Ling An.

They could not go out, not even to fetch water, for they knew that their footprints in the snow would lead anyone who might see them straight to the cave. So they stayed huddled in their quilts at the back of the cave the whole day. It was during this day that they ate the last of the peanuts. Bao Erh strained his eyes in the dim light to read the

Gospel of St Luke in a low voice. Sometimes they listened, sometimes they slept; and so the day went by.

About three o'clock in the afternoon they were startled by the sound of voices on the hillside a few yards below them. Two men were arguing.

'I know I saw smoke coming out of the cave yesterday evening,' said the first.

'It must have been a wisp of mist,' replied the second man.

'It was smoke,' said the first. 'There must be someone there.'

'The cave is haunted,' said the second man.

'Haunted it may be, but ghosts and devils don't cook meals.'

'Ghosts and devils don't leave footprints,' said the second man. 'Look at the snow in front of the cave. Not a footprint in it. There's no one there.'

'Ah!' said the first. 'You're right.'

'Let's go.' And they made off down the hillside, in great haste. Those in the cave could hear the stones slipping and sliding under the men's feet and rolling down the hill.

'We must go,' said Bao Erh. 'It's no longer safe for us here. Others may come.'

'How can we go?' said Ling An. 'Every step we take will be seen in the snow.'

'Listen!' said Mulan, 'It's raining!'

Mulan was right. The heavy grey clouds which had hung in the sky all day were at last pouring the rain down and melting the snow. In an hour most of the snow had vanished.

They gathered up their few possessions, rolling them in their quilts. The cooking pot was too heavy and too bulky to carry, so they left it behind, burying it at the back of the cave under a pile of rocks. The kerosene tin they filled with the last of the carrots and the sweet potatoes, and Ling An and Mulan carried it in turn. Bao Erh put the Gospel of St Luke into his pocket.

‘Where are we going?’ said Mulan as they left the cave.

‘Home,’ said Bao Erh.

‘Where is home?’ said Ling An.

‘In the east,’ he replied. ‘Perhaps my father will receive me again like the man in the story we were reading today.’ As Ling An trudged along in the dark, she wondered where home would be for her. She had no home. She did not know whether she had any family left; but to the east she must go, for somewhere in the east country was the inn by the pass where she had left the two little girls, the last of her family. She must find her way there and see what had happened to them during her long absence, and on the way she must bring Mulan to her father’s people.

They walked all night, avoiding villages where dogs would bark and warn people that strangers were about. Early in the morning they came to a dry deep river bed. In summer this river was a raging torrent with great waves foaming white around the huge boulders it had brought down through centuries of storms; but in the winter it was just a sandy course with a narrow stream meandering among the stones in the middle. They found a hiding-place among a group of enormous boulders, and here they made a meal and then rolled themselves in their quilts and slept two at a time while the third watched.

‘One more night journey,’ said Bao Erh, ‘and after that it will be safe to travel by day.’

They walked and walked. It may have been two weeks or two months. Afterwards, Ling An could never be sure. To her the journey was a long blur of aching feet, frostbitten ears and cheeks, hunger and thirst. Even Mulan was never sure how many days they had been walking. The weather grew colder and colder as Candle Month wore itself out. ‘Nobody travels in Candle Month,’ Ling An remembered. But they did, on and on, day after day. Their shoes wore out completely, and they had no time to make new ones and nothing to make them with anyway. For food they stole what they needed as they went along . . . a chicken here, a few sweet potatoes there, some corn cobs left dangling from the roof of a gateway, a bunch of beans from a barn, sometimes (greatly daring) a segment of bread left in the pocket by the handles of an unattended wheelbarrow; but after the first week, they felt that they were safe and began to beg for food and shelter.

Towards the end of the month, there was a day of bitter weather. The sky was grey and lowering. There was no wind, but the chill air penetrated to the very bone. The sun did not appear once the whole day. They were crossing a great flat plain where villages were so widely scattered that they had not been able to get anything to eat all that day. The fields they passed were empty of everything but the winter wheat, stiff and black in the bitter cold. They had met few people on the way, and in such weather no one lingered. Tired, cold, and hungry, they came in the late afternoon to a great dyke by a wide river. Here there was a tiny village. Bao Erh looked back at the women trailing behind him and decided that they at any rate could go no further that night.

The village was poor and mean. There were scarcely more than twenty houses huddled at the foot of the dyke.

Bao Erh stood in the gateway of the first house and called, 'Is there anyone at home?' A lean dog lying on the ground by the entrance to the shed which was the kitchen rose to its feet and bared its teeth in a growl, and then as Bao Erh did not move away, the dog burst into a frenzy of barking. An old woman feeding the fire with dry leaves called out in a high cracked voice, and an old white-haired man came out of the house.

'Who is it?' he said.

'We're travellers. Have pity on us and give us something to eat.'

'Tell them to go away,' said the old woman.

'Wife,' said the old man, 'it's Christmas Day; and one of them is a child.'

At that the old woman came out and looked at them

There was an open shed joining the house, and in front of it a millstone with a little heap of golden millet on it waiting to be ground on the grey stone. Ling An went to the mill and she said, 'I and my daughter will grind the millet for you if you will give us something to eat and a cup of hot water.'

'Not so,' said the old man. 'Come in and rest a while, and my wife will bring you some tea.'

There was only one room in the house. Quilts were piled on the *k'ang* which occupied the wall on the kitchen side. It was to heat this *k'ang* that the old woman had been feeding the fire inside it with leaves. The old man bade Ling An and Mulan sit down on the *k'ang*. He and Bao Erh sat down in the two armchairs which stood one each side of the table opposite the door. In the fourth wall of the room there was a door opening into the shed.

Bao Erh was ready with his story. He mentioned a small village they had passed about fifty miles away, and said that bandits had attacked it, killed his father, burnt the village, and stolen all the stores; and now he was taking his mother and sister to his elder brother who lived in the city which he knew was about twenty miles down the river.

The old woman said, 'Aiyah!' and brought the tea and hot water to wash their feet; and the old man said, 'It is twenty miles to the city. I will spread some straw on the floor in the shed, and you can sleep there tonight.'

Then he and the old woman went to the millstone, and together they ground the little heap of millet. Then the old woman said, 'This millet was for our morning meal and our evening meal tomorrow.'

'I know,' said the old man. 'But it is Christmas Day, and these are poor travellers.' So they ground the millet, and the old man cooked half of it in the great cooking pot, and he added sweet potatoes to make it more, so that what was enough for two became enough for five.

Then they both took great armfuls of straw and laid them on the floor of the shed, and Ling An unrolled their

quilts and spread them on the straw. Because it was col
and there was only one light in the house, and that was
wick floating in a dish of bean oil, they all went to be
early. The straw was thick and warm, and their stomach
were full of warm food. It was not long before all thre
were fast asleep.

In the middle of the night Ling An awoke. Somethin
had awakened her. She lay and listened. From the room i
the house there came the murmur of voices. The old ma
and his wife were talking.

'What are the names of God?' he said.

'Oh, I've forgotten again,' said the old woman.

'Come now,' he said, 'you said them just now.'

'Oh, now I know,' said the old woman, 'Old Heaven
Grandfather.'

'Yes,' said the old man, 'that's one name. What are th
others?'

'Who knows!' said the old woman.

'The Ruler Above,' prompted the old man.

'The Ruler Above,' repeated the old woman, 'God
Heavenly Lord,' and, in a rush, 'he is sometimes calle
the Old Heavenly Grandfather.'

'That's right,' said the old man. 'You can say it. Now sa
it again.'

She said it again.

'What is the nature of God?' said the old man.

'What is the nature of God?' repeated the old woma
under her breath. 'Without beginning, without end, with
out shape, without appearance . . . '

Ling An drifted into sleep. After that she woke agair
and the old man was asking the old woman, 'Who is Jesu
Christ?'

'Jesus Christ is God's only-begotten Son,' replied the ol
woman, without any prompting.

'There, you can say it!' said the old man. 'Now, who wa
his mother?'

'The Virgin Mary,' replied the old woman.

'Where was he born?'

But this was beyond the old woman's power to remember. Her tongue got tied up with the strange name, Bethlehem.

'I can't say it,' she said. 'But I can say, born in a stable.'

'Good,' said the old man. 'But the priest will want you to say all the answer.'

'Aiyah!' she said. 'When will I know this catechism? I shall be like Mrs Lo, who died before she could be baptized.'

'It won't be so,' said the old man. 'Come now, let's begin again. What are the names of God?' And so they went on through the long night.

No one stirred in the house the next morning until the sun was high in the sky. By lying abed late in the morning, people kept themselves warm. They were also able to make do with two meals a day instead of three. The old woman gave each of her three guests a bowl of hot porridge, and after they had breakfasted, they thanked their hosts and set off again on their journey.

'Those people,' said Ling An, 'were kind.'

'Those people,' said Bao Erh, 'were Christians.'

'How do you know?' said Mulan, who like Bao Erh had slept like a log without waking all night and had not heard the old people talking in the dark.

'Because they were kind to us,' said Bao Erh. 'They have to love people. It is written in their Book. They even have to love their enemies, I have heard.'

'I do not love the people who killed my father,' said Mulan.

At that time, there was nothing they could say, so they trudged along in silence.

They were nearing the end of their long walk. Another twenty miles and they would reach the city, where there was a railway. There Bao Erh planned to stop only long enough to earn sufficient money to get all three of them on to the train. He did not know how he was to get the money.

As he walked along, well ahead of the two women, various schemes came and went through his mind.

Ling An followed, thinking of the old man and the old woman and their conversation in the depth of the night.

'I wish I could read,' she said to herself. 'That book in Bao Erh's pocket is all about this Jesus. The old man who gave it to me told me it was precious. But what good is a book to a man who cannot read? It is like money in a locked box when a person has no key to it.'

'You are the Son of God,' she said, looking up at the grey cloudy sky. 'You are in heaven. We are your poor sheep,' she said, remembering the picture she had seen so many years ago at the fair. 'Oh have pity on your poor sheep.'

Mulan stood waiting in the path for her to come up.

'We are the poor sheep of Jesus,' Ling An said.

'What?' said Mulan.

'I have remembered,' said Ling An; and as they walked along she began to tell Mulan about the picture of the Good Shepherd she had seen long ago at the great church at the fair.

21

THE REUNION

The little city lay among the flat wheat fields of the plain. Away to the south, and yet not so far away, the gentle brown hills rolled to the sky like the waves of the sea. To the north, the mighty river flowed with a current so swift that to the travellers on boats in midstream those same hills appeared to be racing madly away from them. On such a boat, even without a good wind to fill the sails, they could reach the great city in a day; but to return upstream against that current a boat took three or four days, or even as much as a week.

The city was some distance from the river, which was known to be treacherous and liable to flood and spread its waters over the fields, drowning all the crops and the labour of many months. For this reason many of the fields, especially those near the river, were planted with sorghum; for the stalks of sorghum are high enough to hold the ears of grain above the water. While millet and corn rot beneath the surface of a flood the farmers are able to row among the sorghum stalks and harvest a crop. A poor food it is, and fit only for domestic animals, but in times of dearth it is better than nothing, and even human beings are glad to eat it then.

When the water crept across the plain to the very walls

of the city, the magistrate would order his men to shut the gates and put bags of sand against them inside so that the water could not come in under the gates. Every household was obliged to send its young men out to the dyke to repair the breaches which had let the raging water surge out of the river. In the meantime, while it was still possible to get away, the women and children fled to the higher ground at the foot of the hills.

Such floods occurring in the late summer often left water in the fields all through the autumn and winter. Flocks of wild duck flew in the sky above the water, endlessly wheeling and turning in their V-shaped formations, then fading away on the horizon like drifts of grey smoke. In the winter, the water froze, and people who had been marooned in their villages for so many weeks were able to walk dry-shod over the ice into the city. In the spring, when the water receded the ground was left sodden, and as it dried a white deposit of salt lay upon its surface.

Although there had been many such disasters in the history of the city, they had occurred with such long intervals between them that they were accounted rare. Generally the city lay quiet and safe under the pale blue sky, amidst the fields of yellow loess, its grey walls merging so unobtrusively into the landscape that from a distance it was almost invisible. Around the four massive stone walls of the city there was a moat, and on either side of the moat was a row of tall poplar trees. In the autumn, when the poplar leaves turned gold and red, mothers sent their young children out with wooden needles threaded with string to gather these leaves for fuel. The little boys and girls stuck the needle through the leaves and came home like young dragons, trailing glorious tails of gold and crimson behind them.

There were four gateways in the city walls, one on each side, manned by city police who took note of all who came and went and shut the gates at night and in times of trouble when there was need to keep intruders out.

From these four gateways four main streets ran into the middle of the city. They were quiet streets, wide enough for the wheelbarrows and ox-carts which constituted the main traffic. On either side were open-fronted shops and the entrances to dwelling-houses; and in the middle of the city where the four roads met there was a monumental arch commemorating the virtue of a pious widow who had lived more than fifty years after the death of her husband and never remarried.

Outside the city, around the entrances on the east, west and south, suburbs had grown up; but beyond the unpropitious north entrance there was no suburb, only a temple with a ferocious idol in it to frighten away demons and other undesirable intruders. Beyond that, the flat fields stretched away to the river.

Bao Erh's family lived just within the south gate of the city. Many courtyards led one out of the other to an innermost yard where his parents dwelt. Here Bao Erh had brought Mulan and Ling An, after many adventures and much hardship. They had arrived in time for the celebration of the New Year, and Bao Erh's father had forgiven his son and welcomed him home, much to his mother's relief, for she had been fearful that her husband would take a stern view of their son's behaviour and send him away again. Mulan was sent to her father's family home, which was in the same street, and there she was kept in the strict seclusion becoming to a young maiden, which after her life of freedom and adventure would have been a trial to her if it had not been such a novelty. Ling An was welcomed by Bao Erh's mother as the woman who had saved her son's life on two occasions, and so was given a place in the household where she soon made herself useful in the kitchen.

After the New Year holiday, Bao Erh told his father that he wished to marry Mulan, and asked him to make arrangements. Bao Erh's parents were doubtful whether a warlord's daughter would have been well enough educated in domestic duties to make them a good daughter-in-law. His mother, however, having heard Ling An sing Mulan's praises, thought again, and decided that Mulan was still young enough to be trained by herself in the right ways, though it was a pity that she had such big feet. Bao Erh's father reflected that his son's jilting of the squint-eyed maiden whom they had chosen for him would make the parents of any other maiden they might consider very wary of dealing with them. Mulan's family were old friends, and her father, the warlord, in accepting Bao Erh as one of his men, might be considered as having aided him in the matter of escaping from his fiancée . . . a fact which would probably make negotiations easy. So, when all things had been considered, such as the young people's horoscopes and Mulan's dowry, a propitious day was chosen, and Mulan came to Bao Erh's home, riding first all around the outside of the city in a red sedan chair, preceded by all her new household possessions displayed in baskets.

Ling An was delighted. Mulan had become like a daughter to her, and she rejoiced to see her so happily and safely settled in life, just as she would have done if such a thing had happened to her own two daughters.

Her own two daughters . . . where were they? The last of her children . . . what had become of them? Day and night she thought of them. She must go and find them, but in the winter she could not go. The long journey to the east and the many hardships on the way had taken toll of her strength. To have made such a journey on foot at such a time of year would have been a severe test of strength for any woman. Ling An, who like all women of her generation had had her feet bound with the toes bent under the sole of each foot since childhood, had performed this journey on crippled feet in worn-out shoes. The effect of such hard treatment did not wear off until several months after her arrival at Bao Erh's house, and it was high summer before she could begin to think of making the journey to the inn where she had left her daughters.

During the spring the defeated army of one of the warlords had been disbanded in the district, and most of the men had taken to brigandage and were infesting the hills to the east of the city. It was some distance away in the heart of these hills that the inn lay, and it was for this reason that Bao Erh's parents, though willing to help Ling An in her search for her daughters, were unable to offer her any means of conveyance. No man would dare to push his wheelbarrow through that region, and the mere sight of a mule on the mountain tracks would have been an invitation to robbery.

So it was that early one summer morning before the sun was up, Ling An set off on foot alone. The journey was uneventful: no one thought twice about the plain peasant woman hobbling along the stony paths. The countryside was full of such women, making their way from their villages to their fields, hobbling along on the heels of their tiny bound feet. Ling An looked just like one of them, and so although she passed many a bandit along the way, not one of them thought of stopping her.

On the fourth day of her journey, at midday, she came to the inn. At first it seemed to her to be as quiet and as deserted as it had appeared to be the first time she had seen it, when she had stood at the top of the pass with her children around her. As she drew near, she saw a middle-aged woman working the bellows beside the stove, heating the kettles of hot water. There was no sign of the old woman, nor of Ling An's daughters. She drew out one of her coppers, asked the woman for a pot of hot water, and sat down at one of the rickety tables.

Through the torn paper of the window at the back of the room she could see a man working in the stony fields. Clearly there had been changes. Ling An sipped her hot water slowly and considered the situation. Her eyes darted all over the room, looking for something that might indicate the presence of a child; but they found nothing. She watched the woman covertly and decided that she did not like her. She looked like a hard woman. Would she tell the truth when Ling An enquired about her little girls? Ling An could not be sure and dared not begin to ask her.

Presently the man came in from the fields. He sat down at one of the tables and mopped his face with a dirty towel hanging on a hook behind the stove. The woman poured him a cup of hot water. He took out his little brass-bowled pipe and, putting a pinch of tobacco into it, began to draw the smoke up through the long stem of the pipe.

'That girl,' he said, 'didn't weed that field. It's full of *chili*.'

'Lazy little thing,' said the woman. 'I'll send her out to do it when she comes in from the hills.'

Ling An listened. So there was one child here at least, a girl too. Was she her child, or the woman's? The woman's next remarks enlightened her.

'She eats enough,' she said. 'It's time we made enquiries about a husband for her.'

'She's only eleven years old,' said the man.

'Well,' said the woman, 'her sister was nearly twelve when we sent her off to her mother-in-law. We could say she's twelve years old.'

'She doesn't look ten years old,' said the man.

'Well,' said the woman, 'she's not our child. Why should we go on feeding somebody else's child? There's little enough for ourselves.'

Ling An's heart leapt in her side. Surely this child and her sister must be her children! This one must be Anming. Anping had been married and sent away. They were both alive. Oh what a thing to be thankful for! After all this time, she still had two little daughters left!

She got up, and saying good-day to the woman, she went out and began to hobble up the road towards the pass. She did not go far, however. A huge boulder lay beside the path, and in its shade on the side furthest from the inn she sat down in such a way that she could see the road in front of the inn and the slopes of the hills around it.

The heat shimmered like water over the dry brown grass. Lizards darted in and out among the stones. No birds flew in the hot pale sky. The short shadows lengthened. No one came along the road; but at last the mother's sharp eyes espied a large basket piled high with grass and weeds moving slowly down the hillside to the left of the pass. Beneath the basket was a child, small for her age, carrying a bamboo rake nearly twice as long as she was tall. It was Anming.

Ling An got up and went to meet her. Stumbling among the tussocks of grass and the loose stones, she hurried to meet her child before she could reach the inn. At last they saw each other face to face.

'My little daughter,' she said. Anming stood still. There was no look of recognition in her face.

'Anming!' said Ling An. 'My little daughter! Anming!' But the child did not recognize her.

'I am your mother,' said Ling An.

'My mother,' said Anming, 'has gone away.'

'Well, now she has come back.'

'My mother has gone,' said Anming. 'My sister has gone away too.'

'Where?' said Ling An, but Anming could not tell her.

'Well, now your mother has come back. I am your mother, you are my little daughter.' Ling An sat down on the stones and pulled the child down beside her. Her mother's heart smote her as she took stock of her daughter. She was small for her age, and so thin there seemed to be scarcely any flesh on her bones. Under the sunburn of her face there was no healthy colour in her cheeks, and the dark circles around her eyes made them look unnaturally large. Thin scanty hair falling about her face told plainly of ill-nourishment. The toes of her still-unbound feet poked through a pair of ragged cloth shoes. She was wearing only a pair of trousers, faded and torn. Through the sunburnt skin of her body the ribs were clearly to be seen. All this was shocking, but could be remedied. What worried Ling An was the unchildlike apathy and lack of expression in the child's face.

'Come,' she said, taking Anming's hand. 'Let's go back to the inn. I'll ask about your sister, and then you shall come home with me. How will that be?' she asked, searching for the smile of joy on the child's face. But there was no smile, nor any change of expression.

The man looked up from a bowl of noodles as they came into the inn.

'What's this?' he said. 'Wife,' he called, 'here's our guest back again, with the girl.'

The woman came out of the inner room.

'What's this?' said she.

'This is my daughter Anming,' said Ling An, 'and I am going to take her home; but first I want to know where my elder daughter Anping is.'

The woman looked at her husband. He got up and followed her into the inner room.

'Shall we let the child go?' said the woman.

'How do we know that this woman is the child's mother?' said the man.

'Does that matter, if we get rid of the child?'

'Well, but if she isn't, and the child's mother returns . . . ?'

'Why should that worry us?' said the woman. 'Anyway, how does she know about the other child if she isn't their mother? She's their mother all right. Now then, how much shall we ask for?'

'Ask for?' said the man.

'Yes. How much shall we make her pay for looking after the children all this time?'

'Well,' said the man, 'if this woman is their mother she must be the woman who took care of my old mother after the bandits robbed her. We can't ask for anything. Anyway, the woman looks too poor to pay more than a few coppers.'

'That's true,' said the woman.

'Besides, if we let the child go, we shan't have to feed her,' said the man. 'The millet in that field isn't going to be much of a crop this year.'

'There's no help for it,' said the woman.

So they came out of the room and sat down at the table opposite Ling An and her daughter. After much talk and a pot of tea and bowls of noodles all round, it was agreed that Ling An should depart the next morning and take Anming with her. The man told her where Anping was and all that he could remember about the circumstances of her marriage. Ling An listened and forbore to comment, except with, 'How good you have been!' For these people had at least kept her children alive.

The next morning, holding Anming by the hand, she set out on the return journey to Bao Erh's house.

22

THE UNHAPPY WIFE

Truly it was wonderful to see the little starveling responding to good treatment. Good bowls of millet and vegetables soon put flesh on Anming's bones and filled out her cheeks, making them round and rosy. Her hair, neatly braided with red string, grew thick and glossy. Bao Erh's mother, with much indignant clicking of her tongue, searched through her bundles on the top shelves of her cupboards, and found a piece of red cloth for a jacket and a length of gaudy flowered cotton for a pair of trousers. The servants petted Anming and made her little shoes with butterflies and flowers embroidered on the toes; but in spite of all this loving-kindness, it was very rarely indeed that a smile brightened the heavy apathetic expression of the child's face. She did not seem to know how to play; and now that she was expected to do so little work, she would sit quietly doing nothing. It grieved Ling An to see her like this, and rather than watch her looking so miserable, she would bring the spinning-wheel out into a sunny place in the courtyard and set the child to spinning.

Bao Erh's mother shook her head, and said to her husband when they were alone, 'That child is a fool. Misery has destroyed her brain.' She was wrong, but not entirely so. Anming was no fool, but misery and malnutrition had made havoc of her body and personality. Although she would never be very bright, she was able to learn, albeit slowly and laboriously; and in time, but only after many weeks, she began to respond to her mother's love.

Meanwhile Ling An was making enquiries about her other daughter, Anping. This child was already married, and Ling An could not hope to have her with her again, but she wanted to satisfy herself that the girl was happy and that she had enough to eat and wear. Such information was difficult to come by. The village of South Pass was remote, in the heart of the mountains; travellers rarely passed through it. Few people seemed ever to have heard of it, and those who had pursed up their lips and narrowed their eyes as they said it was a poor place with a bad reputation. All through the time of the summer rains, Ling An's enquiries met with no more success than this. Then, after the autumn crops had been gathered in, the draper's wife told Ling An that her son was just about to set out with a barrowload of cloth to sell in the villages in the mountains. He would be travelling through South Pass village and could make enquiries about Anping.

Yang Jen was a tall youth, married, and the father of two children. As the eldest son, he would inherit his father's business. In the meantime he obeyed his father in the shop. He had stayed at school long enough to read, write and do accounts. Then he had gone to work with his father, learning first how to store the bales of cloth so that they did not turn mouldy in the heat nor fade through unskilful displaying in the sunshine. Then he had to learn how to measure the cloth, and how many inches to add on to the measurement required by the customers. He accompanied his father to the great city where he bought his supplies and, returning with him by road, had helped to push or pull the big wheelbarrow piled high with bales of cloth.

In the inns along the way he had listened to his father's tactful questions for information about the journey which lay ahead of them: the condition of the road, the presence of bandits, and suchlike necessary knowledge. He had sat with his father sipping tea in the inns listening to travellers' tales of encounters with bandits and warlords' soldiers, of ghosts and haunted houses, of wolves that tugged at people's jackets in lonely passes of the hills, of profits made at fairs and markets. Finally he was sent out on a pedlar's itinerary to take a barrowload of cloth to the villages in the eastern hills.

This he had been accustomed to do regularly several times a year, until the disbanding of the warlord's army in the spring. Then it had become so dangerous that the draper had refused to allow him to go, for although his business was now so prosperous that it could stand the loss of a barrowload of cloth, the draper did not wish to run the risk of losing his son.

However, at the end of the summer, it had been rumoured that the bandits were no longer active in the eastern hills. They had even been seen gathered on the banks of the river not far from the city, where they had boarded junks and sailed away to join their lord in another part of the country. Now, after the harvest had been gathered in, women would be unpicking last winter's padded clothes and quilts, washing the cloth, and remaking it into next winter's garments and quilts, if it were still not worn threadbare; but much new cloth would be required to replace that which had worn beyond repair.

So Yang Jen piled his barrow high with bales of cloth, skeins of thick red cotton for girls to tie around their plaits, skeins of fine cotton — blue, black, red, and white — for sewing, packets of sewing needles, a box of embroidery silks, and a few odd remnants of satin and silk for making babies' hats or brides' shoes.

In the deep pocket between the handles of the wheelbarrow were a large segment of circular bread, some pickles, and a knife. Across the top lay his pedlar's drum ready to his hand as he entered a village. When he turned its handle and the clapper struck the drum, this characteristic sound brought the women hobbling from their houses. They gathered around the barrow, some to buy, and others, who had no money, to feast their eyes on the goods. Others came to hear the news which Yang Jen had brought from the city and added to as he came through the villages along the road. When his mother told him to enquire about Anping in the village of South Pass, he agreed to do so without demurring. It would not be difficult, he thought, to ask a few indirect questions of the village women as they bought his cloth and listen to the comments they made among themselves.

As it happened, his task was easier than he had imagined. For as he entered the village of South Pass, he saw a group of people standing in a field not far from the track. They seemed to be considerably disturbed; and while he stood hesitating whether to start clapping his drum or not, a man came running across the field with a long rope in his hands. The group seized it and tied it around the waist of a young man who stepped into a well and began to go down. At this Yang Jen, contrary to his father's orders, left his barrow unattended in the track, and went to join the group at the well. He had judged, and rightly so, that no one would even see his barrow while there was a so much greater attraction around the well.

Much advice was shouted down to the man in the well, and then, with much heaving and straining on the part of those playing out the rope, it was pulled up, and the young man came up supporting a young girl. Both were covered with mud, and they were cold and shivering.

Women immediately surrounded the girl and carried her off to a house a few yards along the road.

'Who's that?' asked Yang Jen.

'Li Anping,' was the reply spoken in haste. 'Come, there's another over there.'

And sure enough there was another, much smaller,

group around a second well at the other end of the field. Rescue operations here were proceeding in a slow and leisurely manner.

'Why don't they hurry?' asked Yang Jen.

'No danger here,' was the reply; 'the well's dry.' In due course an elderly man came up, supporting a middle-aged woman with a sharp face like a ferret's. No sooner was she above ground than she began to curse and to swear, and it was with considerable difficulty that the man who had brought her out of the well led her back to the same house into which Anping had been taken.

'Who's that?' asked Yang Jen.

'That's the mother-in-law,' was the answer.

After that it was easy to gather all the information he needed. People gathered around the barrow, talking freely as people do when they are excited about something that has shocked them. Yang Jen soon learned that Anping's mother-in-law had been offended and had chased Anping with the vegetable chopper. Anping had fled from the house and jumped into the nearer well. Her mother-in-law, mad with anger, had then thrown herself down the other well.

'They say she washed her face in the water before she took it to her mother-in-law to wash in,' said one woman.

'Well,' said an older woman, obviously another mother-in-law, 'she didn't show respect to her elders. No wonder Sister-in-law Li was angry.'

'True,' said the first woman, 'but she had put some water into another bowl for her mother-in-law, but that fool her husband came and drank it, so there was no water for her mother-in-law except what she had just washed in herself.'

'Why didn't she go and draw more water out of the well?' asked Yang Jen, measuring out a foot of black cotton serge for the older woman. 'There are two wells near enough.'

'Those wells are no good,' said the woman. 'The first

has run dry, and the other has only mud at the bottom of it. The nearest water is two miles away. We all have to get it from the next village.'

'Well, her husband had to pull her up out of the well. He won't drink his mother's washing water again, I think!'

'That wasn't her husband. That's her brother-in-law. Look, here comes her husband.'

They all turned their heads and looked up the road.

'Does Sister-in-law know he's out?' said the older woman.

'I'll go and tell them.'

Yang Jen looked at the ungainly figure shambling down the road. He saw the huge misshapen head, the vacant eyes and drooling mouth. Anping's husband was indeed a fool.

23

THE RUSE

The steamy heat of early September had given way to the cool bright days of October. The people said, 'The days are thick at the two ends,' because they needed to put on warm clothes in the morning and again in the evening; but in the middle of the day it was so hot that men took off their blue jackets and worked half naked in the fields, their bare backs gleaming like burnished copper in the sunshine.

Outside every house beds were brought out, and laid across them were the blue covers of winter quilts and the heaps of new white cotton with which the women were patiently lining them, with a deft action of the thumb which they said could only be acquired early in childhood. They would work all day in the hot dry sunshine until the quilt was finished and could be folded up and put away ready for use in the long cold nights of winter. The next day they would start work on another.

Hanging from the lintel of the door the golden cobs of corn were drying in the sunshine, and on the persimmon trees, stripped by the nightly frosts of all their leaves, the bright persimmons hung like lamps of golden light.

The dates had been gathered from the thorn trees, and Ling An, turning them one by one as they lay drying in the hot sunshine, suddenly thought of a way to rescue Anping from the misery of a marriage which was in reality no marriage at all and never would be. In Candle Month it was the custom for young brides to return to their maiden homes and eat dried dates. The visit was a short one, for as daughters-in-law they were needed by their husbands' mothers to help with all the preparations for the New Year holiday at the end of January. Ling An would send for her daughter, and then she would devise some means of keeping her with her at least for a little while.

So towards the end of the year, Anping, escorted by her nephew-in-law, a young lad of sixteen, came riding on a mule into the city. The nephew, who was not very bright, though not a fool like his uncle, was easily persuaded to return home alone; and for that he was soundly berated by his bad-tempered grandmother when he got there.

By one excuse and another, Anping's return was delayed while Bao Erh's mother persuaded her sister, who had married a well-to-do tea merchant in the capital city, that she needed another servant in her household. After the New Year holiday Anping was sent to her, and there she learned many things and, growing in health and strength, blossomed into the comeliness of youth and happiness. After a while, Anping's mistress arranged a marriage for her with a young farmer who lived a short distance from the city; and there she settled down and brought up a family of eight children.

When her former husband's mother, impatient at the delayed return of her daughter-in-law, sent her elder son to bring her home, Ling An informed him that Anping had died of pneumonia. It is unlikely that anyone believed this story, but everyone's face was saved, and Anping's mother-in-law was advised to pursue the matter no further.

24

THE MAN IN THE DOORWAY

The years went by. Ling An was growing into the middle years of her life. Her two daughters were happily provided for, for even little Anming had been comfortably settled in a village in the plain and had a kind mother-in-law and stalwart young husband who did not expect a great deal of intelligence in his wife as long as she was capable of ordinary domestic duties and able to bring up a family of healthy children.

Ling An herself had enough to eat and drink, clothes to wear, and a roof over her head as long as she remained in Bao Erh's family; and it was unlikely that she would ever be cast out while Bao Erh's parents lived, and while Bao Erh himself and his wife Mulan remained in the family. She had nothing to worry about. Then why could she not be happy?

At night, when all the other servants slept, she alone lay awake, and felt a hunger gnawing in her heart. Sometimes she was aware of a tension, as though some power were pulling her up and plucking her away from the comfortable security in which she seemed to be so settled.

'Well,' she would say, 'I am like a widow. It may be that I am truly a widow, so why should I not feel like this?' But when she imagined her husband's return she realized that she would not be able to greet him with true joy.

'It cannot be that,' she would said to herself. 'That is not what I lack. Then what is it?' And the hunger gnawed in her soul and stretched the emptiness of her heart until she heard the cocks crowing in the dawn. Then she would rise and light the fire and boil water, and make tea, and take it to Bao Erh's parents and to Mulan and her husband, and waken their children and dress them, and after that the day would be so full that she would forget the strange hunger for a while. But at night, when she lay down, it would come again.

One New Year's holiday, in early February, a company of actors came to perform in the theatre outside the South Gate of the city. This theatre was nothing more than a raised platform built of stone with a small stone-built shelter at the back of it. In this there was a room at ground level and another above it on a level with the stage. A large threshing-ground of well-trodden earth provided a space where the audience could stand and watch the plays, and come and go as they pleased. Long before a performance began, the actors assembled and banged their cymbals and drums, played upon their flutes, and twanged their stringed instruments, making a great noise which could be heard all over the city. As few people possessed a clock, this was the only way to inform them that a play was about to begin. Then the women came, hobbling on their heels, carrying benches so that they could stand on them and see over the heads of the people in front.

The plays, which were usually stories taken from the history of the country, were highly moral, and as there was much emphasis on filial piety to parents and elders, Bao Erh's mother had given all the servants permission to attend.

So it came about that Ling An was alone in the house one morning in early February. It was one of the mild days of winter which justified the people who said that spring began with the New Year, although it was often the coldest time and the ground was generally frozen as hard as a stone. Ling An, preparing the meal for the late afternoon, was chopping one of the huge winter cabbages into tiny pieces. The two doors of the room in the west wall and the south were open to the mild spring air. Hens were pecking on the bare soil outside.

Sometimes one came into the room crooning and clucking and pecking boldly at a bit of cabbage which had fallen on the hard earth floor. Then scuttling outside to join her sisters, she was pursued with a great flurry of flapping wings by all the others when they saw what she had in her beak.

The plays had begun, but the house was too far from the theatre for the sounds of the actors' singing to come to Ling An, although loud music betokening the changing of a scene sometimes floated over the city wall, the edge of its stridency dulled by distance. But this only happened at long intervals; and so except for the soft cluckings of the hens and the gentle tapping of the chopper on the board, there was no sound in the room. Within the south doorway the sunshine lay golden on the floor, and the cabbage gleamed fresh and green under the sharp blade of the knife.

Suddenly Ling An was aware of another presence in the room. She looked up from her chopping board across the room to the doorway in the west wall. A man was standing there looking at her. He looked at her, and his eyes went past her and through her and around her, sweeping into the dark corners of her soul, and filling it with such light that the pain of it was almost unbearable, for all the love of heaven and earth and the universe looked out of that man's eyes. 'Lord!' she said. 'Good Shepherd!'

He stepped into the room and walked through it, and the leaves of the cabbage on the table glowed like translucent jade as he passed. He went to the doorway in the south wall, and there he turned and looked at Ling An again. Now all the pain of that healing love was concentrated in Ling An's eyes, and she felt the tears stinging as they spilled out and flowed down her cheeks. She dropped the knife and went to the door and out through the yard. The man was going towards the East Gate. She rubbed her eyes on the sleeve of her blue jacket. The man was walking towards the East Gate: he was through it, and she could no longer see him; but follow him she must. On the heels of her feet she hobbled as fast as she could go; but when at last she too was through the East Gate, there was nothing to see but the empty stone-paved road, stretching up the hill towards the hospital.

25

THE ENTRY IN THE REGISTER

The one-armed gateman at the hospital had died long ago, and his place had been take by another man. This one had only one leg, but the doctor had fitted him with a wooden one, and he stumped about his duties receiving patients and leading them into the clinic as blithely as many a two-legged gateman — perhaps even more cheerfully than some, for this man was a Christian whose life had been harder than most people's even in that place where life was hard for everybody; and now at last he had regular employment in work that he could do.

He had come from a remote village in the depths of the mountains, and the loss of his leg, he said, was the result of exposure on the mountains one severe winter when he had been shepherding the villagers' sheep on the hills and had lost his way in a snowstorm. Most of the sheep had been lost too, and their owners were very angry. Somehow or other his family had carried him to a mission hospital on the other side of the mountains, where he lay for many weeks while the doctor did what he could to save his leg but in the end was barely able to save his life by amputating it.

Young Li, during the months he spent in that hospital, found a new life and became a Christian, and a very zealous one too. He was often discovered leading the patients in the ward in prayer. The doctor found work about the hospital for him to do, and the catechist taught him to read. There were hopes that he might become a catechist himself and use his zeal in spreading the gospel; but alas, this good work was not able to proceed in peace. A warlord and his army descended on the village, killed the doctor and the catechist, and burned the hospital. Young Li fled for his life. He did not know where to go, for his own village, full of neighbours still smarting at the loss of their sheep, would not welcome him.

Then he remembered what he had heard of another hospital, in the east suburb of another city on the other side of the great mass of mountains, and slowly and painfully he begged his way from village to village until he got there; only to find when he arrived that that hospital, although still standing, had also been ravaged, and there was no one there to welcome him.

He sought work in the city; but it is hard for a one-legged man to find work at the best of times, and these times were very bad. Moreover, young Li's livelihood during his long trek through the mountains had been by begging, and he was ill-nourished, and his face marred by a fine crop of recurring boils. Rumours went around that the loss of his leg had been caused by leprosy. The boils on his face were noted as additional symptoms of that disease. Once this rumour had spread, everyone was afraid to employ him, except one man. He was the owner of a business which manufactured paper horses and furniture and other objects thought to be useful to departed souls, to be burnt at the graveside for their use in the next life. Young Li, as a Christian, was extremely loath to occupy himself in such work; but hunger is a strong master, and at last he gave in, accepted the work, and finally became an expert at making paper horses, two of which always stood in the doorway of his master's shop, advertising his goods.

In pursuing this work, young Li had cut himself off from his fellow-Christians, and although he never reverted to the customs of his youth, he did not continue to gather with other Christians in their church. Marriage for him was out of the question, and he spent his spare time, when he had any, in a little derelict house just within the north wall of the city, where he had for a companion an old blind man with an enormous tumour on the back of his neck who spent his days begging from door to door.

Many years went by, and the hospital in the east suburb re-opened; but young Li, now grown middle-aged, was too ashamed to go there. It was not until the old blind man lay dying of pneumonia that Li at last overcame his scruples and, summoning one of the city's six rickshawmen, put his companion into a rickshaw and set off for the hospital.

The old man's bronchial pneumonia did not carry him off immediately, and during the weeks that he lingered, Li visited him whenever he could; and it was not long before it was discovered that he was a lapsed Christian. When, a few months later, the old gateman died, Li was given his job. His wages were less than his wages at the shop of the maker of funeral furnishings, for Li had risen to the top of his trade and was a master-craftsman. His paper horses were famed for miles around. His master was angry at losing such a valuable workman, and his fellow-workers called him a fool; but Li was happy because now he would be able to earn his living in a good Christian manner and could once more associate with fellow-Christians.

It was this gateman Li who was sitting in his room in the hospital gateway on that same February morning. There had been little to do all the morning, for although many people might be ill, only emergencies and accidents forced them to leave their homes during the New Year holiday to go to such a place as a hospital.

Li looked up from the Bible open on the table before him and, reaching across it, opened the window and looked out; and there he saw Ling An coming up the steep road to the hospital steps, just as long ago the one-armed gateman a generation before had looked out and seen her in her mother's arms upon that same road. This gateman, too, knew the signs of trouble, and he knew that no woman walking at such a pace on her tightly-bound feet could be ill. She came up the steps and looked into the room through the open doorway.

'What is it, Sister-in-law?' said Li, rising from his chair.

'Has he come in here?' gasped Ling An.

'Who?'

'The man.'

'What man?'

'The Good Shepherd.'

'I didn't see him come through the gateway,' said Li. 'But he's here all right.'

'Take me to him.'

'Wait here a moment,' said Li. 'I'll go and enquire.'

He stumped across the outer yard, past the doors of the clinic to the inner courtyard where the rooms for sick people were, past the kitchens and the wash-house where the old washerwoman was hanging long strips of bandages on the leafless branches of a lilac bush to dry in the sunshine. He passed the open door of the chapel.

'That's where he is,' said Li to himself, looking in; but he went on to a house at the far end of the courtyard. Here he opened the door, and standing in the doorway, called, 'Elder Sister, there's a woman here who wants to learn the teaching.'

A tiny old woman came out of the inner room of the house. Her straight black hair was drawn tightly back from her forehead into a bun at the back of her head. She wore a long blue gown that reached to her ankles.

'What is it?' she said, for age had made her a little deaf.

'A woman. She says she wants the Good Shepherd.'

'What kind of woman?'

'A poor woman, but neat and clean.'

'Is she sick?'

'No, she's not sick. She's come to learn the teaching. Such a woman,' said Li, 'might be a good cook.'

So it came about that Ling An left Bao Erh's family and went to live at the hospital. There she cooked and cleaned for the old woman catechist, and in return was taught to read.

Learning to read after the age of forty for one who had never been to school was by no means easy; but Ling An, unlike many women of her age, had good eyesight and was able to see the strange black characters which were words; and although she was never able to learn enough to read a newspaper, she did succeed after many years in recognizing the three or four thousand necessary for reading the New Testament; and as she never possessed any books other than a Bible, hymn-book, and prayer-book, she never felt the necessity for learning more. But first she began with the catechumens' catechism, a thin book of coarse paper so flimsy that all the pages were made of double paper, on which the characters were printed large and black.

'How many gods are there?' the first question began.

'Of gods, there is only one true God,' came the answer in the next column.

Ling An read the characters one by one, pressing her finger under each as her eye passed it on its way down the page. Aloud she read the question again and again until she knew it by heart. It was not until then that the characters began to stand out as different from each other. She pursued this study with such vigour that even in the coldest weather the sweat would run in rivulets down her face.

After many months of such laborious study, the old woman catechist took Ling An to the parish priest and said, 'This woman has learned all that I can teach her. She can read her catechism and answer its questions by heart. Please examine her and see whether she can be received as a catechumen, so that she can begin to prepare for baptism.'

The parish priest was old and rather hard of hearing. During the past year he had been ill and unable to travel about to the fourteen widely-scattered churches of his parish. These he had been obliged to leave to the ministrations of the young priest whom the bishop had sent to help him. He, in the meantime, with gradually returning strength, found time hanging heavily on hands which before had been so busily occupied.

With few books beyond a Bible and prayer-book and those few Christian classics which had been translated into his language, he could not spend much time in study; and so to while away the tedium of inactivity, he set himself to writing a history of his parish. With the memories of his own long life and those stories he had heard from his parents and his aged men and women parishioners, and with such a written record as his parish register provided, he was able to delve back to the time when Christianity first came to the city. Many seekers after truth had he welcomed first into the catechumenate and then on to baptism and confirmation, and rejoiced with a full heart when they knelt before him at their first communion.

Now, as Ling An stood before him, he asked her kindly, 'What is your name?'

'Wang Ling An,' was the answer. It was an unusual reply. Whereas every other woman replied with her husband's family name and her maiden family name, this woman had replied with her husband's family name and a personal name of her own. Women did not have personal names as a rule, especially poor peasant women like this one. Perhaps, the priest reasoned to himself, she is a member of some other church, and this name Ling An is a baptismal name. There were no other churches in the district nearer than the Roman Catholic church fifty miles to the west. Perhaps her maiden home was somewhere in that district; but when Ling An told him where she had been born and brought up, he knew that that was impossible, for the reputation of the village had not improved with the passing of the years, and everyone knew of its evil character.

'Who gave you that name Ling An?' he asked.

'It was a nurse in this hospital,' she replied, and she related the story her mother had told her so many times in her childhood.

'Is it not a good name?' she asked, suddenly troubled that it might be taken from her. 'My mother said it was a good name that would keep me from harm and bad luck and illnesses.'

'It is a good name,' the priest replied. 'It may be even a better name than you know,' he thought to himself, resolving to search through his registers and read in the church records again that curious story of the baptism of the peasant woman's baby forty-odd years ago, This, after examining Ling An and finding her ready for the catechumenate, he hastened to do, and was truly convinced that Ling An and the peasant woman's baby were the same person. She had been baptized and so could not be baptized again.

When Ling An was told, she said, 'Now I know who has been leading me all my life.'

And the old woman catechist said, 'Truly it has been so. The Lord be thanked.'

26

THE CATECHIST

Now at last, for the first time since her childhood, Ling An was really happy and contented. She grew plump and rosy. The wrinkles disappeared from her face. Gradually, as she learnt more and more about the Good Shepherd, the old woman catechist called upon her to help teach other women who also sought him. In fine weather Ling An would accompany the old woman when she visited the Christian women in the villages of the parish.

They rode on a wheelbarrow, sitting on top of their bedding piled on the narrow seats, one each side of the wheel. The wheel squeaked endlessly; the fine yellow dust blew into their eyes and hair, up their noses, and down their throats, and felt like grit between their teeth. Under the cloudless sky in the hot dry sunshine and in the bitter cold of winter, they trundled along the narrow paths from village to village, taking news of salvation to those who had never heard it, teaching those who, having heard, were eager to receive more.

When they reached the village, the dogs would start barking, until the children who had been grubbing the grass on the hillsides saw them and came running as fast as they could to tell their parents. Then the women of the houses they were visiting would come out and, shouting

'Dog!' in stern voices, silenced the dogs, who generally went back to their former resting-places and put their heads on their paws but kept their ears pricked until they were sure that these two women were really harmless.

Usually they went to the same household every time, and having greeted the people of the house, drunk a cup of tea as they sat in the wooden armchairs on the east and on the west of the square table facing the door in the south wall, and exchanged news and a little harmless gossip, Ling An would go out into the yard and pin a white calico hymn sheet onto a door, and begin to sing. The old woman and the people of the house would join in, and as they all had very strident voices and sang through their noses, the sound rapidly went through the village, and it was not long before all the women, old and young, and all the children, and even a few men who hadn't too much to do at that moment would be crowding into the yard.

They sang hymns for some time as Ling An, with an improvised pointer made of a stick of sorghum plucked from the bundle propped against the kitchen wall, pointed to the characters one by one. Then the old woman would explain the meaning of these hymns, for they were not only songs of praise: they had been specially composed for the teaching of the salient facts of Christianity.

Praise God, the Holy Father,
Who blesses me abundantly upon this earth.

ran the first verse of one of these hymns;

Praise our Lord Jesus Christ,
Who came down from Heaven to save me.

ran the second;

Praise God the Holy Spirit,
Who makes me holy.

ran the third; and

Praise God the Holy Trinity.

ran the final verse.

This was sung to such a lively tune that, many years later, an officer drilling his men on a threshing-ground outside the city, having furnished it with patriotic sentiments, was to teach it to his men and set them marching to it.

As Ling An became more skilled in reading, she became expert in telling the stories she had read in her Bible. Since she knew nothing about any country or any people other than her own, these Bible stories had a distinctly local flavour. In telling the story of Adam and Eve's disobedience, for instance, when Ling An related how the serpent was to crawl henceforth on his belly, she would remind her listeners that all the pictures of dragons in the local temples showed that serpents used to have legs; but all of them knew that the serpents they found in their fields had no legs, and crawled on their bellies, even as that first serpent in the Garden of Eden.

Again, in describing the work of the Spirit of God, she would tell her listeners how she had noticed that the wheat growing in the corner of So-and-so's field was much more vigorous and flourishing than in the rest of the field, because it was just at that corner that Farmer So-and-so's cesspool overflowed into the field. These illustrations, shocking perhaps to fastidious western Christians, were not so to these people. They readily understood them.

In such a way the years sped by as the seasons came round. The old woman catechist grew feeble and unable to undertake the long journeys into the distant villages of the parish. Ling An went in her stead and returned bringing her news of those whom she had led to the Good Shepherd, who were as precious to her as her own children. For they were her own children, having been born of prayers and tears, and aching journeys on wheelbarrows, and long hours of patient teaching. In this way Ling An became a well-known visitor, much beloved in all the villages within a twenty-mile radius of the parish church. Everyone knew her, and she knew everyone.

She even went further afield and braved the journey to the village in the East Mountains whence she and her children had been cast out so long ago. At first she went there only by making a detour from the road to another more distant place to which she was bound, and with the instinctive tact of her race, made only a short visit.

The villagers, when they saw that she had not returned to live among them again and bore no resentment towards them for their former indifference in her time of need, welcomed her with open arms, cups of tea, and bowls of noodles whenever she passed through, which she did as often as she could. Her plump rosy face, shining black hair under the neat black velvet head-band, and decent blue jacket and trousers spelt prosperity to them. Moreover, they talked to the barrowman who brought her and heard how she lived; and when she untied her Bible from a large white handkerchief and read it, their amazement knew no bounds. Casting their minds back to the poor harassed ignorant woman she had been when she lived among them and comparing that with her present state, they thought, 'If this is what the church does to people, then let us all become Christians,' and pressed around her to hear what she read to them out of the small black book.

From such an unworthy beginning, a few people grew to a better understanding of the church; and it was not long before a number of them were baptized, and that village was added to the fourteen others in the parish as a place to be visited regularly by the priest on his rounds.

The people in what had been Ling An's own house at the end of the village naturally felt very embarrassed and would have nothing to do with her, until one day she happened to be in their neighbour's house after tragedy had struck them in the form of that dreaded disease of childhood known as white-throat. Even the strongest of children could be choked by the white webs that grew in their throats and lie gasping for breath from blue lips before their helpless parents' eyes. This disease had been epidemic in all the villages of the plain that summer; but the mountain villages in their isolation had for some time escaped. However, after the fair in the city before wheat harvest, it had invaded first one remote hamlet, then another, having been brought there by people returning from the fair.

At the end house, it ran like fire through all the seven grandchildren in its most virulent form. Five had died, and neighbours told Ling An that the remaining two were not expected to recover. Nobody dared approach the house, for fear of infection, and nobody knew what to do anyway. Needling and herb medicines seemed to be no use against such a disease. Ling An, however, had not lived on the hospital premises without learning a little and she did know what could be done, although she had never done it herself. She walked down the street to her old gateway and banged on the gate with her umbrella.

'Is anyone at home?' she cried.

The dog barked; a woman called 'Dog!' and came to the gate. She looked through the crack.

'Go away!' she cried. 'We've got this pest of white-throat here!'

'I know. Let me in. I may be able to help. Let me in.'

'Nobody can help,' said the woman.

'Good,' said Ling An, 'but I will try.'

The woman, who was one of the daughters-in-law, went away and consulted her mother-in-law, and after a while the two of them came to the gate, unbarred it, and let Ling An in.

'There's no way,' said the mother-in-law. 'We took the children to the Needling Woman. We got medicine from the city. We prayed to the gods in the shrine; but the children died. There's no way. Fine children . . . all dead, and four of them boys.'

'Are there any others?' asked Ling An.

'Yes, two; but they are dying even now,' was the reply. And even as she spoke, the sound of wailing broke out from the room on the right.

Ling An hobbled to the door and went in. A young woman sat on the bed, holding a blue-faced baby in her arms. It was dead; but on the bed beside her lay another child, almost as blue in the face, gasping for air as its throat was closing in the horrible white web stretched across it.

'Fetch me a knife,' said Ling An.

The women, not understanding, stood amazed.

'Fetch me a knife,' she commanded, 'and a candle.'

The young woman who had unbarred the gate went to the kitchen and bought a knife and a red candle.

'In the name of the Father and of the Son and of the Holy Ghost,' said Ling An as she held the knife blade in the candle flame; and, 'Lord, have mercy upon us,' she said as she put it to the child's neck. The women gasped. The child gasped too, and drew a long breath of air. They watched as the blueness vanished from its face, and its breathing grew normal.

'The Lord be thanked!' Ling An said, and fell to her knees on the earth floor, as much to still their trembling as in reverence.

Ling An was no doctor. But she had common sense and she knew the value of cleanliness. She also knew that the villagers' common sense at such times could be obliterated by superstition, and that their standards of cleanliness came nowhere near her own. So she sent for her bedding and stayed in the room with the sick child, tending him carefully until his throat was clear and the wound in his neck had healed. The family's gratitude knew no bounds, and from that time, whenever Ling

An visited that village, they always pressed her to stay with them.

One year in early spring after the New Year holiday, when the intense cold of winter was beginning to give way to the gentle spring rains, Ling An, who had arrived in dry weather, was held up at the end house by the first rain of the season. She was sitting in the main room of the house, opposite the gate, teaching the mother-in-law her catechism.

'What must a person who desires to be a Christian promise to perform?' she catechized.

'To live in peace with her neighbours. To go to church regularly. To study the doctrine. Not to gamble nor smoke opium,' faltered the mother-in-law as she pushed her blackened fingernail down the column of characters on the page. The gate was barred for the night. The daughters-in-law were in the kitchen preparing the evening meal. The last of the seven grandchildren stood watching his grandmother as she laboured at her catechism. Two new brothers and a cousin were toddling in the yard outside. The light was fading fast, and the air was getting chilly.

Suddenly the dog growled. The hair on his hackles rose. He got up, went to the gate, and stood before it barking loudly.

'Dog!' shouted one of the daughters-in-law, and she went to the gate and looked through the crack.

'What is it?' she cried.

'Oh Niang, let me in!' came the strange reply from a man standing outside.

Now, everybody who belonged to that family was already home for the night, so the daughter-in-law said, 'Go away. You can't come in.'

'Oh Niang, let me in,' cried the man.

'Who are you? What's your name?'

'Wang Lao Da,' was the reply.

'Wang Lao Da? We're all called Li in this household,' said the daughter-in-law, recoiling as the man fell against the outside of the gate and collapsed in a heap on the threshold.

Ling An had heard her. She leapt to her feet and hobbled as fast as she could to the gate, and as she unbarred it, 'My son!' she sobbed. 'It's my son! Oh my son, Lao Da, I'm coming . . . your mother. Oh my son! Lao Da!'

27

THE CALM

'Just like the prodigal son,' was what Ling An always said with bated breath whenever she told the story of the return of Lao Da.

He was alone, and in a state of utter exhaustion. They dragged him across the threshold and laid him on a bed in one of the rooms. For a while, he was too feeble to speak; but a bowl of hot soup and a good night's sleep strengthened him enough to tell Ling An that her husband, his father, had died many years ago, in one of the great cities they had passed through in their wanderings through the land. What they had done, where they had been, and how they had lived he kept to himself.

All he would say was that, having fallen ill of typhus in a northern province, lost his job, and been deserted by his fair-weather friends, he suddenly felt sick of city life and decided to return to his mother. Having no money, he had begged from village to village as he walked the long way back to his old home.

When Ling An told him that the house and land were no longer theirs, he accepted the fact without comment; and when, after a few days of rest and food, Ling An judged him fit for the long journey back to the church outside the city, he went with her willingly enough, sitting on the other side of the barrow-wheel, balancing Ling An's weight easily, since although he was a full-grown man of no mean stature, illness and privation had reduced him to little more than a skeleton. Ling An got him admitted into the hospital, where the doctor diagnosed his case as one of severe malnutrition bordering on tuberculosis. There he stayed for many weeks, while Ling An planned for his future.

Ling An was astute. Her wages through the years had been carefully hoarded. Now she counted her silver and began to make enquiries about pieces of land, and finally bought a small house with a well and a millstone in the yard and a few terraced fields on a hillside to the west of the city. Then she made enquiries about eligible maidens, for her son must have a wife, and she at last would have a daughter-in-law.

This was much more difficult than finding the land. Lao Da was not young, his health was poor, and nobody knew what he had been doing during his long absence. There were those who thought him lacking in filial piety, and those who argued that he had been filial towards his father and in the end had come back to his mother, and anyway it was not unusual for young men to go away from home and never send a word for years on end, or even not at all. Grass widows in the villages were by no means uncommon.

But then, it might even turn out that Lao Da had left a grass widow waiting in vain for him in one of the cities where he had wandered, or even more than one grass widow, ventured some of the mothers of maidens in their inmost hearts but not in speech. What had he been doing all those years? Would the consequences of some dire deed committed in the past pursue him into this new quiet life which his mother was planning and wreck his life and any one of their daughters who might have been given to him as a wife? Why had he returned to his mother? Was it truly as he had said, because he was sick of city life? Was he escaping from something? These thoughts were certainly not openly expressed in words, but they filled the minds of parents when Ling An's middleman approached them.

Lao Da himself did not need to hear these things stated. He knew that there was truth in their fears. He was escaping and hiding from the consequences of evil living. He even had a wife and three children left desolate in the alleyways of a great city. But of these things he kept silent. Yet there remained some vestige of the goodness which had been his in the days of his innocence before his father had led him astray; and so when his mother told him of this maiden and that, he would have nothing to do with them and said that he had no desire to marry. This to Ling An was a sorrow, for like all women of her generation, she longed for grandchildren and a daughter-in-law. Lao Da did not tell her that she had them already. Such a piece of news was so bound up with the secret of his past life that he felt it was too dangerous to tell even his own mother. So he kept silence.

The farm prospered. Lao Da worked hard and scarcely ever went to the city. Ling An was delighted. A less loving mind might have wondered how Lao Da could be so content with such a solitary life after the hustle and bustle of the big cities and perhaps guessed that Lao Da was hiding; but such a suspicion never entered his mother's mind. It was enough for her that her son had come back to her. The prodigal son had repented of his former wickedness. When he had got everything in order, he would marry. There would be a future generation. What more could any mother want? What more could any woman want? Ling An thought that she could say with the Psalmist, 'My cup runneth over.' She had her livelihood, work which filled her soul with joy; she had good health and strength. Three of her children had survived and were happily established, not too far away for frequent visiting. She had grandchildren: although it was true that they were only grandchildren that her daughters had borne and could not be reckoned as members of her family. Above all, she dwelt in the Good Shepherd's flock; and never was there a sheep that followed him so closely.

She was no scholar, and any self-styled theologian could have considered himself victorious in a discussion of doctrine with her. But she stood her ground firmly in matters of belief, trusting those who had taught her and deepening her faith in continuous fellowship with the Good Shepherd. On one occasion the 'old spinster' from the Roman Catholic church fifty miles away, passing through the city, was obliged to spend the night on the church compound; and being a zealous woman and a good Christian, sought to deliver Ling An from what she considered to be a 'state of error' by discoursing on the apostolic succession as they sat over a pot of tea and a plate of peanuts in Ling An's room. Ling An rose from her chair, took the old spinster by the hand, and led her into the church. There she showed her the bishop's chair, carved with the arms of his diocese, which included his mitre.

'There,' said she. 'That's our bishop's chair. How can you say that our church has no apostolic succession?' Faced with such visible and tangible evidence, the old spinster was silenced for the time being. Ling An, being human, made use of this episode with a certain air of victorious pride when she needed an illustration to explain to some country woman why she could be confirmed only by a bishop and not by the priest who had baptized her.

The years went by uneventfully in that remote region. One year would be remembered by its unusually cold winter, by the deep drifts of snow, by the river covered by huge plates of ice so that men ventured to cross from one side to the other and fell in and were drowned, or by a summer of excessive heat, or by swarms of locusts that ate the standing crops, or by floods, and sometimes by something that became more and more frequent — the passage through the district of soldiers disbanded from some warlord's army.

These men, often penniless, turned to banditry as they journeyed on foot through the country to their own homes, looting and killing as they went. For the whole country was in the turmoil of civil war. North fought with south, up and down the length of the land. Yet the sound of battle rarely came near them, and the rumours and news which reached them seemed so remote from the peace and quiet of their days that they seemed to come from a world which did not concern them, like the old plays which were performed in the open-air theatre every spring by the travelling players.

Then suddenly there was a new enemy, an invader from outside. The Japanese had arrived.

28

THE REFUGEE CAMP

The Chinese soldiers in their grey cotton uniforms and cloth shoes, who flashed their long curved swords on the village threshing-grounds in daily drilling sessions which were more like sword dances done in unison than military drill, were no match for this new enemy with their khaki battle-dress, their thick hobnailed leather boots, their modern arms, tanks, aeroplanes, warships, submarines, and all the recent paraphernalia of war. The Chinese were not lacking in courage and they did what they could; but the enemy drove them from one end of their country to the other. City after city fell before the victorious Japanese; and those Chinese who were not killed fled into hiding in the remote villages, to sally forth as guerrillas in due time to harass their conquerors. War on such a scale could not be unknown even in the most remote of hamlets. Survivors from burning villages came fleeing to the city and were housed in temples, sleeping on the floor at the feet of the hideous statues of gold.

Many came to the church and were housed in the church rooms, sleeping as well as they could on the benches and sometimes on the brick floor under them. But these refugees never stayed long. Directly it was known that the enemy was no longer in their villages, they crept back to the blackened walls and the burnt beams of their houses and set about repairing them, for the seasons would not wait. Fields had to be ploughed, sown and harvested, otherwise there would be nothing to eat. Young women were married as quickly as possible. Their younger sisters were left in the care of Ling An, who lost no time in teaching them about the Good Shepherd. So far there was nothing new in all this. Similar things had happened in the days of the warlords, and through the years Ling An had acquired much experience and wisdom in coping with such emergencies.

But now there came a most alarming rumour. Five thousand troops were on their way to be billeted in the city and in the neighbouring villages. People hastily hid away their stores of grain as best they could. Pits were dug in their yards, and their most valued possessions buried out of sight. Daughters and young daughters-in-law poured into the church compound. Grown sons were sent away hastily to hide in the hills. Mules and wheelbarrows disappeared without a trace.

The city gates were hastily closed; but when the five thousand soldiers arrived, they turned out to be a well-disciplined troop of their own countrymen under a Christian general whose beliefs, although they may have been somewhat unorthodox by usual standards, were the source of behaviour which would have put many other Christians to shame. All his men were set to doing work useful to the citizens. The road from the city to the pass was paved with great blocks of stone which the men gathered from the hills. Breaches in the city wall were repaired, the moat was deepened, and latrines were built on the far side of it and in other places along the road. Across the plain to the river, a high causeway was built so that people could walk through the fields when they were flooded. The dykes along the river were strengthened. Trees were planted on the hillsides.

And every morning the soldiers drilled on the threshing-grounds, marching and singing to hymn tunes furnished with patriotic words. One threshing-ground by the hospital was always in use because there was a cemetery next to it. Immediately the distant hum of an aeroplane was heard, the soldiers dived into the shelter of the cryptomeria trees, where they remained hidden until the plane had passed. In the long dark evenings the men were gathered into groups and taught to read.

The citizens soon lost their fear of them and accepted them. Some people who had been alarmed by reports of atrocities committed by the Japanese invaders now began to relax. 'For' said they, 'these are good men, and they will defend us if the enemy come here.' Others said, 'The enemy will never come here. That is why the soldiers are here. It is a safe place to train them.' And others said, 'Well, but when they are trained, they will leave us to go and fight elsewhere, and then we shall have no one to defend us.'

And that was exactly what happened. One morning when the citizens awoke, they found that the soldiers had all gone, silently marching in their soft-soled shoes over the new causeway to the river. Whether they had crossed it or how they had crossed it nobody knew, for nobody had seen them. The city elders met together and discussed the matter. There must be a reason for this sudden withdrawal of the troops, and everyone knew in his heart that the most probable reason must be the imminent arrival of a large contingent of well-armed Japanese soldiers. What should the city do? It was impossible to defend it with the handful of sentries at the gates and the few police in the city. There was nothing to do officially but wait until the enemy came and then try to placate him if they could.

While the elders were sitting in council, the citizens who had no doubts about the reason for the military retreat from their city began to put their own plans into action; and while the morning was still early, every man who had a relation in a village at a safe distance from the city piled his household goods on to whatever vehicle he could find and fled with his family. Those who had no such places of refuge decided to remain in their homes until the Japanese soldiers were seen descending the pass towards the East Gate. Then everyone would pick up his bundle and make for the church compound or the hospital compound, where they should be safe, at least for a time.

Watchers were posted on the city walls, the city gates were shut and barred, and every household gate was shut and bolted by sunset. Few householders slept that night except by turns with other members of their families. No lamps were lit, and people spoke in whispers. Even children, infected with their elders' fear, did not cry.

The long night passed slowly; but with the first light of day, there was a shout from the watchers on the wall. They climbed down and ran through the streets, banging on the doors and crying, 'They're coming! They're over the pass! Hurry! Hurry!' and the people opened their gates and streamed out into the streets, some going to the church, and some to the hospital.

When the Japanese soldiers arrived half an hour later, they found an empty city. The gates were open. They marched from one end of each of the two main streets to the other and then all around the inside of the wall, but they did not see a soul. There was not a single dog, and only one or two cats who, being highly independent, had escaped from their owners, in spite of attempts to catch them. Hens, ducks, geese, and mules had all gone with their owners.

There was not a living thing left in the city, and it was not long before they discovered that there was nothing edible either. Then they sallied forth in parties to look for vegetables and eggs in the three suburbs outside the South, East, and West Gates; but those inhabitants had also fled. So they returned to the city and satisfied themselves with army rations.

The citizens meanwhile settled themselves in the church and hospital compounds. Some were accommodated in the boys' school and the girls' school, the preaching hall, and the women's class-rooms. The gatehouse was full of the gateman's relations, which included some very distant cousins.

Babies were born and people died. There was sickness and quarrelling, and a great deal of hardy cheerfulness and fortitude; and if time hung heavily for some, it was not because they were idle, for everyone was kept busy providing the necessities of life for himself and the weaker members of his family. They made huts and shelters out of straw mats on the school playing-fields, but as summer passed into winter, these afforded no shelter from the cold; so they dug holes in the ground and made themselves homes underground. Cosy they were, too, with the earth beaten to a smooth flat floor, a raised platform of earth at one end for the family bed, and a flight of steps cut in the earth leading down to the room, which was roofed with straw matting. It was a little dark perhaps, but who wanted light for sleeping? Cooking, sewing, and daylight activities were conducted above in the air and sunshine.

The Japanese lost no time in coming to visit the church and hospital. They knew that the city had been occupied by Chinese soldiers, and it was of prime importance that they should find out where they were hiding. So they banged on the great gate of the church compound, demanding admittance.

The gateman reluctantly unbarred the gate and let them in. Holding their bayonets before them, they marched up the avenue of trees to the church, the sound of their hobnailed leather boots echoing in the sudden silence which had descended upon the refugees when the gate was opened. They opened the church door and marched through it and out through the door in the apse behind the altar. They marched on to the playing-field, and there they divided, some going into the schools to the right and left of the church, others marching across the field to the women's yard.

Da Go, the pensioned gateman who had a room outside the gate of the women's yard and did odd jobs for them when needed, saw the soldiers coming and shouted through the barred gate to Ling An, who was sitting in her room with a great crowd of women and children. In the garden there was a group of husbands, fathers, and older brothers who had just brought their womenfolk into this place of shelter and were now standing about, uncertain where to go or what to do. When they heard Da Go shouting, 'They're here!' these men rushed to the bottom of the garden to hide in the lilac bushes; for well they knew that even if they escaped with their lives, they could be forced to fetch and carry for the Japanese soldiers; and then they would be punished later by their own soldiers, if they should ever return, for consorting with the enemy.

Ling An saw them running for shelter. She called after them, and bade them run into her room and take refuge with their womenfolk. This they did, crouching low on the floor and covering their faces with their arms. Then Ling An went to the gate, looked through the crack between the gates, and saw a Japanese officer coming towards them.

'You can't come in,' she said. 'This is a women's yard.'

At this Da Go, standing beside the officer, said, 'It's all right. I'll come with them. It would be better to let them come in.' So Ling An unbarred the gate, and the soldiers came in.

'I will not lead them anywhere,' she thought, 'but I will go where they go and do what I can for these poor women and children. So she stood waiting for the officer to take the first step; and Da Go stood beside her. The soldiers went to the room where country women stayed for a month when they came in the spring and autumn to learn their catechisms. Although it was crowded with women and children, there was not a sound to be heard, but when the door was flung open and the soldiers tramped in with their bayonets, one small child lifted up its voice and howled.

'Stop that,' said the officer. 'We shall not hurt you. There's nothing to cry about.'

'Nothing to cry about, indeed!' thought Ling An as she followed the soldiers to her own house. 'Nothing to cry about, when your own country is taken over by invaders, when soldiers force you to flee from your own home, when your brothers, husbands and fathers are killed by enemy bullets, when young wives and girls throw themselves down wells rather than live in shame, when whole villages are burnt so that nothing is left but smoke trailing across the blue sky? Nothing to cry about, indeed!'

The door of her room was thrust open and the soldiers tramped in. They saw the men crouching on the floor, and 'Stand up!' the officer shouted in Chinese with a Japanese accent. The men stood up, and for one moment Ling An's heart stood still, fearful that the soldiers were about to kill them with their bayonets; but all they wanted was a clear passage to the cupboard behind the men. This they opened, and they thrust their bayonets though a large bag of millet and a bundle of bedding which they found inside it. 'Well,' thought Ling An, 'it's only grain that's spilled. At least it's not blood.' Then the officer, looking around on the terrified faces of the women and children, commanded his men to depart, and they went as noisily as they had come. They listened in silence to the noise of their feet clumping along the path to the gate and receding across the playing-field.

'Leather shoes,' said one of the women. 'Yes, leather shoes,' repeated another. 'They were all wearing leather shoes,' and they sat there thinking about the leather shoes because they were afraid to talk about what lay uppermost in their hearts.

For most of the day, they sat quietly talking and hushing their children. Nobody ate anything because nobody could cook anything. Mothers and grandmothers who had them took carrots or circles of griddle bread or a few peanuts out of their bundles and gave them to the children. Even the dogs who had come with their families knew better than to bark at each other. A mother cat wandered around looking for her kittens until she found them, three gingerish tabbies, under a hollyhock in the garden where a little girl had hidden them for safety. A woman gave birth to a baby in the school, an epileptic boy fell down in a fit, and an old man had a heart attack. Ling An was kept busy coping with these and many other emergencies through that day.

In the evening, space had to be found on the floor so that everyone could lie down and sleep before darkness closed in, for it was not safe to light candles or lamps in such crowded quarters. When everyone was settled, and every inch of floor space was occupied, Ling An, lying on the table with the refugee girls under it, silently gave thanks that so far no one had been hurt, indeed not as much as the sound of a shot from a rifle had been heard. Then she wondered how long these people would have to remain with them and where food to satisfy so many hungry mouths could be found; but remembering the story of the feeding of the five thousand, she thought, 'It's all right. The Good Shepherd will think of a plan,' and pulling the quilt up over her chin, she soon fell asleep.

She was awakened by the two girls under the table. 'Listen!' said one, 'Listen!'

'Leather shoes,' said the other. 'They're going.'

Ling An leaned up on her elbow and listened. Beyond the wall at the end of the garden, there came the measured tramp of an army of men marching along the road under the willow trees. The sky was already pale in the early light, and the oriole fluted his four notes across the garden. There was someone knocking at the gate.

'They've gone,' said Da Go when Ling An opened it. 'They've all gone.'

'Thank the Lord for that!' cried Ling An, and she went to tell the refugees the good news.

After a hasty consultation, some of the men ventured out, and crossed the road, and peered through the empty gateway of the city. There was no one inside. Two, greatly daring, entered and crept up the silent street. No one was in sight. Others, when they heard no shots, climbed up to the top of the wall, and crouching low as they went, surveyed the inside of the city. It was empty. Then they came down and traversed the streets and lanes. They went into their own homes; they looked over their neighbours' walls. There was no doubt about it, the enemy had left, taking all their arms with them.

So they returned to their families in the church compound and told them the news. The refugees did not return. The wiser ones decided to wait and see what happened. Others, more foolhardy, ventured in, but were so appalled by the strange silence that hung over the city that they soon returned, carrying their cooking pots and other cooking utensils, which they told each other were what they had returned to get.

Soon after midday, the church gateman, looking out, was amazed to see that the city gate was shut and that there were two sentries standing on guard on the city wall above it. He could not believe his eyes, so he called his twelve-year-old son and asked him to look and see whether the men were Japanese or Chinese. The boy peered fearfully from the gatehouse window.

'They are our soldiers,' he said.

The Chinese soldiers who had left two nights ago were back again. They stayed for three weeks, and then as mysteriously as they had returned they vanished again; but this time they did not get away without casualties. There was the sound of distant firing, a quick burst of rifle shots in the south suburb, and the smell of smoke from burning houses; and then the girls who still slept under Ling An's table wept because they lived in the south suburb and feared it was their homes that were burning.

In the evening the Japanese were once more occupying the city. This time they had come to stay. The refugees at the church and hospital had made good use of the three weeks' respite. Some had departed for distant villages across the river where they had relations; but these had been replaced by refugees from other villages harried by the enemy. All who could had gone out and harvested their crop of wheat, and brought it to be stored in the church compound. They sallied forth every morning and came back laden in the evening.

Booths made of straw mats were erected all over the playing-field, so that each family could have its own home. Young girls in the women's yard tended their silkworms, gathering mulberry leaves from the trees in Ling An's garden to feed them. There were classes in the long afternoons to teach them to read the Thousand Character Gospel. If you read a new page every day, you learned ten new characters. So if you read the whole book of one hundred pages, you would have learned one thousand characters. But who wanted to live like this for one hundred days? They all thought they would be able to go home long before that.

But the days went by, and the autumn came with its crisp cool mornings. The autumn crops of millet, corn, and sorghum, and later the sweet potatoes and peanuts and cotton, and last of all the carrots had to be gathered in. The refugees sallied forth from the back gate of the church compound every morning and returned in the evening as they had done in the early summer. Then when everything was gathered in, they began to prepare for the winter.

In the city, grass grew in the silent streets, for the city had become a fort, manned by the Japanese, who were to be seen on guard at the gates and walking along the top of the city wall. At night, guerrillas would creep through the south suburb and attack the guards on duty there.

Then hand-grenades flew across the church compound, and once two landed in the school playing-field, but exploded without harming any of the refugees cowering under their quilts in their underground homes. Rifle shots were exchanged from either side, but generally the Japanese waited for dawn and then sent charges from their mortar gun after the fleeing guerrillas.

Often after such a night, Ling An would go down to the bottom of the garden and peer cautiously through the drainage holes in the wall by the road between the willow trees that went away to the south. Was there a wounded man there? What should she do if one should be there? Fearfully she peered, hoping that she would see no one, for well she knew that if she did, she would have to help him.

One day there was a man there. He was lying unconscious behind a great boulder which hid him from the road, but which could not hide him from the parties of Japanese soldiers who would be sallying forth from the South Gate before the sun was much higher in the sky. Quicker than she could think, Ling An hobbled to her room, seized the key of the back gate, opened it, shut it behind her, and hobbled around the east wall to the south wall, seized the man by the shoulders, and dragged him to the back gate. As she did so, the guerrillas attacked the guards at the city gate. The air was full of the staccato of rifle shots. Then the Japanese in the early morning light replied with their mortar fire. Ling An dragged the man to the back gate, pulled him inside, locked it, and dragged him down the garden path to a little shed at the bottom where she kept wood and charcoal. She dragged him inside and then saw his face for the first time. It was Lao Da.

29

THE GUERRILLA

Lao Da had never been communicative about his life from the time he had left home with his father until his return alone to his mother. Sometimes he would mention the name of this city and that which they had visited; but he never said what they had done there, and Ling An, supposing that it would be a tale of gambling and robbery and even worse, had not dared to pursue him with questions. There were things that were better left unknown. The past was done, and as far as she could see, Lao Da had left it behind him for ever.

But Lao Da had met something in that dark passage of his life which had enslaved him far worse than the ancient vices into which men fall could ever do; for these which corrupt both body and soul are a man's own choice, and if he was free to embrace them, he is still free to cast them off if he desires and is strong enough; and there is help for him if he is too weak to do it alone, as every repentant sinner knows from his experience. But this thing which enslaved Lao Da was outside himself, and he could no more escape from it than an unarmed diver who has unwittingly swum into the seething mass of tentacles of a giant octopus in the depths of the sea.

It had happened that one day when Wang and his son

were travelling from one city to another, they had met a merchant on the road. He was travelling alone, since his village home was not far from the city, and although the way was rough and lonely, he had not anticipated any danger in broad daylight. Wang and his son set upon him and robbed him of a good fat purse of silver dollars which they found stuffed in his belt. They had used violence, but not enough to kill him; but the merchant was elderly and suffered from his heart, and their rough treatment was too much for him. When they let go of him, he sank to the ground apparently lifeless. Lao Da and his father left him where he lay and fled. The merchant was not dead, and when another traveller found him a few minutes later, he was able to give a good description of the two robbers.

Father and son, thinking that man was dead and could tell no tales, skirted the road for some distance and then returned to it and made their way to the next city.

There the police found them in an inn, gambling with the merchant's money. It was not long before Wang and his son found themselves being led through the main street of the city with ropes around their necks, on their way to execution outside the gate.

They were not the only ones in this dire state, for marching with them were the leader of a band of guerrillas and several of his men who had been captured in a recent skirmish in the hills.

Twenty citizens, members of an underground organization known as the Comrades, had mingled themselves in the crowd who pressed around the prisoners and their escort. This crowd was so dense that the police had difficulty in keeping the way clear for themselves and their captives. Lao Da, shocked by the sudden change of circumstances, was walking like a man in a dream. Suddenly there was a sharp staccato sound as of bullets all around him. The Comrades were letting off strings of fire-crackers. People, supposing that bandits had come to rescue their comrades, rushed hither and thither in panic as they tried to escape from what they thought were rifle shots. In the mêlée, the Comrades seized as many prisoners as they could. Wang had already dashed into the crowd as he tried to save himself. Lao Da felt himself firmly gripped by a stranger who flung his own jacket over his captive's naked back and pushed him into the jostling crowd, where they were soon lost to sight.

Police in the meantime recaptured Wang, and the mob of angry and righteous citizens pressed on to the city gate to see justice done on one of the robbers at least.

As the crowd surged past the road that went all around the city inside the wall, Lao Da's captor drew him out of the mob on to the deserted road, and thence, twisting and turning in a labyrinth of alleys, they came to a small house in a yard behind a tinker's shop.

'That was well done,' the Comrade said as he pulled the double doors together and barred them shut. 'A dollar well spent on fireworks and nobody hurt, and we shall soon know how many heads have been saved from hanging over the city gate.'

Lao Da stood speechless before him. 'What is he going to do with me?' he thought.

Then from the North Gate there went up a great roar of satisfaction from the crowd as they saw justice done.

'So,' said the Comrade, 'someone was not saved.' At that moment, there was the sound of footsteps outside and a stealthy whisper through the crack between the doors. The comrade, recognizing the password, opened the door and let in his leader and all the comrades with those whom they had managed to save.

'Call the roll,' said the leader. 'Many were saved. Let us know how many!' So they called the roll, and each man as he answered stepped into a line before his leader, until no one was left but Lao Da, who stood alone at the back of the room.

'What's this?' said the leader. 'This man is not one of

us! Who are you?' he asked Lao Da. Lao Da, deeming that silence was his only refuge, said nothing.

'Who brought him here?' demanded the leader of the men lined up before him.

'I did,' said Lao Da's captor. 'Is he not one of us?'

'He is not. He knows our meeting-place. He knows our faces and our names. We are no longer safe. He must be killed.' At this Lao Da threw himself on the ground at the leader's feet and knocked his head upon the earth floor.

'Have pity upon me,' he pleaded. 'I do not know you. I do not know the name of this place. I will never tell anybody about you. How can I tell what I do not know? Have you not saved my life? Am I not your man from this time for ever?'

The leader hesitated. Lao Da's captor said, 'He could become one of us. We need new men to replace those whom we have lost. This one looks young and strong.'

'Is he not one of those two men who robbed the merchant?' said an older comrade.

'We want no criminals in our ranks,' said the leader.

'True,' replied the older man. 'But he is young and could be taught. It may be that he has vices which could become virtues. Such a man could be useful.'

The leader thought for a while. Lao Da with his head on the ground shook with fear.

'Very well,' said the leader at last. Then, turning to Lao Da's captor, he said, 'You saved his life. He is your man. Train him.'

There was food and shelter and rest and safety of a kind. Stunned as he was by the shock of his father's execution and his own escape from the same fate, Lao Da accepted everything without comment. The secret underground organization known as the Comrades, of which the guerrillas were members, took charge of Lao Da's life. He was to them as a brand plucked from the burning. They probed the veneer of viciousness which Lao Da had acquired, and penetrating to the real Lao Da beneath, they found courage, fortitude and loyalty: good virtues which could be used for their purpose. Moreover, since he had been rescued by them from execution, he was completely in their power and utterly dependent on them, at least for the time being. Meanwhile, he could be indoctrinated so that eventually he might become one of themselves.

Lao Da at first supposed that he had fallen into the hands of a gang of bandits, and was surprised at the puritanical conduct which they demanded of him. Gambling and similar vices were forbidden. Drunkenness was not tolerated. Honesty in material matters was insisted upon. Quarrelling was not allowed. There was a spirit of comradeship among them which was attractive to Lao Da, who had been an outcast for so long; but he soon discovered that brotherly love did not extend beyond their ranks. All who opposed them and had a different philosophy were hated with extraordinary violence; and this hatred was also directed against those of themselves who deviated and left their ranks. Such men disappeared in a mysterious manner, and their names were never mentioned again.

The man who had rescued Lao Da took him to his own house and kept him there until the next market day when, hiding him under sacks of sweet potatoes and cabbages in a cart drawn by an ox, he smuggled him out of the city and handed him over to one of his comrades in another city. Lao Da now became another person; trained and indoctrinated, he eventually became a trusted member of the organization. After a few months of good feeding and rest he looked so different from his former self that it was deemed safe to get him a job as a water-carrier in the city governor's household.

Now Lao Da began to flourish. Life was good; he had health and strength which he delighted in using. He had a steady job with reasonably good wages. It was time to marry and get himself some sons. This was not easily accomplished, for since he had come a stranger to the city, and nobody knew anything about his family, not even about his life before he had become the governor's water-carrier, parents were chary of binding their daughters to such a man.

Finally, after many months, his middleman found a young woman whose widowed mother was willing to allow her daughter to marry him, for she was in desperate fear that her daughter would never wed anyone. The daughter, Da Chieh, was the eldest of her family of ten. At nine years old, when her mother should have pushed her toes under the soles of her feet and bound them tightly with long strips of cloth, Da Chieh had fallen under an ox-cart and broken her leg.

This accident had delayed the foot-binding; and when it became obvious that the leg had been set badly and the girl would always be lame, her mother had never had the heart to inflict further pain on her daughter, so she had grown up with large feet and a lame leg. As if this were not enough, a heavy infection of ringworm had taken off every hair of her head; and although by the time she was fifteen, this disease had cured itself, as it often does, the new hair was frizzy and rust-red, instead of being smooth and shining black.

Added to this affliction was a complexion pitted with smallpox. The rust-red hair ran through the whole family. It was probably inherited from some remote Mongolian ancestor, but it could be hidden with oil and dye. But nothing could be done to hide the lame leg, the large feet, and the scars of smallpox. Da Chieh, twenty-five years old, still wore her hair in a plait down her back and a fringe across her forehead. She herself had begun to wonder what would become of her, for now age was being added to her other disabilities. Her widowed mother was even more worried, for she blamed herself for being so soft-hearted in the matter of foot-binding.

So when Lao Da's middleman came, Da Chieh's mother seized upon this chance of marriage as a drowning man seizes a straw floating upon the sea. Lao Da, of course, would have preferred a better-looking wife; but by this time he knew that he would never have much choice in this matter. Da Chieh was healthy and capable, and if her looks were poor, at least she would never be coveted by any other man.

The marriage turned out well. Da Chieh was a dutiful wife, and it was not long before the two of them were united with a quiet steady bond of affection. Three children were born, two sons and a daughter. Lao Da was delighted with his sons, but when his daughter arrived, his joy knew no bounds.

'She shall have a name,' he said.

'Girls don't have names,' said his wife.

'Well! But she shall have a name. Some girls have names. My mother had a name. A good name it was, too.'

'Good,' said Da Chieh. 'What will you call her, then?'

'Jun. She's a little beauty. She shall be called Jun.'

'Little Beauty! A good name: but she will not be beautiful, husband. Look, her hair is too light. It will be rusty like mine and that of her brothers.'

'True. But that does not matter. She will be beautiful even with rusty hair.'

'It can't be helped, husband; but we will call her Jun even so.'

So, with his wife and three children, Lao Da lived in great contentment in a tiny house in the lane that ran along the back of the governor's residence. The Comrades noted this with satisfaction. Such an apparently innocent and harmless water-carrier was an excellent tool in their hands. They had made their plans and one of the preliminaries essential to success was the assassination of the governor.

For the governor was that rare official in China: a man of incorruptible integrity. A Hanlin scholar, he was steeped in the precepts of Confucius, and modelled his life and work on the teaching of that sage. Although he was over sixty years old and wore a sparse beard beneath his chin, he was still very alert and active. He knew all the officials working under him and dealt sternly with any who were found taking bribes or indulging in any other corrupt practices. The result was a well-governed city and a content and prosperous population. Even the beggars were provided for. The governor was therefore much respected and even beloved by all but the few men of inferior morals who are to be found in every city.

So far, the Comrades' efforts to gain control of the city had been completely unsuccessful. The governor's impeccable reputation was proof against their accusations of bribery and corruption. It was impossible to tamper with the local currency to produce inflation and upset the prosperity of the citizens by ruining their trade, because the governor kept such strict control over every department that no official could be bribed or cajoled into dishonest practices without his knowledge. Even the Comrades' attempts to get him promoted to the governorship of another city already so corrupt that he would have been comparatively harmless to their schemes proved fruitless. He was so beloved that the citizens were unwilling to lose him, and successfully pleaded to keep him. The governor himself had no desire for promotion. He was already old and was looking forward to an honourable retirement among his chrysanthemums in his ancestral home in the country.

The Comrades saw only one possibility of getting rid of the governor, and that was by assassination. When their plans were ripe, they called Lao Da to their meeting-place in a village about two miles from the city and told him what they intended to do and how he was to help them.

The governor, like many elderly Chinese gentlemen, was in the habit of performing certain ancient exercises early every morning in the open air in his private courtyard. These exercises were supposed to promote such muscular control that the body could be made light enough in weight to enable a man to walk like a fly on the ceiling of his house. One sage was said to have been so successful that on one occasion, needing to cross the Yangtse River at a place where there was neither ferry nor bridge, he balanced himself upon a straw floating on the surface of the water and steered himself across the water to the opposite bank.

While the governor was occupied in exercising his body according to these ancient precepts, one of the maid-servants waited at the gate for Lao Da. Once he was inside, she barred the gate and returned to the house to prepare an early cup of tea for her mistress. Lao Da then drew buckets of water from the well in the middle of the courtyard and proceeded to water the chrysanthemums which stood in ranks around the sides of the yard.

The Comrades, knowing this, told Lao Da that on the morning of the next day three of them would come to the gate, which he would open and guard while they killed the governor, who could expect no help from the womenfolk who were the only other people living with him.

Lao Da was most unwilling to have anything to do with this plan. He had nothing against the governor, who seemed to him to be a kindly old gentleman and much to be respected by all decent people. Although Lao Da and his father had handled people roughly when they robbed them, Lao Da himself had never killed anyone.

Moreover, he knew that such an act would be the end of his present job, his family life, and personal security. He was between the devil and the deep sea. The Comrades made it clear that if he did not help them kill the governor, then they would kill him. He had lived among them long enough to know that he must not show any signs of unwillingness to conform to their plans; so he said, 'Good, I will open the gate when you come tomorrow,' and when the would-be assassins began to discuss the details of their part in the matter, he excused himself, saying that the city gate would be shut earlier than usual that night as there were reports of a warlord's disbanded army in the district.

As he walked through the fields between the village and

the city, he pondered how he could avoid his part in this plan. He knew the Comrades well enough to realize that he could do nothing to save the governor. If they did not get him one way, they would get him another. As he thought of this plan and that to save himself and his family, his steps grew slower and slower until at last he found himself standing in the middle of a path through a field that extended to the moat around the wall of the city.

'There is no help for it,' he said to himself. 'I am like a fly that is caught in a web. There is no one to take me out, and I cannot get out myself. I do not wish to do evil, but evil pushes me and I cannot save myself from it. If the Old Heavenly Grandfather cared about what happens upon this earth, he would stretch down a hand from heaven and lift me up and away from this terrible choice. But why should he trouble himself for me, a small fly caught in a web? Men must help themselves, and when evil is too strong for them, there is nothing they can do.'

As he stood there disconsolately, he lifted up his eyes towards the city wall and saw that the gate was closed. He would not be able to get in until it was opened the next morning.

'Now what shall I do?' he said to himself. To bang on the gate and clamour to be let in would be of no use. The gatekeepers would suppose him to be one of the disbanded soldiers, and the city police on the wall above the gate would shoot him. There was nothing for it but to find himself a shelter for the night and return to the city in the morning.

He turned and walked slowly back to the village. All the doors were barred and people were abed. Only the dogs barked as they cocked their ears to the sound of his footsteps in the dusty road. So he walked through the village and on through the fields until he came to the river; and there he found a boat moored to the bank. He stepped aboard and descended into one of the three holds which were waiting empty for the grain which would be loaded into them the next day.

There, with his knees drawn up to his chin, he attempted to sleep. That, however, was impossible. Rats came out of their holes and ran over his feet, and cockroaches crept out of the cracks between the timbers and crawled up and down his body. In the middle of the night the boat was suddenly manned by its crew, who rapidly steered it into the midstream current.

'We can't wait to load the wheat,' he heard one of them say. 'If we leave the boat moored here, the soldiers will take it. Let's get away while we can.'

By morning they were twenty miles downstream. Lao Da, having convinced them that he was not one of the war-lord's men, could not persuade them to let him disembark at one of the villages beside the river. The crew would not stop until they reached the capital city of the province at noon the next day.

There Lao Da went ashore and stumbled up the muddy street that led to the town. His head ached, all his limbs felt stiff and heavy, his eyes smarted, and nausea rose in his throat. The ground beneath his feet seemed to rise up and down, trees and people vanished and reappeared grotesquely.

'What is the matter with me?' he thought. 'Am I ill? I must not be ill. I cannot be ill now.'

But ill he was. By nightfall, he was so hot with fever that he could no longer walk. He stumbled into the entrance of a deserted alleyway and collapsed. How he was discovered, who took him to a hospital in the city where he was nursed through a bout of typhus fever, he never knew. He only knew that this illness was a crisis in his life. It marked the end of all that had gone before and was the beginning of whatever might lie ahead. When he was strong enough, he set off on his journey home to his mother. He would have nothing more to do with the Comrades.

It was no wonder that he was so uncommunicative about

his former history. His life depended on his silence. He thought at first that he had truly escaped from the Comrades. He settled down on the land which Ling An had bought for him and gradually began to enjoy a feeling of security. His mother's love warmed him and melted the hardening of his heart, and when she told him of the Christian way of life, he began to hope that he might be set free from the torture of his guilty conscience. Was not the dying thief forgiven at the last moment? And what about the Prodigal Son that Ling An was so fond of telling him he was like?

Yet in the night he would wake and remember the wife and children of his former life. What could he do about them? As far as they knew, he was dead; and for his own safety, dead he must remain to them. And then he would think of his two little boys and their little sister, and he would wonder. 'How are they faring now, with no father to earn money to buy food for them?' Then he would groan aloud and say, 'What can a man like me do? There is no one to help me.' Night after night he would waken in the deep silence and think of these things, and toss and turn until the cocks crowed in the morning. At last he could stand it no longer and resolved to take his mother into his confidence, for he knew that she was a wise woman and loved him well. He made up his mind to do this on the next market day, after he had sold his load of winter cabbages and carrots.

Alas! As he squatted by the straw mat on the road where his goods were displayed, a shadow fell across him, and a heavy hand was laid upon his shoulder, raising him to his feet.

'Comrade! At last I have found you.' Lao Da's eyes met the eyes of the man before him, and he recognized the Comrade who had originally saved him from execution. There was no escape for him now.

'Well, here you are,' said the Comrade. 'There's work for you to do.'

'Work?' said Lao Da.

'Yes, work. We know what happened last time. We do not blame you. Nobody can help being ill.'

'How did you know that?'

'We know everything, Comrade.'

'Nobody knew, not even my wife.'

'We knew. Did you think we would let you go, Comrade? Surely you know us well by now.'

'My wife and my children?'

'Well. All of them.'

'Then I will go back to them.'

'No, Comrade, you will stay here. We need you here. Have you not a house and some fields on the hillside? We need a rallying-point for our guerrillas.'

'Then my wife and children must come to me here.'

'No, they will stay with us. You can visit them. You can stay with them when we call you to our meetings.'

So Lao Da was dragged back into the ranks of the Comrades. That his wife and children were hostages he quickly realized, but at least he could return to them, and he lost no time in doing so.

Da Chieh was sitting in her courtyard, making shoe soles for Koko, her elder son, who was now five years old and could wear out a pair of shoes in less than six weeks. The two little boys were playing outside with other children, but Jun who was now three years old was sitting with her mother, half dozing in the winter sunshine.

Lao Da came softly through the gateway.

'Wife!' he called.

'Aiyah!' cried Da Chieh, turning as white as snow.

'I have come back.'

'Oh Husband! You have been gone so long.'

'Well, here I am,' said Lao Da, giving no explanation for his absence, after the manner of Chinese husbands.

'I'll cook you some noodles and eggs.' Da Chieh got up and went into the kitchen. Lao Da picked up his little daughter and carried her into the house.

His heart was too full to overflow in words. Here at last he was reunited with his family. As for Da Chieh, she could scarcely believe that it was really Lao Da sitting in the house, with Jun on his lap.

In a little while the little boys came in, and the noodles being ready, Da Chieh set a steaming bowl before her husband. As Lao Da took the bowl into his hands and looked at Da Chieh and the three children standing before him, tears filled his eyes and ran down his cheeks.

'Oh Husband!' cried Da Chieh, weeping with him. 'Eat while the food is hot. You have been gone so long. Oh my husband!'

The children stood around them silent, round-eyed with wonder.

During the years the Comrades had gathered themselves together under a military leader. Now, when the country was overrun by an alien enemy, the Comrades formed themselves into bands of guerrillas which harassed the Japanese soldiers without mercy. Night after night, they crept through the silent fields to attack the enemy guards at the gates of their cities, so that the enemy dared not go out by night. They dug ditches across the roads and lay in ambush. Their attacks were so frequent and so formidable that no buses ever travelled singly. They all went together in a convoy, raising such a cloud of dust as they went that they were quite invisible. Even so, buses were overturned and burnt. All this activity cost money, and this the Comrades obtained by kidnapping the sons of rich farmers and holding them for ransom. Everybody feared the Comrades, but most people had a sneaking regard for them. To young people, students especially, they were heroes, for were they not fighting the national enemy and would they not drive him out in the end?

So, Lao Da, drawn back into their ranks, became a guerrilla. He still worked on the land which Ling An had bought for him and lived in the house there. When there was little to do in the fields in the slack times of the farmers' year, he would go to the city and stay with his wife and family.

From time to time guerrillas met in the house in the fields and sallied forth to attack the Japanese in the early hours of the morning. Lao Da went with them. He told Da Chieh nothing of these activities. Nor did he tell his mother Ling An. It would have been impossible to do so anyway, for the Japanese army made travelling very difficult for the inhabitants of those cities which were occupied by Japanese soldiers. All sensible people stayed at home. Lao Da stayed away and his mother supposed that, like everyone else in the villages around, he was avoiding the city and its near neighbourhood.

As for Da Chieh, although she had been told nothing, she knew that her husband was a Comrade and a guerrilla.

30

THE CONVERSATION

As Ling An stared amazed at her son, he opened his eyes and looked at her.

'Niang!' he said, 'Hide me!'

'Good, my son,' she said. 'You are safe here.'

'Do not tell anyone,' he said.

'No one shall know you are here.'

She took some bundles of sorghum stalks and leaned them against the wall so that they covered him. Then she fetched water and bathed the wound in his shoulder. A bullet had gone right through, and she knew that if she could keep the wound clean and give him time to rest and eat and make up the blood he had lost, he could recover. But how could she keep him hidden?

'Listen,' she said, 'this shed is always locked, and I have the key. I will bring you food at night, but all day you must wait with patience and not make a sound.'

'Good, my mother,' said Lao Da. 'You are a good woman.'

Even as he spoke, there was a loud banging on the gate of the garden.

'Open up! Open up!' shouted the Japanese soldier, kicking the gate with his boot, 'Open up! Open up!'

Ling An hastily locked the padlock on the shed door,

and hobbled away to the gate. Slowly she drew the bars back and opened the gate.

'Good morning, Brother,' she said. 'Have you eaten yet?' The blustering Japanese soldier marched into the garden, holding his bayonet horizontally before him. He marched all round the yard, and when he came to the shed, 'Open it!' he said; but at that moment Ling An said, 'Aiyah! Aiyah! Oh, whatever is that?' putting one hand to her mouth like one in terror; with the other hand she pointed to the far end of the garden where a cat had just run into a bush of mountain lilac.

The leaves were still shaking. The Japanese, convinced that he was about to catch a guerrilla, ran to the bush and thrust his bayonet into it. The cat leapt out on the other side. The soldier laughed. Ling An laughed. Two little girl refugees watching from the window laughed. Everybody began to call the cat, 'Mi-mi, come here! Mi-mi, Mi-mi!' but the cat jumped into the apricot tree and glared at them with its eyes afire.

'Only a cat,' said the soldier, and went off, swaggering though the gate in a good humour.

Late that night, when all the young refugee women were sound asleep on the floor of Ling An's house, she stepped carefully between their sleeping forms, and silently opening her door, she slipped out of the house and made her way to the shed. As she opened the door and slipped inside, Lao Da sat up and looked out between the bundles of sorghum stalks that hid him.

'Wife,' he said, 'you're late. Where are my sons? Have you brought them and my little daughter? Is she safe?'

'Wife!' thought Ling An. 'He must have a fever.' She knelt down on the ground and unwrapped the wound. It looked clean. There was very little inflammation. 'Well,' she thought, 'perhaps it's a bout of malaria, and he will be better in a few hours.' So she sat down beside him, prepared to watch through the night and keep him from talking so loudly that the Japanese sentries would hear him.

Talk he did, all through the night, rambling on and on about the events of his past life. Ling An listened in horror at first, and then with great pity. Gradually she came to understand that the wife he had thought her to be was a certain Da Chieh, a woman whom he had wed in the years he had been away from home. The little girl Jun was his daughter and her grandchild, and she had two brothers.

'These are my grandchildren too,' thought Ling An, and joy was mixed with the shame and horror she felt.

An hour before dawn, the fever went, and Lao Da slept. Ling An set a pot of tea and a cup beside him, and some griddle bread, and crept back to her own house, fearful lest some of the young women should wake and find her missing.

The next night when she went to the shed, Lao Da was much better.

'Mother,' he said, 'I must go.'

'Good, my son,' said Ling An. 'But first you must eat,' and she set before him a bowl of millet porridge with beans in it. As he ate, Ling An said, 'My son, you have been talking about a woman who is your wife, and has borne you two sons and a daughter. I must know who she is and where she lives, for these are my grandchildren, and your life may be taken from you at any moment.'

Lao Da, chopsticks in his hand, stopped eating.

'Niang,' he said, 'Niang, I am an evil man, and I have done many evil things.'

'True it is,' said Ling An, 'but every sinner can be forgiven. The Good Shepherd rejoices whenever one lost sheep is found. Eat first, and then tell me your story.'

So Lao Da ate, and after that, in the shelter of the sorghum stalks against the wall in the darkness of the shed, he and his mother talked in whispers for a long time. It was a terrible tale that he told, so long and involved and so disjointed that Ling An soon lost the thread running through it. It sickened and shocked her so that she could hardly bear to listen, but she endured for the sake of the three grandchildren.

'What happened to the woman, their mother?' she asked.

'She washed clothes for a living,' he said, for this he had found out from the Comrade who had found him, 'but now I am able to keep her.'

'And the three children?'

'They are with their mother.'

'Aiyah!' said Ling An. 'That I should never see my grandsons!'

'Who knows?' replied Lao Da. 'It is not impossible.'

'Well, and how would I know them if I did see them?'

'Ah, you would know them. They all have rusty hair,' he said, smiling wryly, 'and the little girl has a name, like you, Mother. I called her Jun.'

'Ah,' said Ling An. 'Perhaps I will see her one day.'

'If they are still living. A child's life is uncertain,' he said.

'So is an adult's life in these days,' sighed his mother. 'But we can meet in heaven.'

'Ah, heaven!' said Lao Da. 'But I am shut out of heaven. The Comrades do not believe in heaven, nor in God.'

'But you do, my son?'

Lao Da said nothing for a minute. Then, 'When I think of you, Mother, I do. Oh Niang, Niang!' he cried, 'I am caught in a web and I cannot get out! There is no help for me!'

'There is help, my son. Turn to the Good Shepherd and follow him.'

'It is easy for you, Niang. You have always been good.'

'Not so, son. Only by the grace of God. The Good Shepherd has kept me all my life and guided me through many troubles.'

'All your life, Niang? You did not know the Good Shepherd when we were young.'

'True, I did not know him then, but he knew me. I have been a sheep in his flock from the time I was baptized, a poor sickly lamb of a baby, and was given my name. The Good Shepherd keeps his lambs and follows them when they stray and calls them to come to him. He keeps me close to him, and while he looks at me, how can I do anything he does not like?'

At that moment the silence was broken by the sharp sound of rifle shots in the road on the other side of the garden wall. The guerrillas were attacking again.

'Quick, Mother! Let me go. The Comrades are here and will help me.'

'Can you not wait one more night, my son? Another day's rest and food would give you strength.'

'No. After tonight the Japanese will come again to search the place and they will find me. I must go.'

'Then I will go with you.'

'No! You cannot come with me.'

'Well, but I will go with you until you meet someone who can help you.' Lao Da found that he could not stand alone and walk without stumbling, so he put his hand on his mother's shoulder and let her lead him to the gate in the east wall. This she unlocked silently, and the two slipped out into the dark fields.

'They will be hiding near by,' said Lao Da. 'If we creep through the fields, I can wait there till they finish the attack and return with them.'

It was pitch dark, and a very still night. As they walked through the fields along the narrow beaten paths, their soft-soled shoes made no sound. A mile from the city they turned to the right along a path that led them to the road. There they stopped and crouched low on the ground.

'I will wait for them here,' said Lao Da, 'but you must return at once, for it will soon be morning.'

'Good, my son. I will go.'

Ling An hobbled away in the darkness as fast as she could go, for the cocks were crowing in the villages, and she knew that the sky would soon grow pale in the east. It was still dark, and Ling An was passing through a field of sorghum near the church, when she heard the sound of rifle shots again. She dived between the sorghum stalks beside the road for shelter. Soon hand grenades landed on the path where she had been standing, and exploded. 'The Japanese must have heard me moving,' she thought as she crept further into the sorghum field. The exploding grenades set the sorghum stalks ablaze. Ling An fled further into the field, pushing her way through the tall stalks to the other side. There with eyes smarting from the smoke, she found herself standing on the road, and saw that the sky behind the pass was already growing pale.

As she stood in the road, uncertain which way to go, she heard the sound of heavy boots tramping along the road, and before she could turn or flee into any hiding-place, a Japanese soldier came in sight. As he came down the road towards her, she recognized his face. He was the man who had come into the church compound three days before, searching for guerrillas. She knew better than to run, for nothing spurs a soldier to shooting more than something fleeing from him. So she stood still in the road.

'Oh Lord, Good Shepherd,' she prayed, 'have mercy upon us. Deliver me from this man, and deliver him from the sin of murder.'

The soldier bore down on her. 'What are you doing here?' he grunted.

Ling An said nothing.

'Who are you?'

There was no answer.

'Are you not the woman who lives at the church?'

Ling An was silent.

'You are the woman who lives at the church.'

Ling An said nothing.

'I have seen you there, you are that woman. Answer me!' shouted the soldier.

Ling An was as silent as a dumb woman.

The soldier slapped her face.

At that Ling An, who up till then had been paralysed with fear, reached up and slapped the soldier's face. The soldier wrenched the bayonet from his rifle, and held it poised above Ling An's head. For a few seconds which seemed as long as minutes, they stared into each other's eyes. The soldier's nostrils moved in and out like a rabbit's. Anger flared out of his eyes. Then he lowered his arm, clicked his bayonet into the end of his rifle, and tramped on down the road.

Ling An stood stock still until she could no longer hear the sound of his feet. Then moving slowly and deliberately, she moved into the cover of a graveyard on the opposite side of the road. After a while, she heard the soldier return, and soon after that, there came the sound of shots again. Then once more the Japanese used their mortar gun. Bombs and hand-grenades flew back and forth. This was no ordinary sally, but a full-scale guerrilla attack. Had Ling An wished to cross the road and return to the church compound, it would have been impossible to reach it alive.

As she crouched among the graves, almost deafened by the explosions all around her, she tried to decide what to do. She dared not return to the church, for if she did so, she would endanger all those taking refuge there, for that Japanese soldier had recognized her. She had escaped death once by a miracle. Of that she was sure. The soldier's hand had been stayed at the height of his anger. But now from her sound common sense she thought, 'Does he know where I am? Is he watching to see where I go? Am I a snare with which he will catch the Comrades?' And then she thought, 'I cannot go to the Comrades either,' not that she wished to take shelter with them . . . people who had so enslaved her son, who did not believe in God, and who did such evil deeds to attain their own ends. But although she abhorred them, she had no desire to betray them and lead them to execution.

The battle raged all day as Ling An crouched among the graves, the hands of her soul tightly gripping the hem of the Good Shepherd's robe, for well she knew that he was there with her. Then as it grew dark, the shooting stopped.

'Now!' she said to herself. 'Now I will go, before anyone comes out to look for me.' So when it was quite dark, she stood up, and leaving the graveyard, she followed a narrow path between the terraced fields which she knew would lead her to the pass; but where she would go after that she had no idea.

31

THE WARLORD

In those days there was much journeying to and fro. People who had never left their native villages and the surrounding hills found themselves on the roads to places they had never heard of before. A great many fled to the cities, for once these had been occupied by the enemy, conditions inside them were comparatively peaceful. Those who had money could hide themselves and, in the anonymity of a crowded city, escape from the demands of the guerrillas, who needed more and more money to buy arms. Many who were willing to support their own lawful government in its efforts to drive out the enemy were not at all willing to satisfy the demands of the Comrades, who now began to play an increasingly powerful role in the commanding of the guerrillas.

As the enemy advanced across the country from the east, cities fell before them like rows of ninepins, and the government was forced to flee ever further to the west. The country left behind them was ruled by a puppet government set up by the enemy. In the cities occupied and defended by enemy soldiers, this government was able to keep a semblance of law and order at the price of collaboration; but in the distant villages, especially those isolated in the mountains, the guerrillas were in control, and as the war progressed, these came more and more under the control of the Comrades.

For many loyal supporters of their own government there were now two enemies, the alien Japanese invaders and the Comrades, who were their own kith and kin. Collaboration with either was unthinkable. Those who could, in the lulls between battles, fled to the west. As the enemy were in control of the railways, their journeys were taken on foot, stage by stage, from one great city to another.

Mulan and Bao Erh had left their home along with the Chinese army, which had retreated before the Japanese entered the city. Bao Erh could scarcely have done less, since he had become an officer in that army. Mulan and her children and their servants went with him. Ling An had never been told that they were going, nor did she know where they had gone, but she had supposed that they would go, and had a pretty shrewd idea that they would make their way to the western capital.

'Well,' she thought, as she stood in the windy path between the pine trees on the pass in the early light of the day and looked down at the countryside below, rolling away to the west, 'I have been in the west before. I can go there again.' And carefully placing her tightly bound feet in their embroidered shoes between the loose stones of the path, she began to descend.

At first, Ling An's journey was not difficult. She kept away from the roads and travelled on the narrow paths through the fields; and while she was within the borders of the parish, she avoided the villages where she was known, for she did not want to be the cause of trouble to anyone who sheltered her.

However, she did not hesitate to beg a night's lodging and a meal in places where she was not known and where she knew that no one would think of enquiring about her.

One day, in the heat of noon, she came to an inn at the foot of a steep hill. A stone fortress was being built on the summit, and already the walls ringed it like a crown, and from the narrow entrance in the wall to the door of the inn at the foot of the hill there was a long winding black line of men passing the stones from hand to hand as they got them to the top of the hill.

Ling An went into the inn and asked for some water to drink; and while she sat sipping a cup of tea which the innkeeper's wife had brought her, she asked about the work and was told that all the villages around had been obliged to send a number of their able-bodied men to build the fortress on the hilltop, which would protect the district from guerrillas.

'Comrades?' whispered Ling An.

'No,' was the reply, 'not Comrades. There is a warlord's army across the river.'

'My daughter lives across the river,' said Ling An anxiously. 'It is not good to meet soldiers on the road.'

The innkeeper's wife replied, 'Oh, you won't meet them on the road. They are hiding away in the mountains to the north, at a place called White Dragon Mountain. You keep to the road through the villages in the plain and you will not see one of them if you travel by day.'

That was all that Ling An needed to know. She gave the woman one of her copper coins and hobbled off to the river.

White Dragon Mountain was some distance from the river. As she got nearer to it, Ling An grew very fearful. Well she knew that soldiers do not tolerate strangers approaching their hiding-places. Instinctively she knew that an appearance of stealth would be fatal, so she resolved to make as much noise as she could so that the soldiers could hear her coming. She lifted up her voice and sang loudly through her nose.

Jesus is the Good Shepherd
He leads his sheep,
He goes in front,
The sheep follow behind.

Night and day he will protect them all;
Those thieves and robbers
Can never steal them.
He leads them beside still waters,
He leads them on the mountains,
He calls them with his gentle voice,
He keeps them safe.

Two soldiers with guns leaped into the road. 'Stand still,' they said. Ling An stood before them and looked at them. They were not Japanese and they did not look like Comrades.

'You can't come here. The road is closed,' the soldiers said.

'Why are you stopping a poor old woman who has come to visit her daughter?' Ling An said.

'Daughter? What is your daughter's name, Old Mother?' asked one soldier, while the other looking at him with meaning said, 'There are no women here. You should go back to the village by the river and enquire there.'

'My daughter's name is Mulan.'

'Mulan what?'

Ling An did not answer.

'What is her husband's name?'

'Bao Erh.'

'Ah-h!' said the soldiers together, and stepping ahead a little, they conferred in whispers. Then 'Come with us,' they said, and marching one ahead of her and one behind her, they led her to their warlord's camp. The warlord was Bao Erh himself.

32

THE POLICEMAN

They were riding mules across the great mass of mountains that occupied the centre of the province. Mulan rode in front, followed by her elder son, a boy of fourteen, and his brother, who was just ten years old. Ling An rode behind her, holding Mulan's daughter, a child of six, in front of her. The mule was led by an old Mohammedan peasant, whose family had been killed and his house burnt when the Japanese and Bao Erh's men had fought through his village. He had fled to Bao Erh's camp and become one of his men.

The mules were used to being ridden by soldiers. They did not understand how to behave with passive women riders on their backs and men leading them and walking beside them. They played up, Mulan's mule going aside whenever they came to a stream and trying to drink. He could not get any water because all the streams were frozen several inches deep. Ling An's mule had a habit of suddenly putting his head down to smell the path, so that his rider was hard put to keep herself from sliding down over his neck and his enormous ears. Their discomfort was further increased by having no stirrups to rest their feet in. In the hard frost, their cold feet soon lost all feeling. In this Ling An, in whose bound feet the circulation was never good at the best of times, suffered more than Mulan, whose feet were of a natural size.

They had been travelling since just before dawn and they were making their way to the railway which cut through the mountains. Once there, they would wait for a train that could take them down to Shanghai or Foochow or Canton, where they could be lost in the dense population of a great city.

Bao Erh and Mulan had been delighted to see Ling An again and had welcomed her with open arms.

'You are just in time,' Bao Erh said. 'I am sending Mulan and the three children away to one of the big cities. It is not safe for them here, and this is no life for women. Now you are here, you can go with Mulan, and I shall let my heart down.'

In the clear cold mountain air the skin of hands and faces dried and cracked. Their lips were stiff when they talked to each other whenever they stopped to rest the mules. Electricity crackled in their clothing and their hair, making them feel nervous and irritable. Even the children were affected, and the little girl began to whine peevishly. Only old Ma the Mohammedan seemed to be unscathed as he tirelessly plodded along by his mule, loudly commenting on the foolishness of worshipping idols whenever they passed a roadside shrine.

About three in the afternoon, they came to one of the smaller railway stations in a deep valley through the mountains. There were only a few houses standing near it, and as the mules clattered past, half a dozen armed policemen burst out of the first house.

'Who are you? Where are you going? Where have you come from?' they cried. They were police of the puppet government under the control of the Japanese army.

'Mrs Wang and her daughter-in-law and three grandchildren,' replied the old Mohammedan, 'going to Da Cheng. We've come from Shao Shan.' (This was a place halfway along their route.)

'The train comes in another hour,' said one of the police. 'Come inside and warm yourselves.'

'Good, but we are not cold,' said Mulan.

'Lady, if you are not cold, your children are,' said the policeman.

'You had better go in,' muttered old Ma. 'It will seem strange if you don't.'

So they dismounted and entered the police house. It was small but very clean and neat. The walls had been recently whitewashed, and a good charcoal fire was burning in an earthenware pot on the floor in the middle of the room. A policeman drew up a bench before the pot and bade them sit down. Then, pouring hot water into two teacups, he rinsed them, and having run his thumb around the inside of each to remove the tea stains, he poured tea into them and offered them to the two women.

At that moment, the up train's whistle was heard as it approached the station. All the policemen but one ran out to the station to meet it. That one, pouring tea for old Ma, said, 'What time did you leave White Dragon Hill?'

'What?' replied old Ma. 'We haven't come from White Dragon Hill. I told you, we're from Shao Shan.'

'That may be,' said the policeman, 'but when you got to Shao Shan you had come from White Dragon Hill, and your lady is your master's wife, and the other whom I do not know is probably a servant; but do not fear: I shall not betray you.' When the train came in at last, that policeman, to their great amazement, informed the Japanese soldier guarding the entrance to the station that they were Roman Catholics and servants of the German missionaries at a town some distance down the line. Roman Catholics and Germans being in favour with the Japanese at that time, the soldier allowed them to board the train.

Two days later they came to Onsea, and there Mulan rented a small house in a quiet street where she and Ling An were able to live without drawing too much attention to themselves; and there they stayed until at last the long war came to an end, and those Japanese soldiers who had survived guerrilla attacks and American air-raids departed from the city and left it to be occupied once again by soldiers of its own people.

Bao Erh was not among these soldiers, for he had gone with his men long ago to join the free government in the west; and it was many months before he was able to leave his duties there and come to Onsea in search of his wife and family.

33

THE TWO BROTHERS

Da Chieh was making griddle bread.

'Wife,' said Lao Da, coming stealthily into the kitchen, 'where are the children?'

'Oh Husband! I did not hear you come back.'

'Where are the children?'

'At school. They will be home in another hour.'

'I cannot wait.'

'But you have only just come back.'

'Listen, Wife. I have to go away.'

'Fighting?'

'Perhaps.'

'The Comrades?'

Lao Da nodded.

'What shall I tell the children?'

'Tell them I am dead. Tell them a man came and told you this morning that I was drowned crossing the river.'

'Why, Husband, why should I tell them such a thing?'

'Because it is dangerous to belong to a Comrade.'

'Oh Husband, leave them and stay with us.'

'Can the mouse that has been caught by the cat run away again? Just when it seems to be safely away, the paw with all the claws out comes down upon its back. There is no help for it, Wife. Tell the children I am dead, and believe it yourself, for soon I shall be.'

'In the sky there are many stars,' chanted the children, sliding their thumbs down the columns of characters in their readers. The children made so much noise that they could be heard two streets away from the school. The teacher, apparently oblivious to the noise except when it stopped, was sitting at his desk reading a newspaper.

Jun, sitting in the front row near the window, looked out and saw the moon like a pale ghost in the clear sky of early afternoon. Among all the shining black heads of her classmates, Jun's rust coloured hair was conspicuous, and Jun came in for a full share of teasing from her friends, who were firmly convinced that her red hair was due to her having been fed a diet of milk when young.

This was not the case nor was it the reason for the red hair of her mother and her two brothers. It was her father who had called her Jun, which means Beauty. How the children had laughed the first day she had come to school and the teacher had asked her her name, and she had said, 'Jun.' How could anyone with rusty hair be beautiful! they thought.

The pupils' voices rose and fell in a deafening clamour as they recited their lessons. The teacher at his desk at the front of the schoolroom looked up from his paper only when the noise subsided for a moment, for how could any child master the characters of his primer except by reading them again and again at the top of his voice. Occasionally he would call a few pupils out to stand before him and read what they had learned, and if a few of them were able to read without looking at their books, what was the matter with that? It was certainly not harmful for a child to have his mind filled with the good examples provided by the stories of the twelve paragons of filial piety; that child Jun, for example, and her two brothers, with that hideous red hair inherited from their mother.

Suddenly there was a lull in the babble of sound. The most attentive pupils reciting the last words of a sentence were surprised at the unaccustomed sound of their own voices in the silence and looked with their schoolmates across the room to the open doorway. Jun's mother stood there, and behind her were the other women from the lane where she lived, some carrying babies, others holding spools of cotton in their hands. They did not dare to cross the threshold, so they stood in the doorway and shouted to the schoolmaster, 'Send the children out. Soldiers are coming.'

The schoolmaster turned pale and stood up and shouted to the pupils, 'Go!' The pupils needed no second command. They poured out of the schoolroom door, like water through a breach in a dam, and were immediately seized, silenced and taken off by their mothers and grandmothers.

The schoolmaster hastily gathered his books together, carefully concealing anything he thought might be objectionable to soldiers of either of the opposing forces, and made for his home and his wife and family as fast as he could go while still retaining his scholarly dignity. Hampered with age, a long gown, and dignified behaviour modelled on Confucian precepts, he had barely barred his gate and shouted to his wife before he heard the measured shuffle of soldiers marching in cloth shoes through the thick yellow dust of the street outside his house.

In the lane where Jun and her brothers lived, there was silence behind barred gates, as everyone listened to that menacing shuffle of feet along the road at the end of the lane. People held their breath as they listened. Were the soldiers going on, merely passing through the city on their way to billet themselves on some less fortunate inhabitants of another city, or were they stopping to eat their way through all that was stored in this city, to rob and rape, to press fathers and elder sons into their ranks and take them away, never to return to their families again? Jun's mother thought, 'Are they Comrades? Will my husband be with them? Will he come back to me?' and her heart leapt at the thought, for she loved him dearly, and she had never really believed him to be dead.

But they were not Comrades. They were Nationalists, and they did not pass through the city. When the sound of feet stopped, Jun's elder brother, who had had to hide in an alleyway near the centre of the city, came back as soon as the main street was clear and reported that the soldiers had gathered at the crossroads in the centre and seemed to be going to stay for one night at least. Other men hiding with him had told him that they were not Comrades but Nationalists.

To his mother's neighbours in the lane, it made no difference whether the soldiers were Comrades or Nationalists. To them, soldiers belonged to the least honourable of the five callings in which a man could spend his life, and whatever they were fighting about was of no concern to other people. For plain people, a battalion of soldiers was something to be endured, like a swarm of locusts, and doubtless like a swarm of locusts they would depart in due course. Even if they left devastation behind them, something could be salvaged by those who had survived, and after a while life would go on as it did before. In the meantime, if there were good men in charge of the soldiers so that they were made to behave themselves properly, there might be something to be gained from this disaster.

It was not long before their fears were set at rest. Before sunset every house but one in the lane had at least two soldiers billeted in it. Mothers hustled their daughters into the kitchens and kept them busy preparing a meal for the guests, while fathers and brothers stood around the soldiers seated on either side of the table opposite the door, admiring their rifles and other equipment and listening open-mouthed to the tales the soldiers had to tell.

In Jun's house, there being no men but her two brothers, Koko and Titi, it had been deemed safe to billet one soldier alone. This man, Pao Ying, lost no time in ingratiating himself with his unwilling hosts, and it was not long before he and Koko were fast friends.

Jun's mother, who cared nothing for politics and did not concern herself with the merits of either side, was thankful that an older man had been sent to their house and gratefully exercised her skill so that she was able to keep the whole family on the pittance allowed her for one man's lodging.

Nevertheless, when she lay down with Jun in the fading light, she would look at her husband's old blue jacket hanging from the rusty nail in the wall at the end of the bed and wish that the Comrades had come instead of the Nationalists.

Seeing Pao Ying so at ease with her children, she asked him one day, 'How many children have you at home?'

'I have no children.'

'Are you not married then? Surely you are too old to be a bachelor?'

'I was married once. My bride died. On our wedding night. Charcoal fumes.'

'Aiyah! I have heard of such things. But that was long ago? You must forget and marry another young girl. It is your duty to your parents to give them a grandson.'

'Well, perhaps I shall some day, but I shall never forget my bride An Mei.'

'An Mei? My husband's sister was called An Mei.'

'An Mei. It's a good name: Peaceful Beauty.'

'Peaceful! Peace! What is peace? The children ask me, "What is peace? Where is it?" and I cannot tell them. Soldier, tell me, will there be peace again?'

'We are fighting for it, Sister-in-law. There is still peace in the south, they say.'

Spring came and summer followed. Then, when the nights turned cold but the days were still hot, dry and dusty, Pao Ying came home one evening and announced that he and all the soldiers were leaving at dawn the next morning. As they sat eating their supper, 'I will go with him,' said Koko.

'No, my son. You are too young.'

'No, mother, I am a man.'

'A man must take care of his mother,' said Pao Ying.

'That is so, but we are poor, and when you have gone, my mother will wash other people's clothes from dawn to dusk, to get a few coppers to feed us all. A soldier gets money. I will send mine to my mother and there will be enough to keep her and Titi and Jun.'

'Soldiers get killed,' said Titi. At this Jun began to cry.

'Well,' said his mother, 'you cannot go.'

Pao Ying set his empty bowl down on the table and went out of the house. Koko got up from the table to follow, but Jun pulled him by the sleeve of his jacket, while his mother hastily barred the door of the house and stood in front of it.

'You cannot go,' she repeated.

'Well, but I will go, tomorrow or next week. When you open the door, I will go.'

'What shall I do, oh what shall I do?' she thought. 'I cannot keep the door shut for ever. While we sleep this son of mine will open it and go after this Pao Ying, and I shall never see him again. Is it not enough to lose a husband?' With that last thought she knew what she must do.

'You cannot go,' she said. 'Your father might kill you.'

'Father? Father is dead.'

'Did you not tell us that Father is dead?' said Titi.

'Oh Mother!' cried Jun.

'Well, he is not dead.'

'Well, he will not kill me, his son, a good soldier fighting for his country.'

'He might kill you.'

'How?'

The three children stared at their mother. She looked strange to them.

'Why?' they repeated.

And Jun said, 'My father is a good man. He would not kill my brother.'

'He would kill Koko if he went with the Nationalists.'

'Oh, Mother!' cried Titi.

'Is Father a . . . '

'Hush! Don't say it!'

'A Comrade!' whispered Koko.

'Yes, my son.'

'Oh Mother, Pao Ying will kill our father!' cried Jun.

'A Comrade! Oh Mother, why didn't you tell us? How can I be a Nationalist soldier!'

'You cannot go with them, my son.'

'You must become a Comrade,' said Titi.

'No, no. I will not be a Comrade. I will never be a Comrade.'

'Why not, brother? Our father is one of them.'

'No, I cannot be one of them. Comrades are evil men. Pao Ying told me so.'

'Father is not an evil man,' said Jun.

'Your father is a good man. Comrades, Nationalists! There are good ones and bad ones. There are good Comrade fathers and good Nationalist fathers. It is better to be neither a Comrade nor a Nationalist, just a plain man doing his filial duty, taking care of his mother and brother and sister.'

'Well, I will not be a Comrade,' muttered Koko, returning to his bowl.

'I will,' said Titi. 'I will, and I will find Father.'

Jun said nothing. Neither did their mother, who was wondering how she could get money to feed them all now that Pao Ying was leaving them.

She had good cause to worry. The whole country was plunged into civil war as Comrades and Nationalists fought each other up and down the land. When one city was evacuated by soldiers of one side, it was immediately occupied by men from the other side, who speedily executed those who had sheltered their enemies.

In the hearts of Da Chieh and her neighbours fear rose when the sound of soldiers marching through the city was heard the following day.

'Who are these?' and 'What will they do to us?' they asked each other. The younger children were sent to find out.

'They are Comrades! The Comrades have come!' cried Titi triumphantly. 'Now I shall find Father!'

The other children told their mothers, 'Titi's father is a Comrade.' By the evening everyone knew that there was a Comrade's family in the lane. There were whispered conversations up and down the alleyway. Silence fell between people as Da Chieh approached and continued as she passed them, and they stared askance at her retreating back. Suddenly Da Chieh and her family were cut off from their neighbours; nobody would speak to them, for all were afraid of them.

'The children are the most dangerous,' they said. 'Children have no wisdom to bridle their tongues.'

'You are not to play with them,' they told their own children.

Of the three children Koko felt this ostracism most, for he was more of a Nationalist than any of their neighbours, who were only concerned with keeping themselves alive under whatever powers there might be.

The following day, shots were heard outside the North Gate of the city. An hour later everyone in the lane knew that ten householders had been executed for sheltering the Nationalist soldiers.

'They will kill us too.'

'They can't kill everyone.'

'They won't kill anyone here if we keep quiet.'

'We have never had any Nationalist soldiers billeted here. Just say that and we shall be safe.'

'But we must all say the same.' Two men were sent off to visit all the families in the lane. They came to Da Chieh's house.

'Of course I will keep quiet,' said Da Chieh. 'Did we not also have a man here all the winter?'

'And I also am a Nationalist,' said Koko. 'We will keep quiet.'

But Titi muttered, 'I am not. I am a Comrade, and I shall tell.'

'What's that?' said the men. 'What did he say?'

'Nothing,' said Da Chieh. 'He is just a child. It is nothing.'

'No, it is not nothing. A child's idle words can bring death to us all.'

'We will see that he keeps quiet. Do not worry,' said Da Chieh.

'You see that your brother keeps quiet,' the men said to Koko, 'and keep quiet yourself. It is not safe to be a Nationalist now in this city.'

After they had gone, Da Chieh seized Titi by the shoulders and shook him. 'If you do not keep quiet,' she said, 'you will get nothing to eat.' Titi wriggled out of her grasp, ducked under her striking hand, and ran out of the door.

'There's a devil in the child,' said Da Chieh. 'Go after him, Koko, and keep him out of mischief.' Koko found Titi at the end of the alley shuffling his shoes in the dust and moodily muttering to himself. Just then six or seven children came round the corner.

'There he is!' they shouted, and picking up small stones, they began to pelt the two brothers.

The two fled instinctively towards their own house, Titi shouting derisively, 'Nationalist devils!' the others calling 'Comrade devils!' Generally nobody took any notice of the noise boys made playing in the alley, but now everyone was anxious. Only silence could keep them in safety, they thought. Doors opened, women came out and called to their children, grabbed those they could catch, and pulled them into their houses.

As if truly possessed by a devil, Titi stood in the shelter of his own gateway and yelled, 'Nationalist devils!' at the top of his voice. Koko wrestled with him and pulled him into the yard while Da Chieh barred the gate.

'Nationalist devils! Nationalist devils!' shouted Titi.

There was a hammering on the gate.

'Open the gate! Open the gate!' shouted a man outside.

'Take him into the kitchen and keep him quiet.'

'Niang, I can't!'

'You must, my son.'

Together they dragged the screaming Titi into the kitchen.

'Quick, get under the kindling,' said Da Chieh. She piled the dead leaves over them and hobbled to the gate. In the house behind her there was a sudden silence. The man outside was breaking up the gate. Already his angry red face was visible through the splintered panels.

'Open the gate!' he growled. Da Chieh opened it.

'Where are the Nationalists?'

'There are no Nationalists here.'

'I heard someone shouting "Nationalist devils!"'

'It was a children's game.'

'Then I shall speak to that child.'

'There are no children here,' Da Chieh called after him as he marched into the house.

In the kitchen Koko lay on top of Titi under a heap of dry leaves which had been piled up in a corner to be used as fuel. Only by lying on top of him could he keep him still, and only by thrusting his fist into his mouth had he been able to silence him. Titi's teeth had sunk into his hand, but Koko was keeping it in his mouth until his mother should get rid of the stranger. As he heard the man enter the house, he stiffened his body, and with his free hand pushed Titi's head face downwards firmly to the ground. Whether they were fully covered by the leaves he could not tell, nor did he think about that. His whole mind was bent on keeping his brother quiet.

The man came into the kitchen.

'I tell you there are no children here,' said Da Chieh.

Under the leaves Koko pressed hard upon his brother. 'He must be scared too,' he thought, for Titi did not stir beneath him.

The man glanced quickly around the smoke-blackened kitchen and marched out into the yard. Da Chieh followed and barred the broken gate behind him as he went off down the alley.

Not a sound came from any of the other houses, for during the few minutes he had been searching Da Chieh's house, all the neighbours had fled into the next street, where they mingled with the passers-by until they deemed it safe to return home.

'Niang,' whispered Koko under the leaves.

'He has gone, and the gate is barred.' Koko crawled out from the leaves, pulling Titi as he came.

'Well, the man didn't find us, and I kept Titi quiet,' he said as he brushed the leaves off his jacket; but Titi said nothing. He did not even move. When Da Chieh pulled him up into a sitting position, his head lolled and he fell forward.

'It's a fit!' she said. 'Get some cold water. He's been frightened into a fit!'

But it wasn't a fit. Koko had pressed too hard and too long. Titi was dead.

'Aiyah! Niang! What have I done? Aiyah! I have killed my own brother!'

Mother and son looked at each other. They did not see Jun, who had slipped out from behind the stalks of sorghum standing against the outer wall of the house, where she had been hiding, and now stood in the doorway suddenly chilled as the horror that froze her mother and brother crept into her heart.

'You evil thing!' she cried as she flung herself at Koko and beat him with her fists. He leaned against the wall steadying himself against this onslaught, keeping his hands by his sides, making no attempt to fight back. It was Da Chieh who pulled Jun away.

'Stop,' she said. 'There is no help for it.'
'I did not mean it!' said Koko.
'My son, I know it; but what do we do now?'
The silence between them was suddenly broken by a sharp crackling sound from the other side of the house as a whiff of smoke came into the kitchen. They rushed outside. Their neighbours' house was in flames.
'Quick, get the grain!' shouted Da Chieh as she rushed into the house to pull the quilts off the *k'ang*. Dragging the bag of grain and the quilts they rushed into the street outside. It was already full of people hurrying back and dashing into their houses to save what they could before they also caught fire.
Five were already ablaze, and it was not long before the whole alleyway became a fiery furnace. A strong wind fanned these flames and blew sparks on to thatched roofs of houses and shops, and in less than two hours half the city was a blackened ruin and hundreds of families were homeless.
'Who started it?'
Some people said that the Comrades did it, some said the Nationalists did. Some of the alley-dwellers were sure that Da Chieh's Titi had done it. But they were all wrong. The culprit was Da Chieh's neighbour, who had been making griddle bread when the Comrade came hammering at Da Chieh's gate. She had fled with her children, and the wind had stirred the hot ashes under the griddle iron to flames, which had flared out to the pile of dry leaves which had been placed near so that the woman could feed the fire with one hand and ladle the batter on to the griddle with the other. Thence the flames had leapt to the rafters and reeds above, and so the house had caught fire.
Nobody thought of this at the time. Most of the alley-dwellers were sure that Da Chieh's family were responsible for the disaster. Silence and black looks met them wherever they looked. They were driven away from the well which was their only source of water. A neighbour

who had been unable to drag any grain out of her flaming house snatched a bag of millet away from Jun, knocking her down as she ran off with it. This attack broke into the dazed state of shock which had kept them standing about in the ruined alleyway unable to think of the next step to take.

'Niang. Let's go.'

'Where, my son?'

'Anywhere, Niang. Let's go.'

Quietly they slipped away and got into the main street of the city and so to the city gate. Soldiers were still filling buckets of water from the moat around the city wall and passing them along to their comrades, who were dousing the hot ashes of the smouldering houses. In the hubbub and the half light of evening it was not difficult for Da Chieh and her family to slip through the gateway and quickly mingle with the crowd of people who had come from their houses outside the city to watch the fire.

'Stand here,' said Da Chieh.

They stood in the crowd quietly watching the soldiers for a minute or two, then trudged off down the lanes between the houses of the west suburb into the open country.

'Where are we going?' asked Jun, when at last they stopped walking and Da Chieh spread the quilts on the hillside so that they could sleep for a while.

'Somewhere where there are neither Comrades nor Nationalists . . . just ordinary people like us. Where there is peace.'

'Oh Niang, there isn't any peace anywhere.'

'Yes, my son, there is. Pao Ying told me there was still peace in the south. We will go to the south and live in peace.'

'Peace,' said Jun. 'What is peace, Niang?'

'Peace? There was peace here once, a long time ago. I have heard my mother talk about it. We will find it in the south. Then you'll know what it's like.'

They rolled themselves in their quilts and slept, for they were so weary that grief, guilt, and anxiety could not keep them awake.

Towards evening the next day they came to a small city on the railway. The station was crowded with people who had been sleeping and eating on the platform for two nights and days as they waited for the southbound train. There was such a hubbub inside and outside the station that Da Chieh and her two children found no difficulty in slipping past the ticket-collector, who had given up the idea that every passenger should have a ticket: first, because it was impossible with such hordes of people pressing their way through the wicket, and second, because he knew that the tickets he did punch would be passed out again to relatives waiting outside the station, and how could he send one of them back through the solid stream of people pushing past him into the station. Besides, he was a merciful man.

The train came in that night. It was packed with people.

Even the footboards outside were full of people hanging on as best they could. The waiting passengers clambered on to the roofs of the cars. Da Chieh and her two children found themselves standing at the end of the platform opposite the entrance to the last car and managed to wriggle themselves into the solid mass of people who filled it. Each of them carried a small bag of millet, but their quilts they had had to abandon, for there was no room for anything so bulky.

The train moved slowly out of the station and puffed its way through the fields hour after hour through the night and the long hot day that followed. When it reached a city, it gathered speed and passed through the crowded station without stopping. There was no water on the train, and by late afternoon people were so thirsty that they could think of nothing but water. Every time they came to a city their hopes rose of getting out and finding a tap, and then fell as the train rushed past the platforms without stopping.

Late in the afternoon, the train slowed down and came to a halt in the fields miles away from any city. Nobody knew why it had stopped nor how long it would stay, but many people got out to look for water. There were wells in the fields, and although it was not the time for running water from them into the irrigation channels, the men who were working on the autumn crops were soon surrounded by mobs of thirsty travellers begging them for water.

Among them was Koko. Da Chieh and Jun, like most of the other women, had stayed in the train to keep their places and guard their bundles. Koko, scarcely more than a child, found that he could not push his way through to the front of the crowd of men surrounding the nearest well, so he ran to the next one, and finding that equally difficult, ran on to the next. There were fewer people waiting there because no one knew when the train would start again, and nobody wanted to go too far away from it. Even so, it was some time before Koko was able to get near enough to the water to fill the brass bowl he had brought.

He had just dipped it into the bucket of clean cool water which the farmer had drawn up for the last men when the train whistled. Everyone began to run back to it. Koko ran too, the water splashing out of the bowl as he went. Then he stumbled and fell, and the precious water was spilt and soaked up in the dust of the path. He picked up the bowl and ran back to the nearest well which was only a few yards away. The farmer, who had seen his plight, hastily filled his bowl, and Koko ran off; but the train began to move, and before he could get to it, it was going too quickly for him to climb up into it. Forgetting the water in the bowl, he ran along the line frantically following it until it was out of sight.

Da Chieh with Jun wedged so tightly in the solid mass of fellow-travellers that they could move neither legs nor arms nor see anything but the blue jackets of those in front of them did not know that Koko was not on the train. In the stifling heat Jun was no longer able to keep her feet on the floor, and her mother's chief fear was that when the train stopped again, and people began to move, Jun would fall and be trampled to death under their feet.

'He has climbed up in another place,' she thought, 'and he will find us when the train stops again.'

But when the train stopped late in the night, there was no sign of Koko.

'Well, he is sleeping,' she thought, but fear stirred in her heart. 'What shall I do if he has been left behind? How can I find him again?' she said to herself, as she thought of him wandering alone in the fields where the wells of water were. Early the next morning the train reached Onsea, at the mouth of a river; and further than that it did not go. The refugees climbed down from the train and stretched their cramped muscles and rubbed their benumbed limbs, and tottered across the platform to the exit. Da Chieh, laden with the few bundles left to them and dragging the half-fainting Jun, was pushed along in the stream of people jostling past the ticket-collector.

Once outside, the crowd rapidly dispersed. Those fortunate ones who had relatives in the city sought them out; the others disappeared in the alleys. Da Chieh, who had neither relatives nor friends in this city so far from her home, lingered by the entrance to the station scanning the faces of the last travellers coming through it, hoping against hope that she would see Koko come out: but he did not come, and at last she knew that he had been left behind and was lost.

34

THE COLD NIGHT

Winter came early that year. In the middle of November a bitterly cold wind blew in from the sea, sending people scurrying into their houses to open their chests and pull out their warm silk padded robes. Refugees who had nothing but the thin cotton garments which they had been wearing in the summer when disaster had so suddenly sprung upon them huddled blue-nosed and shivering in the doorways of the alleys up which the wind came shrieking like a demon and sweeping leaves and papers before it.

Da Chieh and Jun, who had never ventured far beyond the square in front of the railway station because they were hoping against hope that some day they would see Koko come through the entrance, had found themselves a sheltered place in the gateway of an old cemetery facing the station. It was a very ancient cemetery, and no one had been buried there for several years. Most of the coffins were above ground, covered with mud and white plaster, waiting for filial sons to remove them to their ancestral fields far away in the country. For some of them that day would never come, for the sons themselves had died in distant lands and left no children to perform their filial duties.

A few weedy trees grew around the edge of the cemetery, and some dusty blades of grass struggled with the sorrel and other weeds in the narrow spaces between the graves. City authorities had long ago decreed that no new bodies should be interred there, and the gate was kept locked to prevent the poor men of the city from carrying in their dead by night and surreptitiously burying them in the darkness.It was a desolate place, and even homeless refugees did not care to shelter in the gateway, but for Da Chieh and Jun the roof had kept off the rain, and on windy days the side walls and the wooden gate at their backs had protected them from the wind, while the open space in front gave them a good view of all who came and went through the station entrance.

One of them usually sat in the gateway watching while the other darted in and out of the crowds in the square begging and picking up anything that might be dropped, and sometimes on a lucky day stealing something which could be eaten. In this way they had managed to keep body and soul together; but both mother and child were miserably thin. Da Chieh, who gave most of what she got to Jun, was scarcely more than skin and bone. When the wind blew on this November day, she felt that it blew right through her body, chilling every drop of blood.

When the sun set, the wind dropped, and the air began to freeze. After the last train of the day had come in, Da Chieh sent Jun out to beg among the passengers in a last attempt to get some morsel of food to stay them through the deadly cold of the coming night. People were too intent on getting themselves out of the cold air into their warm homes to take any notice of the thin little wraith flitting in and out among them. Jun had had so little to eat that even the exercise of running and dodging could not warm her hands and feet. Gradually the crowd thinned. Only a few people were coming past the ticket-collector; they had been delayed by the assembling of their baggage, and when they came through the wicket laden with parcels, they were much too flustered to thrust their hands into their pockets to find something for the beggar child who stood so forlornly before them with eyes that seemed to fill her thin face. Just as she was about to give up in despair, following slowly behind the last of the passengers, Jun saw that there was a large sausage sticking out of the top of the wicker basket which the woman had hung from her elbow because her hands were grasping the two string bags so full and heavy that they touched the ground on either side of her. Jun crept closer and pulled the sausage gently and swiftly out of the basket and fled like a mouse that even as it sits up to eat a crumb senses the presence of a prowling cat.

It was a lovely sausage, about ten inches long and thick as a man's thumb. Through its transparent skin lumps of dark red meat and yellow suet could be seen mingled with the purple brown of liver. Even in the cold night air the garlic could be smelled, it was so strong.

'Niang! Oh look, Niang! a sausage . . . a liver meat sausage!' cried Jun, throwing it down into her mother's lap. Da Chieh tore the sausage into two pieces and handed the bigger one to her daughter. The smaller one, and it was scarcely more than a quarter of the whole, she put into her own mouth.

'Niang, you have given me more than half!'

'No, Daughter. It stretched when I tore it. Sausages do.'

As Jun had never had a sausage before, she accepted this statement as true and lost no time in swallowing her portion. Then feeling sleepy and a little warmer, she lay down beside her mother in the far corner of the gateway.

'Oh Niang! You do feel cold!'

'It's a cold night, child. Put your arms around me and I'll soon be warm.'

They put their arms around each other and so they slept, while in the cemetery behind the gate the blades of grass grew white with frost, and a thin sheet of ice formed on the puddles of water in the square before the station.

Jun slept deeply as children do; but towards day she dreamed that she was clasping an enormous sausage bigger than herself. It was a huge sausage, hard and icy cold. She put her arms around it to warm it so that she could divide it easily, and it stretched. 'Sausages always do,' it said, and began to coil itself like a snake around her legs. She drew up her knees to her chest to shake off the icy coils and so woke herself up.

The sky was light behind the station; the sun was coming up. 'Good,' she said to herself. 'It will warm us.'

She looked at her mother, still asleep with her face to the wall, and edged herself away carefully, trying to avoid awakening her before the sun was up high enough to warm them.

She stood up and stretched, then rubbed her stiff fingers along her thighs in order to send the blood coursing down to her half-frozen feet. After five minutes, as this had no effect, she crept out into the open space and began to stamp and jump and throw her hands behind her, slapping her back, as she had seen rickshawmen do.

Soon the square began to fill; rickshaws and pedicabs were assembling outside the station; the owners of food stalls were taking down their shutters. Fires were lit; there was a smell of smoke and cooking. Travellers were queueing up to buy tickets; people came hurrying past the cemetery gate. The sun came up, casting long shadows across the pale yellow ground.

Jun went around the stalls to see what she could find and managed to snatch a small triangle of a bread biscuit when she thought the stall-keeper was too busy working his bellows to heat up his kettles to see what she was doing. He did see her, but being a kind man who had known how it felt to be hungry, he said nothing. Hiding her prize under her jacket she ran back to her mother in the gateway.

'Niang!' she cried, 'Look what I've got! Bread for our breakfast. We shall be lucky today. Perhaps Koko will come.'

Her mother was lying with her face to the wall just as she had left her. She had not moved, although the sunshine by now had found its way into the gateway and was shining slantwise upon her.

'Niang, how can you sleep so long in the sun? Wake up.' Jun dropped on her knees beside her mother and gently pulled her by the shoulder. It was icy cold and hard as iron under the thin cotton jacket.

'Niang, Niang! Wake up. It's late. The sun's warm. I've got some bread.'

She pulled her mother towards her, and her body came all of one piece like a board.

'Oh Niang! How cold you are! I didn't know you could get so stiff with cold.'

She began to rub her limbs with her own blue hands. Up and down she rubbed, but Da Chieh never stirred. Then she flung herself full length on top of her mother, hoping that the warmth of her own body might melt the icy stiffness of her mother's.

She lay thus, slapping her with her hands and breathing on her face for half an hour or more, but Da Chieh did not move. She did not even open her eyes.

Panic seized Jun. She sat up and shouted, heedless of the crowd of people gathering outside the gateway, standing on the pavement, blocking the sunlight, filling the place with their cold dark shadows.

'Niang, Niang! Wake up! Open your eyes! It's me, Jun! Oh Niang, oh Niang! Wake up! Please, wake up!'

With her little blue fingers she pulled her mother's eyelashes and tried to force her eyes open, but the eyelashes were frozen to her cheeks.

'Oh how pitiful,' the crowd murmured, but nobody did anything to help. Only a policeman who had come to see what the crowd was looking at stepped out into the square and hailed the driver of a Blue Cross Coffin Truck which was cruising around the streets, picking up the dead who had died of cold and starvation during the night.

At that moment Ling An entered the square.

35

THE GRANDDAUGHTER

Ling An was once again almost alone. As rumours of the Comrades' victories in the north became items of irrefutable news, Mulan's husband became more and more uneasy. After the war had ended he had joined his wife and children in the city of Onsea and bought himself an egg-merchant's business which included a factory in which dried egg-flakes could be prepared from those fresh eggs which, having suffered in the journey from the country into the city, were unfit for export to Hong Kong and other distant places. This business throve so well that Bao Erh soon became a rich man, and being honest as well as astute, he was asked to take his place among the city elders. This he did, and it was due to his good influence that many necessary reforms were begun in the city. They were begun but never finished, for time was too short. Catastrophe was advancing surely and swiftly from the north.

After the fall of Tientsin, Bao Erh considered his position and decided to risk losing his business and take Mulan and his elder son to Hong Kong. He could see that Onsea would soon fall into the hands of the Comrades, and under their regime there would be no place for an egg merchant exporting eggs to Hong Kong. Therefore he would lose his business anyway, and his integrity and perhaps his life as well. His daughters were married and out of his care. There remained only Mulan and his two sons, his younger daughter, and Ling An.

With the elder son, who was already helping his father in the business, there was no trouble. He agreed to his father's proposal with alacrity. So did Mulan. To them it was a matter of common sense; but with the younger son there was a problem.

He was a student in his second year at one of the city's great universities, and unknown to his father, he had joined one of the Comrades' underground cells because, being a good lad, his mind was full of lofty ideals. Seeing many social evils around him, with the fervour of youth he wanted to destroy them immediately, and the methods of the Comrades seemed to his impatient fervour more likely to accomplish this than the slower, surer efforts of his father and the city elders. So his secret rejoicing at the fall of Tientsin was suddenly dampened when his father announced his decision to take the whole family to Hong Kong. Bao Erh, who had no idea of his son's secret allegiance and had a very poor opinion of his diligence in his studies, was amazed when Sheng Erh pleaded for permission to remain a few weeks longer in order to take an examination; and suspecting that the real reason might be a clandestine romance, he was all the more adamant in his insistence that the young man should accompany them immediately.

Sheng Erh, bursting with wrath which he had had to contain within himself in the presence of his parents, flung himself on his bicycle and pedalled furiously away to a friend's house where he knew he would get a sympathetic hearing and perhaps some Comradely advice for dealing with this situation. In his anger he did not care how he went and ran straight into a truck. Fortunately the truck was not speeding. Sheng Erh was knocked off his bicycle and thrown several yards across the road where his flight was stopped by the wall of a bank, which he hit head first. He was knocked unconscious and taken to the nearest hospital with severe concussion. His parents were told that a journey would be most inadvisable for several weeks to come.

Mulan in tears besought her husband to put off their flight for another month at least, but Bao Erh feared that that would be too late. He knew that the tickets he had obtained with so much difficulty could easily be sold to others, for there were more applicants than places on the few ships leaving the port. Moreover it was rumoured that there might be no more ships afterwards. So he said, 'We must go. There is no help for it.'

At that Ling An said, 'I shall stay. No one will harm an old woman like me. I shall stay and bring Sheng Erh with me when he is well enough to leave the hospital.'

'But this is probably the last ship.'

'Well, what if it is; we shall come by train.'

'But trains also will stop.'

'True,' said Ling An. 'But only for a time. We shall lie low until we can leave quietly. Anyway, what else can we do? Is it not a right thing to do, to care for the sick? And is not the Good Shepherd guarding his sheep that are walking along the right road?'

'True,' said Bao Erh. 'But I do not like to leave you.'

'You should have more faith,' said Ling An.

So Ling An stayed. In due course Sheng Erh recovered and, leaving the hospital, came home to the tender care of Ling An. Convalescents are generally peevish. Sheng Erh was more so than others, for to the discomfort of headaches and general weakness there was added the perpetually nagging tension of a divided heart and a wobbling conscience. The precepts of his upbringing still tied him to his family, and he knew that in obedience to his father he should join him as soon as possible. Moreover a genuine affection for his old nurse was urging him to get her out of the country while it was still possible to depart; and she, he knew, would never depart without him. On the other hand, a brave new world was just about to begin, and he wanted to have a hand in bringing it to pass. There were even times in the depths of his sleepless nights when it seemed to be his duty as a Christian to support the Comrades, and he would think that he had solved his problem and turn over on his bed and sleep until dawn. But when he awoke, the folly of that argument would stare him in the face, and he would spend the rest of the day in a state of nagging indecision.

Such a condition did not hasten his return to good health, and in spite of Ling An's efforts to tempt his failing appetite, he was getting so thin that she, remembering her own little Lao Erh, was becoming very anxious indeed. For this reason she was abroad so early on that bitterly cold morning, crossing the square to go to the early morning market, hoping to find something that might make a relish for the rice she would cook for Sheng Erh's breakfast.

She saw the crowd around the gate of the cemetery, and when she saw the policeman hail the Blue Cross truck, she knew why; but she thought it strange, for that autumn starving homeless refugees were dying off like flies: every morning there were dead bodies lying in the street; but people did not stop and stare at them. They merely grumbled that some of them were left so long before being picked up and carried away. As Ling An passed the gateway she heard a child screaming 'Niang! Niang!' It was a cry that wrung the hearts of all who heard it. Tears coursed down the faces in the crowd. Some women sobbed aloud, but nobody stirred a finger to help. Only Ling An pushed her way through the crowd, and taking Jun gently by the shoulders, she pulled her off her mother's body.

'Come, child,' she said, as she held the little blue fingers between her own warm hands. 'How cold you are. Come with me to my warm house.'

'No, no! I must stay with Mother.'

'Your mother is dead. It was too cold for her last night. You will die too if you do not come with me and get warm quickly.'

So Jun went quietly away with Ling An. A good meal, a good wash from head to foot, and warm clothes worked wonders.

'What is your name, child?' asked Ling An.

'Wang Jun.'

'And your father's?'

'Wang Lao Da.'

'And your mother's?'

'She was called Da Chieh.'

'And your two brothers'?'

'I didn't tell you I had two brothers.'

'No, but you have. What are their names?'

'Koko and Titi. Titi is dead, and Koko got off the train for water and was lost.' At this Jun started to cry again.

'There is no one left but me,' she sobbed.

'Well, there is still your father, and he is my son.'

'Your son? Then you are my . . . ?'

'Yes, your grandmother. Let your heart down, child. You are my granddaughter and you will live here with me.'

'Koko?'

'We shall go to the station every day to meet the train, and one day we shall find him.'

Little by little, like squeezing water out of a stone, Ling An drew out of Jun the tragic story of the events which had brought her and her mother to Onsea.

Jun was one of the fortunate ones. Hundreds of children died that winter of cold and hunger; but in her grandmother Ling An's house Jun was warmly clad and well fed. After a few weeks she was plump and rosy again, and the rusty hair was shining with health. Once a day she went with her grandmother to the station entrance and eagerly scanned the face of every boy who came past the ticket-inspector, hoping that Koko would come through:

but he never came. By the end of March even Jun had lost hope that he would ever come, and consented to Ling An's suggestion that she should attend school, on condition that her grandmother should go to meet the train every morning and look out for a boy with hair the colour of rusty iron.

So Jun went to school and found it very different from the school she had attended before. Here the pupils were so marshalled and organized that nobody had time to tease anybody else about the colour of their hair. In fact such things were not considered worth talking about. The political teachers stationed in every school saw that every child had plenty of political ideas to think about and discuss. Even the games they played had a political trend.

They spent hours reciting slogans and learning the Comrades' songs. It was the aim of every child to join the Young Comrades and wear red kerchiefs around their necks. Their teachers stirred their hearts with stories of brave Young Comrades who had done wonderful things for the Party, even handing over their own parents for execution. There were dances to learn — peasant dances about planting rice or wheat such as Jun, who had been brought up in the country, had never seen. There were processions to walk in on the Comrades' special days of commemoration. True, these could be rather boring when one had to sit for long hours in the middle of the road waiting for another procession to pass the intersection; but there were sometimes amusing things to watch. Ling An, looking out of her window, saw the young woman in a white gown personifying Peace, having trouble keeping her balance on the globe which represented the world, and drew her own conclusions, which she wisely kept to herself. Then she saw the man leading the white mule at the end of the procession. No one was riding it.

'The Good Shepherd is there,' said Ling An to herself, 'riding after his sheep which are all going astray.' For by this time Ling An knew well that she and the Comrades stood at opposite poles.

'Teacher says there is no God,' said Jun, coming home from school.

'Then who made you?' said Ling An.

'Nobody,' said Jun. 'We are all the great-great-grandchildren of monkeys. Teacher says so.'

'Nonsense,' said Ling An. 'That's a bad idea. You must not believe it.'

Sheng Erh, hearing this, called Ling An aside.

'Take care,' he said. 'You must not say such things to a child. If she repeats it in school, there will be much trouble for all of us. Such words are dangerous.' Then, lowering his voice, he added, 'Children are our greatest danger now. We must be careful what we say in front of them.'

'Well,' said Ling An, 'we are not the children of monkeys. Teachers should not tell children things which are not true.'

'No,' said Sheng Erh, 'they shouldn't, and it isn't true. Darwin never said that we were descended from monkeys. He said that we descend from the common ancestor of apes and men, which is a different theory altogether, and anyway it is only a theory and not proven.'

'Good,' said Ling An. 'God made us. We can let our hearts down.'

'He made Comrades too,' said Sheng Erh with a sly grin.

'Well, what if he did,' she replied. 'There are always some black sheep in a flock.'

'Only,' she thought as the months went by, 'these are not black sheep; they are red sheep.' For the wolves had cast off their sheep's clothing and now behaved according to their true characters. Gone were the words of gentle persuasion. An army of Comrade police descended on the city, and woe betide the citizens who did not toe the line stretched so rigidly before them. Shopkeepers were so severely taxed that those with double-fronted shops took to sharing with others, so that a shoemaker showed his wares in one window while a grocer might display his goods in the other. Yet as the weeks went by even this arrangement became impossible as taxation mounted even higher. Then it became dangerous to walk under high buildings. Too many suicides were jumping off them.

People who occupied positions of authority spent sleepless nights thinking how they could satisfy the Comrades who were demanding accusations against their foreign associates. The latter had long since left the country and were well out of reach, but their loyal partners were unwilling to accuse them of crimes which they had never committed and in many cases found it impossible to fabricate the kinds of 'sins' which would satisfy the Comrade officials. With their days spent in endless hours of indoctrination followed by study groups for confession and long sleepless nights, even the best balanced of minds began to waver. The weaker ones were driven to end their agony by killing themselves. Their humbler associates suffered with them, but were spared the emotional tension of betraying their friends and partners.

'Father is a Comrade, Brother is not,' said Jun. 'What are you, Grandmother?'

'I am a Christian,' said Ling An.

'What is that?' asked Jun.

So Ling An began to teach her and found her an apt pupil.

Yet as time went on she began to feel that all was not well with her granddaughter. She was too quiet for a child, far more self-contained than any child ought to be. Ling An felt that Jun was like a winter stove that has been damped down for the night, the hot embers smouldering until the morning, when they will burst into flames.

36

THE CHANGED HEART

Now that Sheng Erh could see the Comrades in their true colours, he was so disgusted that he could hardly endure another week in the city. He wanted to leave immediately, but that was impossible. The river was mined so that ships could neither leave the port nor enter it. Trains were still running, but tickets were only available to those who had applied for a travel pass, and that was only obtainable after a long and detailed investigation into a person's history, past and present, and a minute discussion of his reasons for departing. Sheng Erh was unwilling to subject himself to such an ordeal, and knew in his inmost heart that as his father's son he would not be given permission to leave. There was nothing for it but to find some secret method.

He now became so moody and melancholy that Ling An was afraid to let him out of her sight. It seemed to her that there were only three courses of conduct for young men like Sheng Erh in those times: they became fiery young Comrades, or else pined away in melancholia and threw themselves off the tops of high buildings, or hid themselves indoors and did nothing.

It was soon apparent that the last course of action would soon be impossible. There were many empty rooms in their house, and Ling An foresaw that it would not be long before they would be forced to accommodate Comrades who were flocking into the city to help with the administration.

Thinking to rouse Sheng Erh from a state of apathy which had lasted two whole days, she said, 'What shall we do? I will not have one of those evil creatures in this house.'

'They are not evil creatures,' said Sheng Erh. 'At least, not all. They are trying to do good. They think they will make this world into heaven.'

'Heaven,' said Ling An. 'You can only get into heaven behind the Good Shepherd, and he will count all his sheep, one by one, as they go through the gate; and there won't be any pushing or trampling on the other sheep or rushing past him without even a look at him standing there. He will call them all by their names.'

'Well, but some of the Comrades are good people.'

'Good people! Nobody is good without God.'

'I would not say that.'

'Well, some people are not bad, but neither are they good. They will never make a heaven in this world. Heaven is in the Good Shepherd's flock. His grace can change the not-bad people into good people who will hear his voice and follow him. These Comrades cannot change people's hearts. They can force people to do this and that, but they cannot change their hearts. That is where they fail.'

'They can wash people's brains and change their thinking,' said Sheng Erh.

'Some people's thinking,' sniffed Ling An.

'They can change the hearts of children. The next generation will have known nothing else but their teaching.'

'Aiyah! We must get my granddaughter away from this evil place before it is too late.'

'I wish we could,' sighed Sheng Erh, and he set himself afresh to devising plans to get himself, Ling An and Jun out of the country.

37

THE STRANGER IN THE ATTIC

'Jun's grandmother is a Christian. She's an American running dog. Jun's an American running dog. Down with American running dogs!' chanted the children in the playground. Jun with her back against the school wall faced them as they advanced and receded in front of her chanting the shameful song.

'I'm not an American running dog,' she shouted. 'My father is a Comrade.' But they would not listen.

'American running dog. American running dog,' they taunted.

'Old red-haired running dog,' they jeered. 'Down with red-haired American running dogs!'

A teacher came out to call the children in to their classes. She was a Comrade herself, and being young and a recent convert, she was extremely zealous. Yet, when she saw Jun standing alone before the mocking children, pity stirred in her heart; and when she had set her class to work, she called Jun out to her desk and asked what she had been doing to make her companions so hostile.

'Nothing,' said Jun.

'Nothing?' said the teacher.

'Yes, nothing,' said Jun. 'They don't like me because my hair is red, and my grandmother is a Christian.'

'Well,' said the teacher, 'are you a Christian too?'

'No,' said Jun. 'My father's a Comrade. I am too.'

'Then you must do something to show them that you are a Comrade.'

'What?' said Jun.

The teacher turned to the class. 'Listen. I'll tell you all a story,' she said. 'Put down your pencils, children, and listen.'

'There was a little boy in Russia. He was a Young Comrade like you children, but his parents were not. They were bourgeois. That boy loved his parents and he knew that they loved him; but when he found that they were bourgeois and would not ever become Comrades, he knew that there was only one thing to do: tell the police. So he went to the policeman and he said, "My father and mother are bourgeois and they are against the Comrades' government." So the police came to his house and took his mother and father away and executed them. The little boy stood in the crowd and watched his parents die, and he never cried one single tear. He just shouted, "Down with traitors." What a hero he was! Don't you think so, children?'

'Yes, we do,' the children shouted back.

'There!' said the teacher, looking at Jun.

They were having supper. Ling An had tossed eggs, green peppers and onions together in the pan, and the room was full of the smell of fried onions. The blue-and-white bowls heaped with rice were set before them, and they were just dipping with their chopsticks into the communal plate of eggs, peppers, and onions, when there was a gentle tap at the door. Ling An went to open it. Jun and Sheng Erh heard her gasp, saw her turn and look at them, then say loudly to the newcomer, 'Go away,' but instead of shutting the door on the stranger, she stepped out herself and closed the door behind her.

Jun got up from the table, but Sheng Erh pulled her by

her jacket and said sternly, 'Sit down! Grandmother will see to it.'

No wonder Ling An had gasped. The stranger was her son Lao Da, Jun's father. She followed him down the road, talking softly behind him as she went.

'Come back later,' she said. 'I am not alone now.'

Theirs was an old house in a part of the city which had once been a foreign concession. There were cellars under the ground floor and attics under the roof. The cellars and the attics were always kept locked, 'So that nobody shall get in and hide there,' said Ling An. Jun had never been inside them and had never wanted to. They were dark and mysterious rooms. She shuddered as she passed the door to the cellar, running down the long dark passage to the kitchen. There it was warm and bright. Ling An, smiling and humming hymns under her breath, was busy with pots and pans.

'My grandmother,' thought Jun. 'I will not let them hurt my grandmother.' Ling An reached up to the line running across the kitchen and pulled down a circle of griddle bread which was airing on it. She wrapped it around a raw carrot and gave it to Jun.

'Eat it, Daughter,' she said.

Jun ate it, crunching the hard carrot with her strong white teeth.

'What characters did you learn today?'

'Three: man, big, and heaven,' teased Jun.

'Ah, man, big, and heaven: such easy ones! Heaven is bigger than man, Daughter.' And remembering little Lao Erh, Ling An wiped her eyes with the corner of her apron.

'Heaven,' said Jun. 'There's no such thing as heaven. Our teacher says so.'

'There is,' said Ling An. 'Your teacher is young. She does not know.'

'She knows everything. She's a Comrade.'

'Ah, a Comrade.' Ling An shut her lips firmly. Such conversation with a child was dangerous.

Jun woke in the night. The moon was shining across the room. Her grandmother's bed was empty. There was a sound in the silence of the house, hardly big enough to hear, and surely just now a line of light had shone under the door. She crept across the room and softly opened the door and looked fearfully up the flight of stairs that led to the attics. There was a red light moving along the upper passage, a light such as one made when a candle flame shines through the hand which is shielding it. Two enormous shadows loomed over the stairway. Jun, terrified, drew back into the room, and as she closed the door, she thought she heard the sound of a key grating in the lock of an attic door.

'Why have you come here, my son?'

'Mother, I have nowhere else to go.'

'Nowhere else to go! Are you not a Comrade?'

'No, I am not. I never would have chosen to be one, and now I have seen what they have done and know what they will do, I never shall be. I have left them, and now they are looking for me. If they find me, they will surely kill me. I must escape.'

'How can you do that? It is impossible to leave this city. The river is mined, trains are few and no one can travel on them without passes. You would never get a pass.'

'No. That is impossible.'

'Then what are you going to do?'

'I have a plan, but I must wait three days. Then a small boat will come down the river to a certain bridge. I will join my friends there, and we will sail down the river in the dark until we get to the sea. There are junks waiting there to take us to Formosa.'

'That will be very dangerous, Son.'

'What isn't dangerous nowadays, Niang? We take our

lives in our hands. We hold them in our tongues, keeping our mouths shut.'

'True, and the Good Shepherd watches over his sheep and keeps them safe if only they will stay close to him.'

'What you say is true, Mother.'

In the morning, Ling An poured tea into a teacup and took it to Sheng Erh when she went to wake him.

'Young Master,' she said, 'someone came in the night.'

'Who?' Sheng Erh sat up, suddenly wide awake. 'Who came?'

'My son.'

'Your son? Grandmother, it can't be your son.'

'I know my own son.'

'But surely he was killed fighting the Japanese long ago, and if he was one of those guerrillas, he could have been a Comrade.'

'He was for a while, but not now. He is escaping from them.'

'Escaping! How? Perhaps we can go too. Where is he?'

'Here, in the attic,' whispered Ling An. 'Be careful. Granddaughter must not know. I will take you to him after she has gone to school.'

Some time later Sheng Erh came into the kitchen.

'Grandmother, where is the child?'

'She has gone to school.'

'Listen: we are all going with him tomorrow night.'

'What, leave the country?'

'Yes, for Formosa.'

'I cannot go without my granddaughter.'

'She will come too. Say nothing to her until the moment we leave.'

'That will be difficult.'

'Yes, but she's small enough to carry.'

'True, but she might scream.'

'Not if we tell her . . . ssh!' Sheng Erh stopped talking.

'What's that?' he said. 'I heard something.'

'Nothing, there's nobody here . . . only rats.'

'Ah, yes, it must have been a rat. The house is full of them.'

But it wasn't a rat. It was Jun. She had crept back to the house because she had seen a gang of children coming down the road on their way to school. She wanted to wait until they were well on their way, because she knew that if they saw her they would shout after her, 'Down with red-haired American running dogs.' So she stood under the open kitchen window, waiting, and heard everything that Sheng Erh and her grandmother said.

'So we are going away,' she thought. 'With that man hidden in the attic. Going in the night secretly, running away from the Comrades. I won't go. I won't go. My father is a Comrade. Grandmother thinks I might scream. I will scream. Carry me! I'll kick and bite. I won't go. If I do I'll never find my father, because he is a Comrade, and the Comrades are here. I won't go to Formosa.'

She crept softly away from the window. There were no children in the road, so she went slowly on her way to school.

'You are late,' said the teacher. 'A Young Comrade is never late. Why are you so late?'

Jun said nothing.

'Tell me, why are you so late?'

Jun stood in silence, looking at the floor.

'Why are you late?'

Still Jun did not reply.

The children stopped writing and stared at her. 'Old red-haired running dog of the Americans,' one muttered.

'Down with red-haired American running dogs,' yelled the class as the children jumped on their desks the better to see what the teacher would do.

'Why are you late? What happened in your home?'

'Nothing,' whispered Jun, almost inaudibly.

'Nothing? Then why are you late?'

'I'll tell you,' shouted one bright boy. 'She's hiding an American spy in her cellar.'

'No! No! No!' shouted Jun, 'I'm not.'

'Is there anyone hiding in your cellar?' asked the teacher.

'No, nobody is hiding in my cellar.'

'Not in the cellar,' shouted the bright boy. 'In the attics. She's got attics in her house.'

'Is there anyone hiding in your attics?' The class was silent, waiting for the answer.

Jun said nothing.

'If you tell a lie, you'll be executed,' said a little girl in the front row. 'You'll be a spy.'

'She's a spy, an American running dog spy! Down with American running dogs,' yelled the children, jumping up and down on their desks. Jun began to cry.

'Answer me,' said the teacher, but Jun would not answer.

A great deal of freedom of behaviour was allowed in schools at that time, partly because it was the policy, but also because most teachers were afraid that if they did not pander to their pupils, they would be accused of bourgeois sympathies. The heads of schools were particularly vulnerable, as they could be caught both ways. If they tried to quell disorder in the classrooms, they were accused of restricting their pupils' freedom. If they allowed disorder to develop into rioting, in which someone might be hurt, they were accused of incompetence and relieved of their posts, and most of them would be thankful that nothing more than that was the result of too much clemency.

The headmaster of Jun's school, hearing the noise coming from her class, came into the room to enquire the cause.

'What's the matter here?' he said.

'Down with American running dogs!' yelled the class.

'Down with American running dogs,' said the headmaster. 'But there are no American running dogs here.'

'Jun is an American running dog.'
'She's hiding an American spy in her attic.'
'No, no, no, I'm not!'
'Yes she is! Yes she is!'
'Down with American running dogs!'
The headmaster took Jun's hand and led her out of the room.
'Tell me,' he said gently, 'what is the matter, child?'
Jun, trembling from head to foot, said nothing.
'Is anyone hiding in your house?'
Still there was no reply.
'There *is* someone hiding in your house.'
Still she would not answer.
'I know there is someone hiding in your house,' said the headmaster sternly. 'Tell me, who is hiding in your house?'
Jun raised her eyes to his face. 'I don't know,' she said.

38

THE WOMAN NEXT DOOR

The street elder came into the police station. Once he had been a fat man, his face round like a full moon, his stomach so far in front of him that when he lay down it rose up like a mountain between his feet and his head. Now, after six months as a street elder, he had lost so much flesh that his skin flapped on his bones like a flag, and his once-so-cheerful round face with its drooping jowls and deeply scored lines looked like an old Dalmatian hound's. He had not sought to become an elder. Who would in such times? It was better to be unknown, wiser to be unnoticed; but the job had been thrust upon him. To refuse would have been to invite criticism, and who knew where that might end? Every suicide in the street, every undocumented disappearance, every unwary whisper against the government would be laid at his door.

'But,' said his wife, 'it may be that nothing will happen here. We are all ordinary people.'

Yet something had happened. There was trouble brewing in Number 26 . . . where one would least expect it. An old woman servant with her young granddaughter and a young master recovering from an accident: how could they do anything to break the uneasy peace of the street? But the schoolmaster had warned him that there was a spy hiding in the attic of Number 26, and now he must report it to the police.

Next door to Number 26, the family had long since fled to safety in Formosa. Only a servant remained to keep the house as long as she could. She was a very old woman, bent almost double as she hobbled about on the heels of her tiny feet.

'No one will want to hurt me,' she had said. 'I am too old, and if they do kill me, haven't I lived a long life already? Nobody can take away the years I have lived, and those that are left are only a few.' So she had stayed, making her home on the ground floor and only occasionally going upstairs to see that nothing irreparable had happened to the property of her master and mistress, for the stairs were difficult for her old rheumatic joints.

That day, just as she was cooking the rice for her supper, three men came to the back door.

'We have come to mend the electricity,' they said. 'We must go upstairs to the attics.'

'Electricity!' said the old woman. 'There's nothing wrong with the electricity. Only it is rather weak since . . . well, but I thought it is weak everywhere nowadays;' and 'Nothing is as good as it was before,' she muttered under her breath.

'What's that?'

'I only said my legs are not as good as they were before.'

'Well, you can give us the key and we will go upstairs and save you the trouble, old Sister-in-law.'

She gave them the key and went back to the kitchen, where the rice was just beginning to burn.

The men went into the attic and locked the door behind them. They went to the wall that divided the attic in Number 25 from that in Number 26. They took out their tools and scraped the plaster away till they came to the bricks. Then they made a tiny hole through the mortar between the bricks and out through the plaster on the other side and thrust through it a long narrow tube. They were so practised and experienced in this kind of work that they had made no more noise than a rat scrabbling behind the wainscot. One by one, each applied his eye to the hole and looked into the attic of Number 26. But very little could be seen except the wall at the other end of the attic. 'But we shall we able to hear,' they said.

Then they sat down on the floor and waited.

The old woman scoured the rice pot and closed the shutters of the downstairs rooms, and she was just locking the front door when she remembered the three workmen in the attic. Cursing them under her breath for causing her to climb the stairs, she slowly went up to the top floor, pausing on each of the landings, holding on to the banisters while she got her breath back, and waiting till the giddiness stopped and she could once more see truly with her dim old eyes.

The attic door was locked.

'The wretches,' she said, 'to take my key. They must have gone out of the front door while I was scouring the pot. I *thought* I was getting deaf.'

39

THE AMBUSH

The chief of police was addressing a squad of men.

'Comrades, you will go to that bridge at 1 a.m. tonight. We know that a boat with twelve landlords on it will be moored under the bridge at two o'clock. Eight men, an old woman and a child will go aboard. Do nothing until all are aboard. Two police boats, lying in ambush above and below the bridge, will intercept the boat so that these American running dogs cannot escape. They will probably leap into the water. Save those you can for execution later. These bourgeois tradesmen need examples. Shoot those whom you cannot reach. Any questions?'

'What about the child?'

'The child is innocent. We do not execute children.'

One o'clock! The sky was cloudy and a light drizzle was falling. Ling An gently rolled Jun in a quilt. She did not awaken.

'She should not wake until morning,' Ling An thought; but there she was mistaken.

Strong arms picked up the bundle and hoisted her tenderly on to a broad shoulder.

'My little daughter,' whispered Lao Da. 'At last, my little daughter!' But Jun heard nothing. Six shadows looming over the stairwell came down the stairs and followed Lao Da and Ling An out of the house. Before Ling An opened the door, Lao Da looked at the six men following and said to Sheng Erh, 'Remember, the first turning on the left, then left again, right, right, right, end left along the river bank till you come to the bridge. Wait for us. We go aboard together.'

They went softly down the street until they came to a turning on the left. Sheng Erh and his companions left them there to join them later at the bridge. Eight men together on the street in the middle of the night would excite suspicion. Lao Da and Ling An went on together to the crossroads.

As they turned into the main road which led to the river, a policeman shouted to them, 'Halt!' They stopped.

'Where are you going?'

'To the hospital. My child is sick.'

'What is the matter with the child?'

'Measles. Bad measles.'

The policeman had five children. 'Pass,' he said. Measles could be bad, he knew. Hadn't he lost his eldest son with measles!

In the shadow of the bridge the water lapped against the wooden piles. Even in the daytime it was black with the filth of the city through which it flowed, and the bottom was many feet deep in slime which had been accumulating there for more than a thousand years. Every morning flat barges, their holds filled with the city's sewage, slowly made their way out to the fields where it could be used to enrich the soil and produce good crops of grain and vegetables to feed the inhabitants of the city. Even at night, the water still stank of what had passed over it and been slopped into it. Hidden among the piles, a boat waited in the shadow of the bridge. Eleven men sat there in silence. The twelfth waited in a sampan under the bank, squatting on his heels, hiding his white face between his knees so that it might not be seen in the darkness.

They were all twelve of them desperate men: criminals guilty of one crime — the possession of land which they had sublet to tenants. Now their land had been taken from them, and they were fleeing before their lives could be taken also.

'Formosa is free,' they said. 'We will make ourselves new homes in Formosa.'

Six men came along the narrow beach, running under the low bank. They were bent almost double, hoping that their heads might not be visible above the top of the bank.

'The bridge,' whispered Sheng Erh.

They got into the sampan, and the man already there stood up with his pole, ready to start.

'Wait!' whispered Sheng Erh. 'There are three more to come.'

'Three!'

'Yes, three. Lao Da, his mother, and his child.'

'A child! We can't take a child.'

'Only a little girl . . . ten years old.'

'Ten years old . . . well . . . perhaps . . . '

Two figures loomed out of the drizzle: Ling An, and Lao Da carrying Jun.

The man punted them into the middle of the river, and thence to the boat waiting among the piles. They went aboard.

The boat pushed off.

Jun opened her eyes. 'Father,' she said. 'Father?'

'Yes, Daughter, Father. Ssh.'

'Halt!'

A boat was standing in their course. Immediately they turned about to go up the river: but there was another boat standing in their course there. They were hemmed in.

'To the banks!' shouted Lao Da; and even as he shouted, shots were fired across their heads by police stationed on both sides of the river.

'Good Shepherd, bring us where you want us to be,' prayed Ling An in the bottom of the boat. There was nothing for it but to leap overboard and swim if they could. Drowning was easier than execution.

Lao Da, still holding his daughter Jun, leapt into the water and swam to the bridge. Wriggling in and out of the slimy piles, he pulled his daughter along with him. Then, half-drowned, he held on to a pile with one hand and supported his child with the other. Jun tried to grab the slimy wood, but her hands slid away from it, so she clung with both hands to her father's neck.

'Hold tight, Daughter,' he said.

The police picked up all those they found in the water.

Then, so that no one should escape, they raked the river with rifle fire, concentrating on the piles under the bridge. The bullets ricocheted from pile to pile. Lao Da ducked and ducked again. The water reddened around him as he was hit, but still he clung to the pile with one hand and to Jun with the other. Finally, a bullet hit him in the head. His hand slid down the pile; his other arm loosened around Jun, but she clung firmly to his neck, and clinging thus, sank with him into the turgid depths of the river.

Of all that company, only Sheng Erh escaped. Swimming as fast as he could under water, he got himself into the central current of the river and there allowed the water to carry him away towards the sea. A fisherman in a sampan picked him up and hid him in the family junk until they reached Hong Kong, where he found Mulan his mother and his father Bao Erh.

Ling An was one of those taken out of the water by the police. As she stood wet and shivering in the police station, she scanned the faces of the nine survivors, and knew that her son, her granddaughter, and her young master were missing.

40

THE HOME-COMING

She saw the crowds on either side of the road: a wall of faces, some blank and some hostile, some bent down so that their pity might not be visible. Though she could not see that pity, she knew it must be there, for well she knew that the presence of all, both hostile and friendly, was a matter of obedience to the same authority which had forced her also to be there. No one spoke, no one stirred. Most of them were too weary to speak; what energy they had must be spared for the Party slogans which they knew would be dragged out of them in a moment.

The signal was given, the crowd roared, 'Down with the traitors!' and the little band of prisoners was pushed forward.

They walked slowly, their faces without expression, as though they did not know why they were there or what lay ahead of them; for long months of imprisonment had reduced most of them to the mentality of beasts. Of them all, only Ling An was able to walk upright, looking before her with purpose: and so it was that she came to be walking a little ahead of them so that she seemed to be their leader; and as she walked, the old habit of prayer asserted itself, and she began to pray for her fellow sufferers, one by one, then for those who were driving them forward to their execution; and finally for the odd face that appeared as an individual in that enormous mass of faces shrieking slogans on either side of her.

Then she saw set in that wall of faces one face that seemed to detach itself from the others and become clear and definite. Surely it could not be Jun. But it was Jun's face . . . Jun's face set on the shoulders of a boy about twelve or thirteen years old, and his hair was the colour of rusty iron.

'It is my grandson Koko,' thought Ling An. 'He does not know me. Poor boy, to be left alone, the last of my family. I will do one thing for him.'

She summoned all her remaining strength and began to sing.

Jesus is the Good Shepherd.
He leads his sheep.
He goes in front,
The sheep follow behind.
Night and day he will protect them all;
Those thieves and robbers
Can never steal them.
He leads them beside still waters,
He leads them on the mountains,
He calls them with his gentle voice,
He keeps them safe.

Then with one last effort she shouted, 'Follow the Good Shepherd. Find him and follow him.'

At this the crowd were urged to another frenzy of slogans.

'Down with traitors! Down with American running dogs! Down with enemies of the People's Republic!'

In the midst of the hubbub Ling An walked in a silence as though she were moving in the eye of a typhoon, and she thought how although she was hemmed in behind and on either side, yet the way ahead was open as it had always been all through her life, leading to the very gates of heaven.

At last they came to the field at the end of the road, and there they were halted and made to kneel in a long row, their hands still bound together behind their backs. The crowd behind them was urged to a further frenzy of slogans, and in the ensuing silence the crimes of each prisoner were recited, and the order given to fire. Ling An did not listen. She looked ahead at the long line of hills to the north. The sky above them was grey and heavy, with no hint of the glory that must be beyond. But so it had always been, and so, she knew, it must always be, for human nature would shrivel into ashes before the unveiled splendour of God. A long time ago she had seen him, walking through the kitchen, and he had turned and looked at her. Now she saw him again, and raising her head, she poised her soul to meet him, and reaching up she felt her whole being glow with the warmth of the love that came down to her.

It was Koko standing in the crowd. At long last, after many mishaps, his long walk through the country had brought him to the outskirts of the city where he hoped to find his mother and his little sister. He had been caught up and pushed along in the crowd surging behind the prisoners. He did not shout when the others rent the air with slogans, and when the shots rang out and the prisoners fell to the ground and lay still, he stood staring in horror.

The crowd began to go away; but Koko could not move. He could not take his eyes away from the old woman who had been singing and shouting about a good shepherd. Surely she had looked at him as she shouted. Now she lay a tumbled heap on the ground.

He felt a hand laid upon his shoulder, and looking up saw the face of Pao Ying.

'Come,' said Pao Ying, leading him away. 'We will look for that Good Shepherd.' So they walked away, and so they will walk through the length and breadth of the land for a long time to come, while the Good Shepherd in his infinite patience waits for his sheep to come to his call. The voices that told of his love, the hands that showed it forth, and the feet that carried him to the uttermost parts of the country are banished from the land or languish in prisons which are not always prisons of bars and walls, but subtler prisons of fears and indecisions.

Yet he is there, waiting, brooding over the clamour and confusion, as in the beginning he brooded over the waste and void that preceded Creation.

THE DRAGON KING TRILOGY
1984 C.S. Lewis Medal Honor Books

Stephen Lawhead

Book 1: In the Hall of the Dragon King

Quentin, a young acolyte serving in the temple of Ariel, is thrust into the centre of a conflict in which the life of the king and the future of the realm of Mensandor hang in the balance. Drawn into the web of intrigue spawned by the Necromancer Nimrood, Quentin, with the aid of friends loyal to the Dragon King, embarks on a dangerous quest.

ISBN 0 85648 859 3

Book 2: The Warlords of Nin

Mensandor is once more in desperate straits. The Wolf Star grows nightly greater and more threatening as the power of Nin increases and black terror reigns. It is Quentin, once again, who holds the kingdom's destiny in his hands.

ISBN 0 85648 874 7

Book 3: The Sword and the Flame

Quentin, now reigning as the Dragon King, is faced with the bitterest onslaught of all. Now Nimrood holds Quentin's son hostage. The Dragon King has lost his sword – Zhaligkeer, the Shining One – and he has lost his way. Will he also betray his vow to the Most High?

ISBN 0 85648 875 5

EMPYRION

Stephen Lawhead

A two-part epic
THE SEARCH FOR FIERRA
THE SIEGE OF DOME
Now in one volume

Eight million dollars for a special assignment, to report on the new colony of Empyrion, ten light-years from earth. How could Orion Treet refuse? But why had Cynetics Chairman Neviss gone to such lengths to track him down?

There was little time to think. Within the hour Treet was on board the transport, hurtling through space with a handful of oddly-assorted companions.

What they saw, streaking through the atmosphere, was a turquoise world, blue-green with vegetation, water and sky. A free and perfect world — or so it seemed. How could Treet know, then, what lay ahead? The Empyrion they had discovered was not the Empyrion they set out to find . . .

ISBN 0 7459 1872 7

DREAM THIEF

Stephen Lawhead

'The dreams had been at Spence again. He could feel their lingering presence like a dimly remembered whisper. They were unsettling in a vague sort of way — haunting. There was a word that seemed to fit. He felt haunted.'

Dr Spencer Reston, sleep scientist on space station Gotham, has become a vital link in a cosmic group masterminded by a mysterious creature known as the Dream Thief.

ISBN 0 85648 838 0

THE PENDRAGON CYCLE

Stephen Lawhead

Book 1: Taliesin

Taliesin is the first book of the Pendragon Cycle: a magnificent epic set against the backcloth of Roman Britain and the legends of King Arthur and Atlantis

'I will weep no more for the lost, asleep in their water graves. The voices of the departed speak: tell our story, they say. It is worthy to be told. And so I take my pen and write . . .'

So begins the tragedy of lost Atlantis, extinguished for ever in a hideous paroxysm of earth and sea. Out of the holocaust, three crippled ships emerge to bear King Avallach and his daughter to the cloud-bound isle of Ynys Prydein.

Here is another world, where Celtic chieftains struggle for survival in the twilight of Rome's power. One heroic figure towers over all, the Prince Taliesin, in whom is the sum of human greatness — grandeur and grace, meekness and majesty, beauty and truth.

This is a tale that spans two worlds, a vision that sings in the heart, and a love that spawns the miracle of Merlin . . . Arthur . . . and a destiny that is more than a kingdom.

ISBN 0 7459 1309 1

THE PENDRAGON CYCLE

Stephen Lawhead

Book 2: Merlin

'Was there ever a time such as this? Never! And that is both the glory and the terror of it. If men knew what it was that loomed before them . . . they would stop their mouths with their cloaks for screaming. It is their blessing and their curse that they do not know. But I know; I, Merlin, have always known . . .'

This is Merlin's story, the story of the Island of the Mighty — of warring battlechiefs and bloody Saecsen invaders, of the hidden Hill Folk and the waning power of Rome.

It is Merlin's story as none but he could tell it — a tale of love and savagery and madness. An all-consuming vision — of the glorious Kingdom of Summer . . . of treachery and death . . . of the saving of a babe new-born, and a sword in a stone . . .

ISBN 0 7459 1310 5

THE PENDRAGON CYCLE

Stephen Lawhead

Book 3: Arthur

Arthur is the third and final book of the Pendragon Cycle: A magnificent epic set against the backcloth of Roman Britain and the legends of Arthur and lost Atlantis.

'Arthur is no fit king. Merlin's pawn, he is lowborn and a fool. He is wanton and petty and cruel — a sullen, ignorant brute.

All these things and more men say of Arthur. Let them.

When all the words are spoken and the arguments fall exhausted into silence, this single fact remains: we would follow Arthur to the very gates of Hell and beyond if he asked it. Show me another who can claim such loyalty.

"Cymbrogi," he calls us: companions of the heart.

Cymbrogi! We are his strong arm, his shield and spear, his blade and helm.

Cymbrogi! We are earth and sky to him. And Arthur is all these things to us and more.

Ponder this. Think long on it. Only then, perhaps, will you begin to understand the tale I shall tell you . . .'

ISBN 0 7459 1311 3

SONS AND BROTHERS

Elizabeth Gibson

By faith and sword divided — a family saga set against the background of the English Civil War.

'The buff and red coats merged, crossed and separated. Which was the enemy? Robert paused, half knowing the danger he was in, half denying it, and steadied himself on a doorpost.

'Then out of the rabble stepped a Goliath of a man, or so it seemed. The man had lost his hat, but the thick, black curls waving onto his broad shoulders proclaimed him unmistakably a King's man. Around them both the rain fell in black curtains.

'Suddenly he knew the other man . . .'

The agony of the nation is mirrored by the brothers — Robert, the hard-line Puritan, Isaac the King's man — divided by love and hate and warring faiths. Passion and tragedy alternate in this richly textured novel of two families, as King and Parliament battle for supremacy.

'In the loves and the tragedies, the frustrations and the joys of ordinary people, Elizabeth Gibson has recreated the frightful and fascinating period of the English Civil War. It's a book that's hard to put down.'
ANDREW GREELEY

ISBN 0 7459 1526 6